By

L. D. K. Johnson

Sale of this book without a front cover may be unauthorized. If this book is coverless, it may have been reported to the publisher as "**unsold** or **destroyed**" and neither the author nor the publisher may have received payment for it.

Copyright © 2013 by L. D. K. Johnson

All rights reserved. No portion of this book may be reproduced in any form without permission from the publisher except as permitted by U.S. copyright law.

For permission, contact **Belen Books, LLC**.

This is a work of fiction. Names, characters, businesses, places, events, locales, and incidents are either the products of the author's imagination or used in a fictitious manner. Any resemblance to actual persons, living or dead, sexy Hawaiian Navy sailors, Scottish lassies, dogs named Brutus, or actual events or places is purely coincidental.

ISBN: 978-1-959715-36-8

Library of Congress Control Number: **2024930952**
Published by **Belen Books, LLC**
St. Petersburg, FL | Winter Park, FL | Chicago, IL USA
Belenbookspublishing.com

Edited by Paul L. Hight
Cover by Belen Media Group

10 9 8 7 6 5 4 3 2

Printed in the United States of America

DEDICATED TO:

Karen, Beverly, & Ally

Three of the strongest Women I know.

CHAPTER ONE

"Congratulations, cuz," Lieutenant Paul Choy said as he gave his cousin, Koa, a firm hug. The 6'7" groom uncharacteristically blushed, hazel eyes glistening under the elegant crystal chandeliers of the ballroom hosting the reception.

To his surprise, Koa Kapahu grinned like a little boy on Christmas morning.

"Thanks, brah."

"You're a lucky man with a beautiful new wife," Paul stated matter-of-factly as he glanced over at Koa's lovely bride in white who was talking with other family members near the table displaying the custom-made wedding cake created by his dad. "Congrats on the promotion too, *Commander* Kapahu! Who thought getting shot and breaking your leg rescuing Coast Guard hostages would be so beneficial to your Naval career?"

"Certainly not I," Koa spoke softly, eyes following his new bride as she walked toward them, long chestnut-locks pulled back in an elegant chignon secured with an antique jeweled butterfly clip. Her curvaceous body enhanced by a simple, yet sophisticated white, A-line, chiffon wedding gown designed by their cousin, Noelani.

"You look amazing, Adrienne," Paul complimented the petite Naval Commander and his cousin's new spouse.

"Thank you, Paul. Now the only one left to settle down is you," the blushing bride replied playfully, and then kissed his cheek.

A sudden rush of heat spread through his cheeks at the thought.

"Hey!" he added teasingly. "If you know of anyone who's looking, send them my way."

"Will do." She laughed as Koa took her left hand in his. "Paul, could I borrow my husband for a while? I want to introduce him to a few of my family members from American Samoa."

Adrienne's father was Samoan while her mom was French. The unique combination made her stunning with feline-shaped green eyes, a pert button nose, and thick, chestnut-brown hair all nestled in a round, flawless peanut butter-colored face.

"Sure, no worries. You two go mingle."

With a twinge of envy, Paul watched the newly married couple walk away. The height disparity between the two made him chuckle. Who would have thought a Goliath-sized, highly trained Navy SEAL would be tamed by a 5'4" Naval Engineer? *Yup!* Commander Adrienne Mathis-Kapahu was surely a force to be reckoned with.

While he stood gawking, Paul felt a hand on his shoulder and looked away from the couple. Turning quickly, he was almost eye-level with the wickedly gleaming amber eyes of his cousin, Kai, younger sister to the groom.

"Aloha, cousin," she said smoothly. "Could you please watch the kids for us while Aiden and I dance? This is my favorite song."

Kai looked radiant in her burnished gold evening gown; the color of the dress bringing out the gold specks in her eyes. Her riotous curls were pulled back in a low ponytail at the nape of her neck, giving her a glamorous, exotic appearance.

"Please," Aiden pleaded, gray-blue eyes focused lovingly on his supermodel-looking wife.

Paul had to admit, although his cousin Kai was a wife and mother, she was still one of the most beautiful women in the Kapahu family, maybe even the entire state of Hawai'i... and that was really saying something. If he weren't related to her, he would have fallen for her as well. The 5'8" beauty was blessed with smooth honey-hued skin, mesmerizing almond-shaped amber eyes, all framed by shoulder length ebony curls.

She was a voluptuous Hawaiian goddess, even if she didn't realize it.

His cousin was also smart as a whip. She and Aiden had been best friends during their four years at the University of Southern California, where Kai was studying for her degree in physical therapy and Aiden was earning his in engineering, but they didn't reunite until almost a year ago. Now, they were happily married with two amazing kids.

"Of course," he replied with a grin as he scooped up Kai and Aiden's eleven-month-old daughter, Aria, and took her now six-year-old, big brother, A.J., by the hand.

"Cousin Paul, can I go play with the other kids?" A.J. asked sheepishly.

"Sure, buddy. Just stay where I can see you, okay?"

He patted the small boy gently on the head.

"No worries," A.J. answered respectfully, looking more like Aiden with each passing day.

With a huge grin, Paul watched as he ran over to the other children who were chatting and stealing icing off of the elaborately decorated, four-tier wedding cake. He couldn't help snorting at their antics remembering when he and the other cousins were children and got into mischief at family functions too. Now, it seemed he was the last single one among the bunch. Even Noelani had recently found a boyfriend.

"I guess it's just you and me kid," Paul whispered to Aria, who was holding onto his formal Navy dress whites like a spider monkey with one hand and sucking the thumb of her other hand. Needless to say, the slurping sounds made him chuckle at the little cutie-pie who looked just like her mother. The only exception being her gray-blue eyes she inherited from her father. Another pang of jealousy pierced his heart, and he sighed sadly as he led his baby cousin to the dance floor.

Several songs later, Aiden came to collect his daughter who had fallen asleep in his arms. Aria was so sweet and well-behaved, he almost wished he had a child of his own. Almost. Swiftly, he shook the idea from his mind. First, he'd have to find a willing female participant to make that scenario possible.

"Thanks a lot, Paul." Aiden took his slumbering offspring in his arms. "Someday when you have kids, I'll return the favor."

"I wouldn't hold my breath on that," Paul dismissed the idea as he examined the Grand Ballroom of the Hibiscus Resort and Spa overlooking Hilton Head with admiration.

Koa's parents had done a beautiful job with the space. The massive room lit by three large, ornate chandeliers hosted twenty-five round dining tables dressed in crisp white linens with royal blue silk organza overlays. Each table was set with full China and silverware wrapped in white linen napkins, crystal water goblets, as well as champagne flutes completed the elaborate scene. Low frosted glass votives, already lit, gave the room a soft, romantic glow, while fragrant floral centerpieces of white lilies, royal blue callas, and sage green gladiolas in varying heights were meticulously placed in the center of each table along with verdant ferns and miniature trees scattered around the space, made the room resemble an enchanted European forest.

The space was large enough to hold all two hundred-fifty guests and looked as if *King Kamehameha* himself would be attending. Toward the front of the main room, a single table, set similarly, just for the bride and groom, topped it all off. Celebrity wedding planner, *David Tutera* would have been proud.

The food tasted amazing as well. The delicious buffet consisted of traditional French foods, in honor of the bride's deceased mother, as well as Adrienne's French upbringing. Dishes such as coq au vin, beef bourguignon, potatoes au gratin, green beans almandine, and an incredible sweet potato and walnut puree. He hadn't eaten so much in an extremely long time and made a mental note to exercise for at least an hour in the morning.

However, the wedding cake was the main attraction, a four-tiered confection with hand-made sugar wildflowers adorning the top layer and cascading down both sides. It could have been featured on some televised cake competition. Paul's father had outdone himself once again.

After the last wedding, when Aiden had to take his dad out on a destroyer as a form of payment, Koa and Adrienne decided it was best for all concerned to *pay* his father for the time and ingredients in making the extravagant edible masterpiece.

The reception passed in a blur with relatives dancing, singing, and having a great time. Champagne flowed freely and the entire event was one they would all remember fondly. Paul, on the other hand, was tired and for some unknown reason... annoyed, so he said *aloha* to his family members on his way to the ballroom exit.

Just as he was about to escape, he heard his name yelled across the still crowded dance floor.

"Paul, wait a minute!"

Startled, he turned back, in time to see Noelani striding toward him with another woman in tow. He gulped as the 5'7", café-au-lait beauty smiled at him, her toffee-colored eyes almost hidden beneath espresso-colored bangs.

Good God Almighty!

She was a knock-out.

Tongue-tied and flabbergasted, he swallowed hard, and waited until they stopped a few feet in front of where he stood gawking like an idiot.

Get it together!

"I'm so glad I caught you before you left," Noelani stated breathlessly. "Paul, this is my friend Meara McBride, the one I met at the Fashion Institute. Meara, this is my cousin, Lieutenant Paul Choy."

"Good evening," the goddess greeted warmly with a sing-song Scottish lilt throwing him completely for a loop. "Noelani has told me a lot about you."

Holy Shit!

Unable to respond, the shy officer admired her from the top of her head, over the subtle curves showcased by her simple, yet stunning little black dress, to the tips of her four-inch matching stilettos, putting them almost at eye level. Long, straight, black tresses fell to the middle of her exposed back like a thick, smooth curtain.

Everything about her was perfection, and to his embarrassment, he couldn't say anything. His mouth felt like he had ingested all of the sand on Waikiki Beach along with his tongue.

Unsympathetically, Noelani rolled her eyes, the action making him want to run from the room as fast as he could.

"Paul." The usually fun-loving, easy-going Noelani eyed him suspiciously before turning back to the heavenly creature beside her who watched him knowingly. "Stop embarrassing me and say something."

His cousin glared at him until he muttered some incoherent nonsense.

"I didn't quite understand that." Meara grinned as she looked him over as well.

"Meara, let me introduce you to some of my *other* family members," Noelani huffed her irritation, and then turned away. "The ones who actually have functional vocal cords."

To his surprise, Meara graced him with a flawless, runway model smile.

"It was a pleasure meeting you, Lieutenant," she expressed with a seductive Scottish brogue that made his cock flex within the confines of his pants. He acknowledged with a faint nod as she turned and headed toward the bar area with Noelani. Paul was even more amazed when the charming female glanced over her shoulder and smiled at him... *Again!*

Damn it! He was such a hopeless idiot!

Grabbing his car keys from the table, making sure he had his wallet along with his take-home container of wedding cake, Paul briskly left the hotel and went to his car, shaking his head in disgust.

No wonder he was still a virgin!

"I'm so sorry, Meara," Noelani apologized again for her cousin's strange behavior.

Meara laughed at her friend's exasperated tone.

"Stop apologizing," she begged with a genuine smile. "It was nice not getting hit on or propositioned at first sight."

"You won't get that with Paul." Noelani giggled.

"Why?" She arched one brow. "Is he gay?"

Noelani's eyebrow arched this time.

"There's nothing wrong if he is," Meara added with a hint of disappointment.

Why were the good-looking ones always gay?

"No! Definitely not!" Shaking her head, Noelani sputtered. "Never in a million years is Paul Choy gay."

"Ahh," the Scottish lady whispered under her breath. "That's good to know."

"He's just never been a player like the rest of the guys in my family," her friend continued. "He gets a little tongue-tied around women. Unless you're related to him, then you can't get him to shut-up."

That made them both laugh.

The lieutenant definitely had potential. He was tall, six feet one inch at least, with thick, inky black locks, deep chocolate-brown eyes, high cheekbones, and the smoothest olive complexion she had ever seen on a man. He was a bit rough around the edges, but with a little cleaning-up he would be incredible.

In fact, Noelani resembled her cousin to the point they could pass for siblings. Both were tall; Noelani was her height, with long, black, silk-like, straight hair, expressive almond-shaped, chocolate-brown eyes, all in a perfectly proportional face. All-natural, cover-girl smile and hourglass figure made her best friend an absolute guy-magnet. Spencer, Noelani's boyfriend of three months, was a lucky bloke.

Meara had no problem admitting her bestie looked incredible wearing one of her own creations: a simple royal blue, raw-silk halter gown with matching wedge heels. The woman's dark hair cascaded like a shimmering curtain over her shoulders down to her waist. As usual, the talented designer looked as if she had stepped out of the pages of a high-end fashion magazine.

"Noel?"

"Yeah?"

"Thanks for asking me to be your 'plus one' tonight. I don't know if I could have taken another night of delivery pizza and streaming movies. I love your house, but I can't wait to be in my new condo."

"No worries." Noelani beamed. "Spencer is on assignment in somewhere in the Middle East, so I needed a date anyway."

Spencer Davis, an undercover intelligence officer for the Army, was a good-looking guy, not as good looking as Paul—*Damn it! Where did that thought come from?* —with his short, preppy-styled, dirty-blonde hair and dark brown eyes. The soldier was built like a brick wall with muscles on top of his muscles, but he had a shy, mysterious nature that sometimes made her uneasy. She, on the other hand, preferred her men on the talkative side.

It was also her wish to be in a relationship with someone who didn't travel a lot. Unlike Spencer, who was always leaving for days, sometimes even weeks at a time on special missions. Noelani tried not to complain about the time she spent alone, but she wouldn't... *No*, couldn't accept it. Her Hawaiian companion had decided that Spencer was worth all of the sleepless nights and dateless weekends. She, on the other hand, wanted... *No,* needed a man who was tied to one place, not wandering all over the globe.

The man she ended up with would be like a rock, settled.

Noelani had only introduced her and Spencer once, but her new boyfriend seemed authentically smitten with her surrogate sister, and that fact made her like him even more. The vivacious Hawaiian beauty deserved a wonderful mate who would accept all of her quirks as well as her flirtatious nature. However, even though Noelani was known to flirt, she was fiercely loyal and accepting. It was these qualities that first attracted Meara to the young woman.

"Well, thank you for letting me be your date." Meara sighed. "Your family did an amazing job with everything. I actually feel like I'm in an enchanted forest. If I ever get married—"

She was cut off in midsentence.

"*When*... when you get married," her friend corrected firmly, grabbing two glasses of imported Champagne from a waiter's passing tray.

Noelani handed her a glass, smiled, and then took a long sip. Meara did the same, giggling when a slew of effervescent bubbles accosted her nose.

Sadly, she shook her head.

"I don't think I'll ever find the right guy," the frustrated Scot stated matter-of-factly. "Look how many duds I've ended up with. Sure, they were all hotties, but they were all no-good sons-of-bitches as well."

"You need to stop choosing the bad boys, that's all," her companion stressed.

In her defense, Roger had definitely seemed like the *opposite* of a bad boy with his clean-cut, boy-next-door good looks and keen insight into the law. He was the kind of man that mothers around the world prayed their daughters would find and marry. Smart, fun-loving, ambitious, handsome, and well established in his career field. Roger had even mentioned wanting children, which had lured her in even more.

"It seems those are the only ones attracted to me, the hot bad boys. I'm a bad boy magnet." She sneered with disgust remembering her ex-boyfriend again. The one who had cheated on her with his dental hygienist... and his dog walker... and the slut who made his sugar-free, extra-foam, skinny, caramel macchiato, and those were the only ones she'd learned about.

Who knew how many there actually were.

Thank goodness she had found out before she'd accepted his marriage proposal.

Meara thanked heaven every day for giving her the uncanny ability to look through someone's facade and find the true person hiding beneath the surface. Roger had appeared to be an upstanding gentleman, but in reality, he had turned out to be a snake, and not a cute little garden snake, but a treacherous King Cobra with extra-long fangs.

What she needed was a break from bad boys. Truthfully, she needed a break from *all* boys. Yup, it was settled. She was going on a *'boy-free'* diet.

"Are you okay?" Noelani's questioning tone brought her back to reality once again.

"Pardon?" She grinned. "Yes. I've just had an epiphany."

"You did?"

"Yes," she replied confidently.

"I'm curious. What was this epiphany?" Noelani mimicked in her best Scottish accent, which wasn't good at all.

"Men." Meara sighed. "I'm taking a break from them."

Noelani choked on her Champagne, before sputtering, "What?"

Amused, Meara scoffed at her best friend's growing frown.

They had met during their two years at the *Fashion Institute of Technology* in New York City and became fast friends and roommates. Noelani Choy was the down-to-earth, high-strung, level-headed one, while she was the fly-by-the-seat-of-your-pants, never-back-down-from-a-challenge one. Together they found balance.

Their close bond was also the reason she decided to move to Oahu to open a boutique together. Over the past year, they had become quite successful with their online store, so it only made sense to open a storefront and hope for the best. Between Noelani's head for business and her strong fashion and design sense, they'd conquer the fashion industry. She hoped.

"It's true." Her resolve grew stronger as she spoke. "I'm taking a break from dating. I'm going to concentrate on all the things I've been putting off and I'm going to start a project."

"What kind of project?" Worry-lines appeared on Noelani's forehead.

"I'm not sure yet, but I'll know it when I see it."

"Did you slip in the bathroom and fall and hit your head on the countertop?" Noelani's eyes narrowed suspiciously.

"No," she chuckled. "I've just realized there's nothing the opposite sex can do for me that I can't do for myself."

"I beg to differ with you," Noelani scoffed and snorted in an undignified fashion.

"Name one thing that I need a man for?" Her friend looked down at her nether regions and waggled her brows playfully, making her laugh out loud. "I have *toys* to take care of that."

Noelani shook her head again.

"I don't think a plastic... *you know*... can take the place of an actual... *you know*."

"I'm going to prove you wrong," Meara stated stubbornly. Her mind was made up as she smiled to herself. Men free and furthering her career in the fashion industry, yes. It was going to be a brand-new day.

A new day indeed!

CHAPTER TWO

Paul woke several times during the night all hot and horny and ready to jump on the bones of the Scottish princess in his dreams. The blasted female had him up... literally, all night with a painful ache in his cock.

Unable to get comfortable, he rose around midnight, watched television, ate his slice of wedding cake, even got a head start on the laundry and cleaning his condominium, but nothing helped. Finally, around three o'clock in the morning, he hopped into the shower and jacked-off *twice*, before he could fall back asleep. Meara would be the death of him.

At six in the morning, he fell out of bed, quickly donned a pair of shorts and t-shirt, ate a banana and some fat-free yogurt then headed downstairs to the gym to get in a quick workout. He of all people knew how much delicious food would be at the Kapahu volleyball game, and if he didn't want to gain weight, he would have to start the day off right.

As he made his way to the first floor, Paul recalled why he bought his unit in the first place. He loved that the complex had several swimming pools with whirlpool spas, its own gym facilities, several professional tennis courts, and even a racket ball court. The multistory building also had its own parking garage, along with two community meeting spaces that tenants could use. In fact, it had all the amenities a young, available, bachelor could want to impress the ladies, if said bachelor *had* a lady to impress.

The location on Wai Nani Way, across the street from Waikiki Beach, in the heart of Honolulu, was close to the Navy base where he was stationed which was extremely convenient. Plus, he was only a few miles away from the local zoo which he held annual passes for and visited often. Lastly, the building was near the major shopping districts, popular nightlife venues, and trendy restaurants.

Paul didn't know how he did it, but he managed to work out for an hour and a half then jogged to the café around the corner from his building for a non-fat latte and an egg white, Canadian bacon, and cheddar cheese on an English muffin. While he waited at the pick-up counter, his gaze unhurriedly swept the area when a familiar brunette with toffee-colored eyes and a body made for sin caught his attention.

The Scottish princess looked gorgeous in a pair of mid-thigh, black running shorts, white t-shirt, and matching black and white sneakers. Her long hair secured up in a high, messy ponytail, and no make-up, only a healthy glow enhanced her features. On cue, his palms began to sweat.

"Not again," Paul mumbled, mentally willing his breakfast to cook faster.

Before he could pretend that he didn't see her, she glanced up, and their eyes locked. Upon recognition, Meara graced him with a sweet smile before returning to her magazine and half-eaten breakfast. Just the simple act of her smiling at him caused his member to instantly harden. Relief flooded him when she stood, waved goodbye and left the restaurant.

Needing to decompress, the young officer decided to walk to a nearby grocery store to pick up a few food staples for the week. Leisurely, he strolled and ate, and by the time he was finished devouring his breakfast, he had arrived at his destination. As he opened the entrance to the small mom-and-pop establishment he had shopped at for several years, he inadvertently bumped into an exiting customer.

"Well," the strong Scottish accent tickled his ears. "We've literally bumped into each other twice in one morning. What are the odds of that?"

She smiled again causing his tongue to melt into a non-working piece of shoe leather inside his dry mouth and the errant appendage between his legs began throbbing inside his shorts. Silently, he whispered a prayer that she wouldn't notice it tenting the material.

Great!

He'd have to think of something, non-sexual, to ease his discomfort. Unfortunately, with the gorgeous female standing so near, it would take something completely boring and complex to get the thought of pushing her up against the building, yanking down her shorts and panties, and burying himself balls-deep in her pussy, in public, like a beast in heat, to distract him.

Swallowing hard, he replied.

"The odds of that are actually rarer than you might think," he babbled. "Statistics prove that the correlations of factors that play into the probability are quite—"

Then nervously he paused, stopping his inane and geeky explanation.

The blushing female's smile grew larger before informing with an air of confidence, "Actually, you'd have to take into consideration the multitude of factors in the equation—since they are in a constant state of flux—are more unlikely to affect the outcome of your probability negatively."

"Good to know," he mumbled, eyes widening to the size of small saucers. "I have to go now."

Then without explanation, he carefully stepped around her athletic physique, avoiding touching any part of her for fear of reawakening his penis, and went inside the grocery store, leaving her to stare questioningly at his retreating form.

With this act of cowardice his suspicions were confirmed. He was a complete moron.

After the morning's unforeseen events, Paul was surprised he'd made it back home before nine o'clock. Not bad for a Sunday morning. He would even be able to arrive on time for his family's Sunday cookout and volleyball tournament.

Wasting no time, he was showered, dressed, and ready to go by nine-thirty. Quickly, he grabbed his keys, wallet, and the fruit salad he made, which was his usual contribution to the Sunday brunch feast, and then made sure to lock the door of his unit securely.

With a spring in his step, he walked to the elevator and within minutes was inside his Acura TSX pulling out onto Wai Nani Way heading to the beach.

"I'm so glad you could make it. When I left you were still snoring away," Noelani teased sweetly while hugging the air out of her best friend's body.

"Thanks for inviting me. Again," Meara's words came out a bit shakier than normal.

"What's the matter?"

"Nothing," she lied as she studied the surrounding beach.

Never in a million years did she expect to be here. In Hawai'i! All around her was soft white sand, aqua-blue water, and warm sunshine making everything seem even more beautiful, more perfect.

Right now, Edinburg would be a cold, wet, dismal place with *crabbit*—grumpy—folk scowling and wishing they were where she was. That thought made her smile.

"C'mon, out with it," her friend prodded.

Exasperated, she sighed then lowered her voice so only her friend could hear.

"Roger called me, again," she confided, her voice laced with unease. "I can't seem to get rid of him."

"As long as he stays in Edinburgh, he can call as much as he wants." Noelani rolled her eyes.

Meara cleared her throat.

"That's the problem," the woman sighed. "He's requesting a transfer to the Oahu branch of his law firm so we can *'fix'* our relationship."

"No, way!" the Hawaiian beauty exclaimed loudly causing some of her family members to turn.

"Yes, way!" Meara returned her horror. Feeling the bile rise in her esophagus, she took another sip of the bottled water Noelani had offered her when she arrived. "I don't know what to do."

"Don't worry," Noelani stated confidently. "I have a family full of huge, muscular men. Navy men. They'll kick his scrawny ass back to Scotland if he steps anywhere near you."

Quickly, she looked around the beach and true to Noelani's words there were at least ten or more large Hawaiian demigods grilling, organizing, and conversing with friends and relatives.

How could so many gorgeous men exist in one family?

Feeling more at ease, she giggled to herself as her friend led the way to the picnic table where all of the ladies were gathered. Believe it or not, the women were even more attractive than the men, if that were possible.

With that said, Meara felt the tension drain from her body. For some reason, the Hawaiian woman always knew exactly what to say to make her feel better. They were the perfect pair: Yin and Yang, hamburgers and French fries, *bangers and mash*.

"Thanks."

"You're welcome," Noelani replied with a gentle squeeze to her forearm.

"Did you leave a fabric swatch on my car this morning, inside a brown paper bag?" Meara suddenly changed the subject.

"No, why?" her partner's eyes narrowed.

"No reason." Meara shrugged it off. "I found it on the hood of my 4-Runner and thought it might be something you wanted to get my opinion on."

Strange.

"Nope." The other woman shook her head. "It wasn't me."

"I wonder who it was." She cleared the image of the beautiful silk fabric that was currently in her vehicle from her mind. *"Ma heid's mince. Am pure done in."*

"Now I know we've been spending too much time together." Noelani belly laughed.

"And why's that?" Meara giggled back.

"Because I understood what you said." Her pal gave her a playful wink.

"By the way, thanks again for the invite."

"Stop thanking me." Noelani pinched her mischievously on the arm. "That's what best friends are for."

"*Aye*... I mean, *yes*." Meara grinned. "They are."

Noelani made quick introductions and immediately Meara felt like an honorary member of the group instead of the girl who kept crashing their functions.

"I love your accent, Meara." Kai Kapahu-Kaplan, Noelani's cousin, complimented as she placed the disposable plates, cups, utensils, and napkins on the table. She was absolutely stunning, but also extremely welcoming. "Where are you from?"

"I was born and raised in Edinburgh, Scotland," she answered shyly.

"Do you miss it?" Mrs. Leilani Kapahu, Kai's mom, inquired as she brought over her world-famous macaroni and cheese, or at least it was world-famous according to the rave reviews Noelani always gave it.

"A little," she admitted. "I miss my family: my mum and dad, and older brothers."

"You're beautiful, Meara. What's your background?" Another lovely Hawaiian, whose name she couldn't remember, interjected.

"My mum's background is West Indian, which, generally speaking, means she's got a bit of everything in her: African, East Indian, and Chinese, but she was born and raised in London's east side. My dad is Scottish."

"No wonder you're so attractive," Kai added, her comment making her blush. "You should have been a model or an actress or something in the media."

"I did do modeling work to pay for university, but I don't like the limelight," Meara stated bluntly. "I'd rather be in the background making sure everything's in order. I guess that's why I love the fashion designing aspect of the industry. Plus, when I get nervous, I tend to be a bit clumsy—"

"A *bit* clumsy," Noelani replied on a snort. "One time Meara almost set an entire medieval castle set on a photography shoot on fire with just a can of hairspray and a dollar-store *Bic* lighter."

Her supposed best friend laughed so loudly all the other women including her, busted into hysterics. It felt good to have a laugh. Even if it was at her expense.

Then the heavenly aroma of well-seasoned meat filled her nose and made her stomach growl loudly. Hearing her complaining tummy, Mrs. Kapahu urged her to help herself, so being polite, Meara helped herself to a plate of macaroni and cheese, grilled sweet and sour chicken, potato salad, and fire-roasted corn on the cob. Seeing her plate, all of the Kapahu or Kapahu-related men stared at her with wide eyes and open mouths.

"What?" she blurted at the entire group; the plastic forklifted midway to her awaiting mouth.

"You eat a lot for such a little person." The Navy SEAL chuckled, but she didn't mind.

"I'm not that little." She blushed, giving a saucy wink.

"You're not that big either," Koa countered with a wink of his own.

"Can I help it if I have a hearty appetite?" She smirked.

"I guess not," Koa added. "But where does it all go?"

"I have a hollow leg." Meara giggled, enjoying the carefree banter. "Does that clear things up?"

"Yes, yes it does." The gentle giant chortled. "Welcome to the Kapahu family. You'll do well."

'This was nice,' she thought to herself then smiled at his reassuring words.

Meara really did miss her family. Her parents, although determined to see her become a barrister, were kind, thoughtful, and most importantly, loving. They would do anything for her. Well, anything except to encourage her dream of being a fashion designer. Her brothers didn't care what career path she followed, they only wanted her to be happy, and designing did just that. It allowed her to be creative, express, and pushed her to think outside the box. It was her passion.

"Look, there's Paul!" Noelani excitedly informed the group as she waved her cousin over, and for some reason, Meara's heart did a little flutter. To cover it up, she took another bite of chicken.

To her delight, the Hawaiian native was striding toward them, casually dressed in navy blue surf-shorts and matching rash guard, looking freshly showered and extremely happy with himself. That is until he locked eyes with her and almost tripped over his own feet. Thankfully, he quickly recovered and sat at the farthest seat from her that he could find.

Sadly, she wondered if the handsome lieutenant just didn't think much of her.

That was just great!

"Paul, you remember my friend from the reception?" Noelani smiled sweetly.

Slowly, he shook his head, but just watched his cousin.

"Yeah," he responded stiffly. "Mia, right?"

"No, her name is Meara," Noelani patiently corrected.

"Good to see you again, Paul," Meara replied, giving her warmest smile.

Paul shook his head.

"Crashing another party, I see."

"Pardon me?" the shocked woman huffed, taken aback by his harsh tone.

"No one even knew you existed until yesterday and now you're an honorary member of the family or something?" He rudely scoffed.

Immediately, Meara's blood pressure rose, and it took all of her self-control not to punch him in the nose.

"Have I offended you in some way?"

"I just don't see why you have to be everywhere, all of the time, that's all," Paul firmly concluded, not fully understanding why he was acting like a complete ass.

"If my presence here is bothering you, then I'll just leave," the furious Scot loudly announced.

"Fine, maybe you should," he agreed, avoiding her poignant stare.

"Fine, maybe I will," she sputtered, her lower lip quivering uncontrollably.

"Great!" His voice rose.

"Fine-bloody-tastic!" Her voice rose too.

Noelani slapped him on the arm, hard.

"What's wrong with you anyway?"

"Ouch! Nothing!" He glared. "I'm gonna get some food before you vultures eat it all."

"Well, *Mahalo* to you too, asshole!" Noelani yelled at his retreating back. "I'm so very sorry, Meara. I've been saying that a lot lately. He's not usually like that. I don't know—"

"Don't worry about it," she interrupted her friend's rant. "It's no big deal."

Then to her embarrassment, she noticed the entire table was gazing at her sympathetically.

"I'm going to take a walk on the beach, burn off some of these calories. I'll be back in a while."

"Do you want some company?" Noelani questioned, watery eyes speaking volumes of her unspoken concern.

Rapidly, she shook her head.

"It's alright," she lied unsuccessfully. "I'm a big girl. Have fun. I'll be back."

The small group watched her trudge away, but she didn't care. She just needed to be alone.

"*What the hell is wrong with you?!*" Noelani hissed through gritted teeth when he returned carrying a plate of lukewarm food.

"What... what did I do?" Paul rested his plate on the table before scooting in beside Aiden at the far end. "Where's your friend Meara?"

"So now you remember her name?" Kai interrogated, both brows arched angrily, fists balled tightly on the table.

"Who said I didn't remember her name?" he chuckled like it was all a joke.

"You said the wrong name on purpose?" Aiden sneered. "Why would you do that?"

"Beautiful girl like that probably needs to be reminded once in a while that she's not the center of the universe."

The young lieutenant grinned smugly, earning a few raised middle digits.

"Believe me, she knows she's *not* the center of the universe," Noelani scoffed in response.

"What do you mean?"

"Her parents are big time lawyers in Edinburgh," his pissed-off cousin explained. "They have their own firm and everything—"

"So?"

"*So*, Meara's older twin brothers, David and Dylan, followed in their parents' footsteps and became attorneys as well. Her parents wanted her to do the same, but she refused."

"Let me guess. She didn't have the grades to get into law school?" He snickered below his breath, and then added. "No wonder she has to look as good as she does. Probably only has her looks to fall back on."

Noelani shook her head no.

"Assume much?" she hissed again. "For your information, Mister Know-it-all, Meara is smarter than you, *'Mister. I-graduated-from-MIT-when-I-was-twenty-then-got-accepted-at-the-Naval-Academy.'*"

With this new knowledge, his whole body tensed as his enraged younger cousin, who was his best friend and who he considered more like a sister, continued her tirade.

"She actually got her B.A. in English at Oxford University when she was eighteen and then was accepted to both Oxford *and* Cambridge University to their law departments... *You dickhead!*"

"Oh."

"Yeah, *'oh'*, she's not some dingbat without any commonsense," Noelani admonished. "And you know what her parents did when she refused to become a lawyer in order to become a fashion designer?"

"What?" he gulped.

Tears welled in his cousin's brown eyes as she sighed, long and hard.

"They disowned her, Paul. They *fucking* disowned her." Noelani sniffled on the verge of tears.

Unfortunately, he didn't see Kai on his right side before it was too late, but her punch landed directly on the back of his shoulder blade regardless.

"*Ouch!*" he yelled. "What the fuck was that for?!"

"You scared her away... *you... big... moron!*"

"How did I scare her away?" His mouth dropped open.

"By being rude and confrontational and just plain... *Mean!*" Noelani continued, flailing her arms. "You're never mean; to anyone. You'd save a poisonous scorpion without blinking an eye, so why are you being so hostile to my best friend?"

"I'm not," he countered, not wanting to be at fault, even though he was.

"You most definitely are!" the woman spat like a viper.

Then, against his wishes, Paul blushed and the whole table, except Noelani, sounded in unison, "Oh!"

"What?" Noelani demanded.

"He likes her," Koa told the table then took a bite of macaroni.

"I don't," he stated calmly, and then realized that his heat was spreading across his features.

"*Brah*, it's written all over your face." The Navy SEAL smirked.

"What?" Paul sputtered indignantly. "You're full of shit!"

"You like her? That's why you're being such a total jerk?" Adrienne asked with confusion. "Why would you do that, Paul?"

That did it. He was done. Done with his family members, and definitely done with the conversation.

"Listen, I don't like her, not like that," he blustered and frowned. "And if I can't eat my food in peace, I'm gonna go home."

Without another word, Paul picked up his plate, walked over to the trashcan to dispose of his half-eaten food, then stormed off toward the parking lot to get his car.

Shit!

When did he become such an asshole?

CHAPTER THREE

The following week went by in the blink of an eye with Information Technology department meetings, APC training for power backup infrastructures, and setting-up new networks along with upgraded PC terminals around the base. Paul was working ten-hour days and was exhausted. Not only from the long hours, but also because of the damn sex dreams featuring Meara every single night.

Even awake, thoughts of her plagued him. He'd be installing a server at work when out of the blue, her face would distract him. Once, he'd almost gotten himself electrocuted when he daydreamed while rewiring a faulty UPS unit. The little minx was driving him to distraction and not in a good way. He was extra grumpy, short-fused, and biting everyone's heads off on a regular basis. Even little A.J. called him a "doody-head" because he accidentally snapped at the boy during a heated game of *Monopoly*.

When the elevator doors slid open on the twentieth floor, his body immediately relaxed at the idea of being in his comfortable one-bedroom unit with the awesome view of East Waikiki Beach. From his balcony, he had an unobstructed view of the Pacific, and it was pure paradise.

"*Shite!*"

He heard a distressed female voice with a foreign accent swearing from down the hallway.

"Bloody! Hell!" The delicate voice swore again, this time the curse was followed by a loud crash.

Instantly, his groin went on high alert, and he knew who it was before seeing her.

Cautiously, he made his way down the tastefully decorated hall to the apartment located three doors down from him. From his vantage point by the opened doorway, he could see the curvaceous creature bent over a broken lamp that must have fallen out of the rather large box she held in her hands.

Paul gulped loudly as his vision was filled with Meara's full, tight ass blocked by her denim shorts. Her plain red tank top hugging pert breasts, which were lovely and ripe and more than a handful. The sight of them made his member grow to painful proportions inside his uniform slacks. If he were braver, he'd walk over, bend her over the arm of the couch and bury his cock to the hilt inside her tight channel. Instead, he cleared his throat hoping to get her attention.

Startled, she turned to face him, and disappointment appeared instantly when she realized it was him.

"Perfect!" She frowned and even that aroused him. "It's you. Well, my day has gone to hell anyway, so why wouldn't I run into you on top of all of this?

She exhaled, sweeping her arms at the messy apartment in front of her.

"Maybe my ceiling will fall in on top of me next."

Simultaneously, they glanced upward at the twelve-foot vaulted ceiling, holding their breath in anticipation. Several tense moments later, they both released their held breaths with relief.

"Did Noelani send you to help me?" The Scottish angel shook her head in disbelief. "I'm not a *quine* who needs help. I mean *a young girl*, especially from the likes of you, Lieutenant Choy. So, if you don't mind, please leave before I *skelp* you."

"Before you do what to me?" His brows rose in confusion.

Meara grimaced.

"*Skelp*... it means *smack*; leave before I *smack* you. Do you understand now, ya bastard?"

Jeez! Her accent was getting thicker the angrier she became.

Suddenly, Paul felt guilty. Sadly, a lot guilty for verbally attacking her the last time they met. It was obvious she needed help. Regrettably, she just didn't want it from him.

"Noelani didn't send me," he clarified, inching forward with his hands up in case she struck. "I live in this building, three doors down on the left, unit twenty-thirty-three."

"What are the odds of that?" Meara rolled her eyes in frustration laughing in a maniacal way that made him want to run away screaming. "Now I know I'm being punished."

"Meara—"

Before he could finish his sentence, she held up her hand like a police officer stopping traffic.

"Don't say another word," she implored. "Just leave me to it. I'll be alright. Thank you."

Then the stubborn female turned her back on him, giving him another mouth-watering view of her backside. His cock hardened a little more and he prayed the insufferable appendage wouldn't break the zipper.

With a solemn expression, she turned to glare at him over her shoulder.

"Please," she begged almost on the brink of tears. "Please, just go away."

"No," he refused calmly, watching her toffee irises grow darker.

Suddenly, she sat down on the floor amidst the broken lamp base, and he worried she would get cut.

"You're right *thrawn*, aren't ya?"

"*Thrawn?*" he pouted; eyes wide. "What does that even mean? Just speak English."

"*Stubborn!* You're *stubborn*, contrary." She sighed with defeat, her expressive eyes glistening with unshed tears.

Finally, he mustered up all of his determination.

"Please forgive me, Meara."

Heat slowly crept across his face, and he knew she could see it.

"I was a total asshole on Sunday," he confessed, still regretting it. "I don't know what came over me."

He lied, trying to spare her feelings. After all, it wasn't her fault her soft, lithe body plagued both his waking and dream world. It was his mistake, and he would never forgive himself for it.

"Will it happen again?" She sniffled.

"I hope not," Paul rambled without thinking.

"Say again?" Meara growled low.

"No, no it will *never* happen again," he promised, crossing his heart, and holding up the *Boy Scout* sign. "I am truly sorry."

And he truly was.

For several long painstaking minutes, she studied him before saying on a sigh, "Apology accepted, Lieutenant."

Then she gave him one of her sweet smiles, warming him from the inside out.

"I'm glad." Paul couldn't help but smile back. "Now, would you like me to help clean-up this mess?"

"*Aye*, yes please," she agreed with a childish grin on her adorable face.

Approximately, two hours later, they had unpacked all of Meara's kitchen and bathroom items as well as rearranged the living room furniture and had even begun hanging a few pictures on the empty khaki-painted walls. Tired, yet content, Paul glanced at the digital display on the microwave. It was almost nine and he was downright starving.

"Do you have anything to eat?" he questioned, as he imagined eating her for dessert.

"I haven't gotten a chance to go out for *messages*," she apologetically informed, shaking her head which caused her high ponytail to swing like a pendulum. "Sorry. I mean... to shop for *groceries*, but I do have granola bars and some Tic-Tacs in my purse."

He groaned at the idea of eating that for dinner.

"No worries. I have leftovers in my fridge if you want to have something better than... those," he teased, grimacing at her choice of pantry staples. "It won't take long to heat up."

She agreed without argument before grabbing her door keys and following him up the hallway to his unit. Quickly, he unlocked the door, turned on the foyer light, and ushered her inside ahead of him. His eyes instinctively dropped to her luscious swaying derriere as she strolled.

Jeez!

He subtly adjusted his crotch.

He was going out of his mind!

Opening his refrigerator, he notified her of their dinner choices.

"Would you like moo goo gai pan, teriyaki beef, or fried shrimp?"

Happily, they decided on all three accompanied by a green salad and a bottle of white wine. While he rummaged through the fridge for the salad ingredients, he watched as Meara wandered around his living room taking in his décor, or lack of décor in his case.

"Well, what do you think?" he dared ask.

"Pardon?" Confusion spread across her beautiful face.

Mischievously, he chuckled under his breath at her unease concerning the loaded question. The condominium unit was a haven for mismatched, hand-me-downs and flea market finds. Nothing he owned could even be called eclectic or shabby chic. It was a home decorator's worst nightmare come to life. The only saving grace of the entire space, in his opinion, was the bobble-head collection of famous sports icons like Joe Namath, Michael Jordan, Kobe Bryant, and Muhammad Ali to name a few. They were his pride and joy.

"What do you think about the apartment?" he clarified.

"It's extremely... *clean*... and... *well organized*." A blush appeared on her bitable cheeks as she spoke.

It was his turn to feel uneasy.

"So, you *don't* like how it's decorated?"

"I do." She smiled, looked away quickly, and then stopped dead in her tracks before she continued. "But I hate the doll collection."

He gasped with mock indignation.

"They're not dolls," he clarified with a roll of his eyes. "They're *action figures*."

Then quite unexpectantly, mimicking him, Meara rolled her eyes at him in that way he was beginning to adore.

"Do you need some help preparing the salad?" she questioned, changing the subject. "Tell me what you want me to do."

That was definitely a loaded question.

Would it be inappropriate for him to say, "Get naked and let me have my wicked way with you?"

He assumed it would be.

"How about chopping the cucumbers and carrots?" he finally asked after careful consideration.

"I can do that." Meara sauntered past him, her butt accidentally brushing his hip as she maneuvered around him in the small, galley-style kitchen. Immediately, his semi-hard cock turned into a full-blown hard-on, and he groaned under his breath at the painful ache. Thank goodness the little she-devil hadn't noticed his condition.

Less than five minutes later, they were sitting at the small dinette eating Chinese food, drinking wine, and talking about everything from the Super Bowl to the current state of Western Civilization. It floored him to know that someone who looked so magnificent could also have such an incredible brain.

Paul was hooked.

"Mmm," Meara moaned, as she rested her fork on her now empty plate. "I never knew leftovers could taste so good. What Chinese restaurant did you purchase this from?"

"Tim-Tam's." He grinned, wiping his mouth with a paper napkin. "It's on the west side of town."

"How did you find this place in a city that has hundreds of Asian restaurants?"

"I didn't exactly find it." He chuckled. "My cousin Keanu owns it. Pretty good, right?"

"It's better than good, it's *bloody fantastic.*" She licked her lips of the sauce, the motion doing strange things to his libido. "I don't know what I would have done if you hadn't stumbled upon me. I've never had a knight in shining armor rescue me before."

She giggled, and the sound reawakened his member like a bolt of lightning.

"Maybe, we could do it again," the hopeful man eagerly suggested. "You know when you're not busy or whatever?"

Her eyes narrowed playfully.

"Maybe, since it's Saturday tomorrow, you could help me with my apartment and then we could go out to dinner and a movie, my treat."

"I accept," he replied smiling at her invitation. "But I have to pay."

She was about to argue when he quickly added with a teasing tone. "It's a Hawaiian law punishable by death or dismemberment."

To his delight, she smirked.

"I wouldn't want to break the law now, would I? And I certainly don't want my work visa revoked or get deported back to Edinburgh."

He noticed her drawl was stronger the more at ease she was and that made him smile even brighter.

"Then it's a date."

"I can't wait. I'm so glad I have another *chum*, I mean *friend*, in Hawai'i," she stated sincerely as she began clearing away the dirty dishes and loading them into the dishwasher. "I've been stitched to Noelani's hip for the last month. I'm really tickled to have another bloke to go around with."

Terrific! The woman of his dreams just used the dreaded *'friend'* term to describe *him*.

Alas, a giant red flag shot up. He may not be a playboy, but he knew what it meant when a beautiful woman called you a *friend* and wanted to hang out with you doing platonic *friend* things like dinner and a movie.

It was the kiss of death in the romance department.

Why did this always happen to him?

Marie's Floral Designs

Unique arrangements for that perfect moment

www.mariesfloral.hi

CHAPTER FOUR

"There is no way, no way... that Koa, my cousin, looks like that guy." Paul laughed at his new comrade's comment.

Meara giggled.

"Yes! Koa looks just like *The Rock*.' Tall, full of delicious muscles, beefy all over."

She waggled her brows indecently, which caused his member to stir to life once again.

"I think I just regurgitated my popcorn," he stated with mock disgust. "What about me?"

"What about you?" The saucy minx tilted her head to the side exposing the long, swan-like neck he secretly wanted to run his tongue over. The image of her moaning and rubbing her body against his made him shift in his seat uncomfortably.

Paul struck a pose he hoped looked sexy but settled for cute instead.

"Who do I remind you of? It has to be an actor or somebody famous."

She thought for a moment before speaking.

"I think maybe a young Russell Wong."

"Really?" he mumbled, smiling to himself. "I can live with that."

"Who do I remind you of?" she urged. "Again, it has to be someone famous."

"Katerina Graham," he answered without hesitation.

"Isn't she the witch from The Vampire Diaries?"

"Yeah," he responded, surprised she knew the actress. "You could be her twin. Except you're a little... fuller."

A cute pout appeared on her full, kissable lips.

"Are you trying to say I'm fat?"

"Hell, no!" He blushed. "You're just right."

"I can live with that too." Meara blushed then grinned, and finally laughed a full belly laugh that made him laugh as well.

Not surprisingly, his new next-door neighbor looked radiant in dark-washed jeans, a white peasant shirt with a scoop-neckline, along with black boots. Her hair was curly now, the long silky strands caressing her cheeks and neck every time she turned her head, and the only makeup she wore was lip gloss and even that wasn't needed. Just being near her he felt an unfamiliar ache in his chest but shrugged it off.

Glancing around the semi-crowded bar area, Paul noticed the men around them admired her from afar, silently leering and smiling in her direction. Meara didn't seem to notice them, but acted as though he were the only person in the room. He felt his chest puff up with pride at the thought of her being his for the night, even if it were only platonic.

"I'm having a really great time with you, Paul."

"I'm glad," he blushed. "You probably do this all the time."

"Do what all of the time?" she quizzed; her head tilted again as she waited for his response.

"You know," he sighed. "Go out for dinner dates and what not. Men are probably breaking down your door trying to get you to go out with them."

"I don't go on many dates." She shook her head.

"I find that hard to believe."

"Men don't usually see me," she explained then elaborated when his brow arched almost to his hairline. "They see the outside, a pretty face. They don't normally want to talk with me or get to know me outside of the sheets."

"Why?"

"I haven't got a Scooby," she said with a shrug.

That was all it took to send him almost off of his bar stool in a fit of laughter.

"What did you just say?"

"Sorry," she clarified, grinning. "'*I haven't got a clue!*' Better?"

He shook his head.

"I see," he said with shock. "They're dickheads. There's so much more to you than just your '*pretty face*' and if they're not willing to look deeper, then they're not worth your time."

The sudden grin that took over her features surprised him. The touch she lingered on his arm surprised him even more, but the fact that the simple gesture didn't reduce him to a babbling fool was the greatest shocker of his life.

He cleared his throat then added, "So, not a big dater. Me either."

It was her turn to look surprised.

"I seriously doubt that."

"Why?" he quickly retorted.

"You're a stud-muffin," she sincerely complimented without shame. "No one in her right mind would let you get away."

"You'd be surprised how many women would disagree with you," he insisted, taking a sip of his beverage.

As they sat at the bar waiting for their appetizers, Meara nudged his elbow and nodded to a table nestled in the far corner of the extremely crowded bar.

"Yon lass is admiring you."

Slowly, he looked around, checking each table for an interested woman.

"Where?"

"Near the facilities." She jerked her chin in that direction again, her smile beckoning him to kiss her.

To his amazement, he spotted the female who waved to make sure he noticed—which being a man—he did.

"Not interested."

"Why not?" she huffed with confusion.

"Not my type." He tipped the bartender who earlier had served their drinks then took a long swig of his *Corona* with lime.

"What's your type then?" Meara sipped at her *Guinness* with a splash of cream.

Boldly he studied her up and down, and then looked away when she arched her brow. He wanted to tell her how beautiful she was, how intelligent, how utterly his type *she* was, but instead he took another long pull on his beer and stared down at the bar top. and Meara was his type: long flowing espresso locks, hypnotic toffee-brown eyes, flawless café au lait skin, and a body that could make the Greek goddess *Aphrodite* jealous.

"I don't know, but *she* is not it."

"I don't understand, Paul. She's pretty and she's been givin' ya 'come hither' looks since we sat down."

"No, she hasn't." His face heated as he peeked at the other woman.

"Yes, she has," Meara claimed.

"Doesn't matter," he debated, peering at the brunette who blatantly winked at him. "I've never been good at picking up women in bars. Truthfully, I've never been good picking up women *anywhere*."

"I don't believe ya," his companion said, her soft lilt tickling his eardrums. "You probably have lasses falling at ya feet."

Indignantly, he shook his head and waited as their waitress rested a large platter of hot wings, fried mozzarella sticks, onion rings, and coconut-crusted chicken fingers between them on the bar. They both thanked her before returning to their previous topic.

"It is true." He motioned to the bartender and ordered two bottles of water.

"I dare ya to go over to yon lass and chat her up." His Scottish beauty chuckled before adding, "Get her number."

"No, Meara," he argued, coyly looking over his shoulder at the brunette who was now joined by a slender blonde and a statuesque red head. "It won't end well."

"Of course, it will." She pushed him off of the barstool toward the direction of his prey. "Have faith, Paul. Be confident. Be assertive."

One of his eyebrows arched questioningly.

"Just do it," she ordered with a stern expression.

"Will you stop hounding me if I do?"

"*Aye*... probably... maybe... we'll see.," she speculated with a grin. "Just go over there ya big stud."

He chuckled but did as she said; slowly moving across to the table and his impending doom.

"This is such a bad idea," he thought out loud as he made his way to certain disaster. "Such a monumentally bad idea."

As her chum strolled away from her, she muttered a quick prayer that he would accomplish his task without incident. All she could do was hope, and as Paul approached, the *hen* who was checking him out boldly licked her lips and straightened in her seat thus pushing out her chest to make it look larger than it actually was.

"Good evening, ladies." The overcompensating male winked playfully. "How's it going?"

The sassy dark-haired vixen beamed.

"Great, now that you're here…"

Anxiously, Meara sat at the bar, nibbling on a deliciously crispy chicken finger, watching carefully as Paul made his way across the room looking ruggedly handsome in dark jeans and a plum polo, introduced himself, then sat down at the table with the brunette and her two friends. Everything seemed to be going well, until the woman's mouth dropped open, her eyes widening to the size of saucers, and then she picked up her white wine Sangria and threw it in Paul's face.

"Jeez!" she whispered as Paul came back, tail tucked between his legs, and asked the bartender for several paper towels.

"Are you happy now?" he grilled, glaring at her like she was a right fool.

"What in the name of all that's decent and holy was that all about?"

"I told you." He growled low in his throat. "I can't pick up women. I suck at it as you can plainly see."

She tried holding in her laughter, she really did.

"What did you say to her to make her so upset with ya?" Her eyes started to tear up as silent chuckles shook her entire body.

Finding her amusement addictive, Paul chuckled too, a deep baritone sound that attached itself to her spinal cord, traveled down to her abdomen, and finally rested in her sex.

What the hell was that? Paul wasn't a guy she wanted to *pump*. *Was he?*

No! He was just a sweet guy that she felt comfortable with and who didn't hit on her or try to seduce her. No, she wasn't going to screw this friendship up by adding sex to the mix. Not again. Not ever.

"We were talking. Everything was going well, so I asked for her phone number—like you told me to do—when I saw a pack of cigarettes in her purse. I told her about all of the ingredients in cigarettes and what the side effects are."

"You had to say something else to get such a caustic reaction." Her eyes narrowed.

He rolled his eyes in frustration.

"I also added that smoking causes wrinkles and ages the skin," he replied robotically. "And since I was sitting so close to her, I pointed out that wrinkles were already starting to appear around her eyes and mouth, and that it wasn't attractive."

"You did not say that to her?" She clasped her hand over her mouth in horror.

"I did. I really did." Paul hung his head in dismay. "I didn't mean to insult her. Honestly, I didn't, but as usual my size twelve foot found its way into my mouth."

"Gosh, Paul," she groaned without humor. "Don't you have a filter on that mouth of yours?"

"I do," he replied sadly. "It just turns off when I'm nervous, and I tend to get nervous when I'm talking to attractive women."

"Really?"

He nodded.

"Why didn't you say something before I sent you over there?"

"I tried to, but you wouldn't listen," he huffed with exasperation.

"How do you get dates if you're so nervous?" Logically, she tried to put one and one together, but she kept coming up with three.

"I don't," he stated flatly.

"I don't understand."

Paul leaned in close to her ear; his warm breath caressing her earlobe did strange things to her libido.

"I don't... get dates... *ever.*"

"You've never had a date... *Ever?*" She gasped in horror.

"I had a couple dates in high school, but we ended up as friends."

"And college?"

"Same thing," he replied emptying his beer.

"So, have you ever kissed a girl?"

"Yes and no," he grimaced as he took a bite of a mozzarella stick.

"What do you mean yes and no?" She followed him and dipped her fried stick into the tomato sauce.

Quickly, he finished chewing, swallowed, and then replied.

"Yes, I've kissed girls, but usually only once each. Apparently, I'm not a good kisser," he stated with indignation mixed with a pinch of humiliation. "But they all wanted to be *'friends'*."

Her eyes narrowed.

"Then when do you have... you know... *relations?*"

He was silent.

"Paul," she spoke again. "When do you ever have relations with women?"

The silence was deafening. Suddenly, the realization hit her like a bullet through the brain, and she whispered, "You're still a—"

"Yup, it's a shocker, right? I'm the only living twenty-seven-year-old... you know—"

"Virgin," she concluded.

Paul glanced around hoping no one heard her high-pitched announcement.

"Damn it, Meara! Why don't you say it a tad bit louder? The table all the way over by the front entrance couldn't hear you."

"I'm sorry, Paul, really and truly sorry."

And she really was, with all her heart.

An hour or so later, they left the still packed bar for the comfort of home. In comfortable silence they rode the elevator up to the twentieth floor and reached it at around eleven o'clock according to the dial on her watch. Paul had been relatively quiet the remainder of the night, and she felt like shite because *he* felt like shite.

"I didn't mean to ruin ya evening, Paul." She tried to apologize for the fourth time in an hour, but he kept looking at her so sweetly and that made her feel even worse.

He laughed softly at her discomfort.

"It's alright, Meara."

"Does anyone else know?" she dared to confront.

"Hell! No!" he blustered with shame. "I'd never live it down."

"I see your point," she hummed nervously.

"Will you be going to the volleyball game tomorrow?" He quickly changed the subject.

"Definitely, and you?" She nodded.

"Yes," he beamed. "I'm going."

"Terrific!" A wave of relief washed over her tense limbs when Paul graced her with a beautiful full smile, his chocolate brown eyes sparkling under the soft overhead lighting.

"Do you want to catch a ride with me, save on some gas?"

"That would be perfect." She released a held breath.

Paul stopped at her door, waited for her to unlock it and turn on the lights.

"Well then, goodnight, Miss McBride," he said with a grin. "It's been interesting."

"It certainly has," she responded with heated cheeks.

"Do you want me to check out your apartment?"

She couldn't help the smile he invoked.

"No, I'm a black belt in Brazilian Jujitsu," Meara proudly boasted. "I think I can take care of myself."

"That's cool," he replied with surprise and admiration. "So, you could probably kick my ass?"

"Probably," she teased, earning her a playful elbowing on the arm. "I guess this is goodnight then?"

"I guess so." He cleared his throat awkwardly. "What time should I get you?"

"I'll be ready by ten."

"Great! See you tomorrow morning, ten sharp... wait a minute." He bent to pick up a standard white envelope he had noticed, placed it in her hand, and then waited while she opened it. "This was next to the doorjamb. It has your name on it."

She read it but didn't know what to make of it.

"*Huh.*"

"What is it?" he questioned with concern.

"A welcome to the building card," she said, grinning at the thoughtfulness of building management. "That's sweet. They must give welcome cards to new tenants."

Paul took the envelope from her, examined the card with her name stenciled neatly on the front before handing it back to her.

"I never got a welcome card," he replied, lips pushed out in a faux pout. "I'll have to complain to the manager."

Tiptoeing, she kissed him gently on the cheek, and he automatically blushed.

"Goodnight, Lieutenant Choy."

"Goodnight, Miss McBride." He still stood at the entrance of her door. "I can't leave until you're safely tucked away inside."

"Thanks." It was her turn to blush. "See ya in the morning."

"Aloha."

Meara closed the door, turned the lock into place, and then quickly peeked through the peephole. Paul, true to his word, heard the lock click into place before heading up the hallway to his own place. The soft-spoken Hawaiian was a genuine gentleman, but he was a virginal gentleman at that.

Well, shite!

She'd have to find a way to help him fix that problem.

Aye!

Why didn't she think of it before? Paul would be her project. She would help him catch a girlfriend and lose his unwanted virginity.

Tomorrow, *Project Lieutenant* will begin!

Meara awoke the next morning exhausted. She had lain awake for hours hatching up a plan to transform the shy, under confident Naval officer into the kind of prize women would cut off their own arm to have.

She'd thought of it from every angle and came up with a plan of action. The guy needed a makeover, but she was certain he would have to be convinced to do it.

Exactly on schedule, the clock on her bedside table switched on; reminding her she only had thirty minutes to get ready. With amazing speed she showered, brushed her teeth, combed her hair into a high ponytail, dressed in a navy-blue bikini with matching beach shorts she had designed and stitched, and a white fitted t-shirt… all in less than twenty-five minutes. Her own personal record.

A loud knock on the door announced Paul's arrival.

"You're ready." Surprise filled his voice when the door flung open.

"*Aye*, I am. Good mornin' to ya, Paul!"

"Wow!" he exclaimed with a smirk. "Your accent is really strong this morning." He smiled with approval, which made her smile too.

"I only got a wee bit o' sleep last night 'tis all." She shrugged, wishing she hadn't drunk three cups of espresso.

Amused by her peppy personality, he laughed.

"I think I'm going to have to invest in a Scottish to English dictionary," he joked. "Are you ready to go? I'm starving."

"Me too."

The drive to the beach was made in comfortable silence. They had to make a pitstop at a family-owned local restaurant near the North Shore for a batch of *Spam* musubi which lengthened their trip, but Paul's convertible top was down, and the warm pineapple-scented breeze played with her hair which made her perfectly at ease. It wasn't until their drive back to Waikiki that Meara caught her travel companion watching her intently with sideways glances.

"What?" she blustered, feeling like a sideshow freak.

"It's nothing." The softspoken man deflected.

"Fine, don't tell me." She puffed her cheeks and made a funny face which broke the tension.

"Fine, I won't." He smirked at her frustration.

"C'mon, tell me," she prompted, poking him playfully in his side with her finger.

"You look incredible today." His face gleamed as he took all of her in before blushing.

"Thank you," she responded with a grin. "So do you."

And he did, with his black basketball shorts and his loose-fitting white t-shirt, his brown eyes hidden by a pair of dark *Ray-Ban's*. He looked casual and carefree, not at all like himself.

"Paul?"

"Yeah?"

"I have something to ask ya, but I don't want ya to get *cross* with me," she rambled anxiously.

"Okay," he hesitantly agreed. "What is it?"

"I want to do a makeover on ya." The words came out in a rushed jumble.

"You wanna do *what* to me?" he begged for clarification.

"A makeover, nothing crazy I promise." The female emphasized with her hands. "I'm calling it *'Project Lieutenant'*. Catchy, right?"

Immediately, his brows hitched.

"Is this like the reality show, Project Runway?"

"*Aye*, maybe... kinda," she said semi-confidently. "But instead of making over clothing designs, I'll be making over *you*."

"Why?" Paul glanced at his reflection in the rearview mirror.

"Because I was thinking about your dilemma all last night," Meara sullenly admitted. "And I've thought of a way to catch you a girlfriend."

"Go on." His interest was piqued.

"You're a great guy," she continued. "Smart, sweet, funny. All you need is a little *tweaking* and you'd be fighting women off with sticks."

"Ya think so?" His Hawaiian lilt grew stronger as well.

"Absolutely!" She nodded enthusiastically.

"What do you want to do to me?"

"Style your hair a little—"

"What's wrong with my hair?" He touched his thick, dark locks. The simple motion causing his muscular bicep to flex against the fitted shirt sleeve, which made her mouth water.

Stay focused.

"It's just a bit too short, and the cut does nothing to accentuate your high cheekbones."

As Meara spoke, she simultaneously reached over and touched his hair. It felt like silk between her fingers, and she had to force herself to stop touching it. Realizing that her mind was wandering to inappropriate thoughts starring the handsome Hawaiian demigod beside her, she yanked her hand back to her lap.

"Ok, *aye*, what else?"

"And I want to beef you up a tad."

"Beef me up," he grimaced. "What the hell does that mean?"

She couldn't help the giggle that escaped her throat.

"You'll need to gain a few pounds, not much I promise; only about ten pounds and it'll be all muscle."

"Well," he replied, seeming to contemplate the idea, "I have been thinking about bulking up."

"Great!"

"Next?" he encouraged, liking what he heard so far.

Truthfully, Paul had always wanted to change his *'look'*. His entire life, women always told him how *'cute'* or how *'adorable'* he was, but that's not what a grown man wants to hear. He wanted to turn people's heads. Especially the woman who was currently sitting beside him explaining her crazy scheme.

"Have you ever considered contact lenses instead of your glasses?"

"Actually, I have some at home," he warily confessed.

"Why don't you wear them?" The Scottish beauty gently smacked his thigh. "They would really show off your eyes."

"I'm always running late, so I can't be bothered," he huffed.

With his new role as chief engineer of the I. T. department on base, he was always going in early and working late. During base inspections, he would often work a sixty-hour week instead of the usual forty. It was grueling, but if he wanted to move up the ranks, he would have to make a few sacrifices.

"Good to know, but I think you should start wearing them, at least during the week."

"Let's hear the rest," he prodded eagerly.

"I want to get you some different clothes, ones that show off the merchandise better."

"Please clarify, Miss McBride."

"You have a great body, lean and sculpted, but you wear such poorly fitted clothing no one can really tell what you've got under the hood."

Meara was correct about that point. He hated shopping, especially for clothes. It had been months since he had purchased anything new to wear, and he had to admit he needed a new updated wardrobe.

"Is that so?" He laughed. "But you can see what's under the hood?"

"Of course," she responded, sitting straighter. "I'm a trained professional. I dress people for a living."

In fact, she had designed and stitched her first formal gown at the age of ten for her *Barbie* doll to attend the toy's first masquerade ball. Her *Ken* doll also got a new suit for the event, but her paternal grandmother ended up finishing it for her. Apparently, a tuxedo has a lot more difficult elements to it.

"I like everything so far," Paul agreed with a nod.

"Bloody fantastic!" she replied, feeling happier than she had when she woke. "There's one more thing."

"Damn! What else can there possibly be?" He rolled his eyes. "Do I have to pluck my eyebrows or something?"

"Yes, but that's not what I was thinking of."

He frowned, still touching his thick, dark brows longingly.

"I want to give you lessons." She held her breath, waiting for his reply.

"*Lessons?*" His lips thinned into a harsh line. "What kind of *lessons?*"

"Picking-up *hens* lessons."

"What the hell are you saying?" He grumbled in confusion. "What the hell kind of '*hen*'? Like a parakeet or chicken or something?"

"A '*hen*' is just slang for a female." She nervously laughed.

"No," he snapped, calmly shaking his head.

"Why not?"

"No," he repeated in a firmer tone. "It's too weird."

"I only want to teach you how to talk to women, how to charm them, how to kiss them and how to... make love to them."

Her voice trailed off and she felt her face heat.

Dumbfounded, Paul was shocked into silence. As his mind spun, his eyes darted from her to the road then back to her again. White knuckled, he clutched the steering wheel and kept swallowing what little saliva he had in his mouth until she thought he might pass out.

"Paul, talk to me," she pleaded, wondering if she had gone too far. "What are you thinking?"

After a long uncomfortable moment, he answered.

"Have you been smoking crack?"

"No!" she shouted in horror and slapped his right forearm. "You're such a *wanker*—"

"And I think you're insane," he interrupted with wide eyes. "I think you've gone out of your ever-loving mind. I think you need to be fitted with a straight jacket."

"So, you want to stay a virgin *forever?*" she countered sarcastically, and she knew she had won the battle. "Is that what you're saying?"

There was a lengthy, pregnant pause as the man driving mulled over her proposal in his mind. Finally, after several more tense minutes he spoke.

"*You'd* be giving me these lessons?" Paul clarified, wanting to make sure he had heard correctly and was not just hallucinating.

"If that's alright, of course?"

Some emotion passed over his face, but he quickly covered it up.

"Of course, *Sensei.*" He grinned like *Dr. Suess's* Grinch as he swindled the 'Whos down in Whoville' out of their Christmas presents. "Go ahead and mold me into your finest pupil... into *a sex Ninja.*"

All she could do is roll her eyes before staring back out at the rolling pineapple fields.

"For heaven's sake. This is going to be one hell of a long project."

"The *'project'* wasn't my idea, remember?" he smugly reminded.

"There is one last, final, miniscule, little thing," Meara added with hesitation.

"I'm afraid to ask." He stared at her suspiciously. "What is it?"

"I need to see how you kiss," she stated under her breath then turned away.

"Why do you need to know *how* I *kiss*?" His voice dropped an octave, and he began squirming uncomfortably in his seat.

"Because..." she began. "I need to know what I'm working with. How much help you need."

"I guess that makes sense." He grinned mischievously as he pulled over to the shoulder of the road, shifted his car into 'park', and turned off the engine, before getting out and moving around to her side.

"Why are you stopping? Is something wrong with the car?" she asked, looking around with confusion.

"No," he replied opening the passenger door, and then diligently helped her to her feet. "You said you needed to kiss me to see what you will be working with, didn't you? Well, there's no time like the present."

I didn't mean right this minute." Her words were almost too low to hear.

"C'mon, Meara," the lieutenant blatantly coerced. "I need to know how much practice I'll need. It's for research."

The man was smart. Too smart. She couldn't argue with his logic. It was obvious that she was being hoodwinked.

"I guess that makes sense," Meara grumbled as she realized she had lost control of the situation. "Alright, let's do this."

"Let's," was the last word she heard before Paul's head descended to hers and then he kissed her.

Warm lips were everywhere at once causing her body to pulsate with pleasure. He was slow, gentle, and for a novice he was surprisingly skilled as he angled his head for better access. She didn't know what to do with her hands, so she leaned against the smooth metallic surface of the car and pressed both palms against it. Trying to curb the sudden impulse she felt to pull him back into the car and ride him like a Brahman bull.

Then suddenly, he pulled back a few inches.

"Am I doing this the right way?" His genuine sincerity overwhelmed her overactive mind.

"Uh huh," she moaned without thought, her voice weak with need as her body came alive. "Try to loosen up a bit. Other than that, you're doing great."

Satisfied at her assessment, he smiled an innocent boyish smile that tugged at her heart.

"Alright."

Then he gently leaned her against the car and took her mouth once again. His lips touched hers, and his large, slightly calloused hands reached up to cup her face; instinctively she wrapped her arms around his slim waist. The unhurried teasing touch of his mouth soon had her moaning and rubbing against his muscular chest.

"Still alright?" he queried, this time only pulling away a few centimeters, his soft full lips brushing over her mouth.

"A little tongue would be nice, if you want to try—"

Before she finished her sentence, he was back, pushing his tongue against the seam of her now swollen lips, demanding entrance. Somewhere in the distant corners of her brain she heard Paul growl low in his throat. The sound causing moisture to pool in her sex. Her traitorous clit pulsed and throbbed for release as she tried desperately not to grind their groins together.

Mindlessly, she opened for him. His talented muscle slipped inside the wet heat of her mouth, licking, and tasting and nipping, driving her out of her mind. Unable to continue, breathlessly, she pushed him away, but managed to smile when he gave her a quizzical stare.

"Did I do something wrong, Meara?"

In a daze, she shook her head.

"No, you actually did *everything* right." Her words were choppy and raspier than usual like she had just jogged a mile up hill.

"Glad to hear it," he stated playfully. "Now, I think we should go before we miss the entire brunch."

Gallantly, Paul helped her back into the vehicle before getting in himself, all the while assessing her as he started up the Acura.

"You look a little flushed."

"Am I?" Meara touched her palms to her cheeks to feel for heat, then fibbed. "It's quite hot today. Don't you think?"

He chuckled in that sexy way she was beginning to love.

"Yeah." His knowing gaze raked her suggestively from head to toe. "It's definitely been a *hot* day."

Completely embarrassed, she groaned, rested her head back onto the cool leather headrest, closed her eyes, and took a deep, cleansing breath.

Yes, it was certainly going to be an extremely long project.

CHAPTER FIVE

Two months later...

"Paul, hurry up!" Meara ordered while glancing at her watch for the tenth time in twenty minutes. "You're walking like a senior citizen and you're gonna miss your appointment."

The irritating male had been dragging his feet all morning. Making up excuses for why he couldn't go shopping. First, he said he didn't get enough sleep and was too exhausted to walk. Next, he pulled a hamstring when he was working out at the gym. The most inventive excuse, however, was one of his bobblehead action figures was missing and he believed that someone had broken into his home and stole it while he was at the gym.

When she questioned if anything else was taken, he simply shrugged his shoulders, and stood looking guilty and out of excuses. At that point, she was so annoyed that she scolded him like a little boy, and practically dragged him out of the door. Right now, she only wanted to get it over with and go out to lunch.

"That's fine with me," he stated matter-of-factly. "I can't believe you're making me do this."

Annoyed by his hostile tone, she planted her hands on her hips.

"Do you want a girlfriend or not?"

The insufferable man actually had to think about it.

"I guess so."

"Then you have to get those *Chia-pets* you call eyebrows threaded," she delivered her retort, trying not to lose her composure.

Paul's right hand moved toward his right brow but stopped a few inches before it landed. Then he stood, glancing between the salon entrance and the mall exit. Meara could only guess that he was about to make a run for it. Thank heavens she was wearing flats.

"Is it going to hurt?"

"No," she fibbed then began motioning him to move.

"Meara?" Both eyebrows now arched to almost his hairline in disbelief.

"Maybe," she amended, not wanting to lose his trust. "But it's nothing you can't handle."

"I'll be the judge of that," he grumbled then took a deep breath.

"Look." She led him to a video of a threading session on a monitor near the entrance of the salon. "This is exactly how the technician is going to do it."

Paul stood staring at the monitor, and then looked through the glass doors of the salon at a lady getting the same procedure done.

Unfortunately, the older woman was wincing painfully with each hair pulled.

Without a word, Paul turned on his heels and started walking toward the parking lot.

"Where are you going?" She ran after his retreating form. "We made a deal. You promised to follow my instructions to a tee."

"But you failed to mention that pain would be involved," he frowned.

"But you're in the military for Pete's sake," she reminded as she pushed him from behind toward the storefront.

"I'm an I. T. geek, emphasis on *I. T.*" He suddenly spun around to face her. "I'm not a SEAL like Koa."

Feeling sympathetic to his plight, she took his strong hands in hers.

"Paul, this is the home stretch. You've bulked up with ten pounds of pure muscle. Your hair has grown out and we're getting it styled today. Then I'm taking you shopping." She pouted playfully at his darkening eyes.

"I can't believe I let you talk me into this," he sighed.

"I promise... this is the home stretch," she repeated for emphasis. "I'm so proud of you. This is gonna get you a girlfriend. I can feel it my bones."

"On one condition." Dark eyes twinkled under his thick, black lashes.

"Anything." Meara crossed her heart.

"You haven't given me my touching lesson, my talking lesson, or my making love lesson."

She gulped, hard.

"Fortunately, you only needed one lesson at kissing, so I figured you could wing the rest of it."

"I don't think so," he disagreed, making a stand. "Kissing you at the side of the highway wasn't a *lesson*."

"Paul, you promised to do this," she whined with exasperation.

"I'll do it if you give me another lesson."

"This is blackmail," she hissed her words through clenched teeth.

"Meara, Meara, Meara." He lowered his voice to that dark, seductive timbre that dampened her panties, and made her breathe harshly. "Blackmail is such an ugly word, but in this case it's totally accurate. I'm not doing anything else if you don't agree."

Then the manipulative donkey of a man, crossed his muscular arms over an impossibly well-chiseled chest, reminding her of an unmovable mountain of granite, and refused to budge no matter how hard she pushed.

Frustrated, she looked at her watch, making a mental note of the time slipping away as they stood in the middle of the mall negotiating.

"Okay," she agreed. "I give up."

The man was becoming a master manipulator where she was concerned.

"You'll have another lesson later tonight."

He smiled, touched her right earlobe before bending to her lips and giving them a feather-light touch with his then quickly took her hand in his before she could protest.

"No welching either," he reminded sternly. "Or the deal is off."

"I agree," she whimpered against her will. "Now, get your *arse* in that salon and suck it up."

"*Arse?*" he asked.

"*Ass*, you're a big ass, better?" She wanted to kill him and throw his limp body into the Pacific.

"I think I prefer *arse* instead." He laughed when she pointed him in the direction of the salon and followed behind him, watching his delicious arse fill-out his faded blue jeans.

"Mmm," she moaned quietly.

"Did you say something, Meara?"

"No, I was just complaining about your behavior, that's all," she lied. "Hurry up!"

He mock saluted with his free hand, and then went into the salon holding onto her other hand the whole time.

As they entered the posh establishment, she noticed another message had been delivered to her voicemail; checking quickly she realized several of the messages were from potential clients, her parents, and her *bampot* ex-boyfriend.

"Paul?"

"Yeah?"

"Do you mind if I stay out here? I need to return a few phone calls."

"Is everything alright?"

"Of course," she answered calmly, even though the butterflies in her stomach said otherwise. "Could you come get me when you're finished with the threading and the hair cut? I've already spoken with Justin over the phone about what I want to be done. Don't worry. He styles my hair and always does a fantastic job."

"I'd rather you be in there with me," he explained nervously.

"Please, this is important too."

He frowned, but nodded and released her hand.

"Wish me luck."

"You don't need luck." She laughed. "See you in a bit."

And he didn't need luck. That she knew for sure.

An hour and a half later, an attractive stylist in his mid-forties came to collect her from the bench in front of the storefront Paul was currently getting coiffed.

"Miss McBride," the man smiled warmly, his French accent reminding her of Koa's new wife, Adrienne. "He's ready for you. Please, follow me."

Filled with anticipation, she smiled back.

"How did he do?" Her heart was beating a million miles an hour at the thought of seeing Paul almost fully transformed.

"He did better than I anticipated," Justin jested, chuckling gleefully. The rich sound easing her nervousness. "Sit right here and I'll get him."

Then he motioned to a plush, white leather sofa in the salon's waiting area.

"Thank you."

"It was a pleasure, Miss McBride." The stylist winked playfully as he turned to leave. "I think you're gonna be surprised."

It was several more moments before Justin reappeared followed by someone who could have graced the cover of *GQ*, *Playgirl*, or *People Magazine*. The demigod was tall, olive-skinned with dark hair and dark eyes. With a newfound air of confidence, he entered the main lobby of the beauty salon and every female within fifty yards stopped, gawked, and listened as the mouthwatering male specimen spoke.

"What do you think, Meara?" Paul turned slowly to give her a view of his new 'do' from every angle. "Do you like it? If not, I'm gonna be really pissed."

Meara sat still.

Unable to blink.

Unable to respond.

Unable to stop the drool that was threatening to roll down her chin.

"Uh... uh huh," she sputtered. "Holy, shite!"

At her obvious approval, he blushed in that boyish way that had her insides melting. She was speechless. Utterly. Unequivocally. Unquestionably, and without a doubt... speechless!

"I'll take that as a yes," the gorgeous male commented. "C'mon, I'm starving." With that said, he grabbed her gently by the wrists, and helped her to her feet which were slightly wobbly.

"Wow!" she muttered at the Hawaiian heartthrob standing in front of her looking too magnificent to be real. He laughed this time, loudly, and led her out of the salon.

Paul liked Meara's reaction to his new and improved look. No! He *loved* her reaction to his new and improved look. Apparently, other women seemed to like it as well including the waitress currently filling their water glasses and taking their lunch orders, the hostess who seated them, and several women seated at the surrounding tables that winked, waved, and stared at him.

But the only person he wanted to impress was currently sitting in front of him texting furiously, trying not to look at him.

"Something wrong, Meara?"

The usually poised female seemed flustered, not at all like her upbeat self.

"Sorry," she apologized mechanically. "Nothing's wrong. Just *hoachin', ken.*"

"I need a translation," he requested with a grin. "I'm at a loss with your Scottish slang."

"Oh," she responded without even a glance upward. "*Hoachin'* is very busy, and *ken* means *'you know'*."

"Could you please look at me?" he commanded, satisfied when she put down the phone and looked him directly in the eyes, toffee to chocolate brown. "I don't believe you. The vein near your right temple has been throbbing since the moment we sat down. What's wrong?"

The lovely, but distracted nymph sighed, the sadness making his heart ache.

"It's my parents," she finally confided with a huff. "They want me to move back to Edinburgh and stop living this *'fairytale of being a clothing designer.'* Their words, not mine."

"What do *you* want to do?"

"Design clothes." She beamed then frowned. "Make people over, make them feel more confident and alive. What's so bad about that? The world has enough lawyers in it. One less won't make a difference."

"I think you should do whatever makes you happy," her lunch companion wholeheartedly agreed. "Life's too short to waste it doing something you hate."

Finally, she exhaled the breath he didn't know she was holding, and he felt himself relax along with her.

"You always put me at ease." Meara sighed. "I appreciate it, more than you'll ever know."

"Enough of that young lady." He blushed as he scolded, his tone playful. "I wonder what's good on the menu."

"I can tell you what today's special is," she responded with a giggle.

"Really?" He glanced toward the *'daily special'* board near the front entrance. "I didn't see anything listed when we were waiting in the lobby."

That made her giggle like a toddler, sweet and innocent.

"Today's special dish is *Paul* with a giant helping of *Paul* and a *Paul*-cake for dessert."

"Funny," he grunted sarcastically. "Real funny, Whoopie Goldberg."

"Dat's nah nice atall!" She smacked his arm hard, her accent severe.

"Are you ready to order?" the perky blonde waitress, Becky, asked them both, but only made eye contact with him.

"I'll have a turkey burger with sweet potato fries and an unsweetened iced tea," he began. "And the lady will have the same except she'll have a sweet tea instead. Thanks."

"No, thank *you*," Becky flirted a little too playfully and he winced uncomfortably.

During his conversation with the waitress, he noticed Meara's cell phone was vibrating. The motion causing that same vein at her temple to jump in agitation.

"Who is that?"

She grimaced and hit the ignore button on the device.

"It's no one."

"Bullshit," he mumbled.

"It's my ex-boyfriend," Meara admitted with heated cheeks. "The one I told you about."

"The ex who cheated on you with a slew of women, and now wants you back, *that* asshole?"

"Yes, that's the one." Her voice was almost a whisper. "I think he's been calling my condo late at night and then hanging up, or just breathing into the phone. It's bloody unnerving. I haven't been able to sleep well."

The cell phone began vibrating again.

"Do you want me to answer it?" Paul volunteered, seeing her obvious distress.

"No! Heaven forbid, no!" she whisper-squealed in mortification. "It'll just make things worse."

"How will it make things worse? Has he been harassing you?"

When she didn't respond, he seized the pulsing phone and hit accept. She gasped at his action, but at that moment he was too angry to care.

"Aloha," he answered calmly like it was within his right to pick up his friend's phone.

"Who the hell is this?" The gruff male voice with the thick Scottish brogue barked on the other end.

"This is the new man in Meara's life."

What? It wasn't a lie.

"Who the hell is *this*?" Paul replied, staying as relaxed as possible.

"This is Roger McVicor III. Meara's my girlfriend, soon to be fiancé, and you, sir, need to remove yourself from this situation before I remove you myself," Roger threatened. "And I can assure you, it won't be a pleasant experience... for *you*."

Both of Paul's brows arched at the unexpected threat.

"Pay attention, you arrogant, cheating, lying, prick. If you come near her again, I'll kick your pretentious ass all the way back across the pond. I hope that's clear enough for you."

Then with a steady hand, he hung up the call and blocked the number from her phone.

Meara could only stare at him but did not say a word.

For the rest of their time at the mall, Meara was unnaturally quiet, and he wanted to apologize for his behavior at lunch, but he didn't think he should have to. After all, he was only looking out for her best interest. Roger McVicor III was a menace to society and she shouldn't have to put up with his shite... *shit... whatever!*

The first store they stopped at was *The Gap*. There, they purchased several pairs of jeans and dress pants along with a couple of button-down shirts in varying styles and colors. At Meara's request, he tried each one on before he purchased them since his body was larger now with more muscles than before. She even made him model each pair for her. Her eyes glimmering with some emotion he wasn't familiar with.

Longing? Lust maybe? Thinking it was absurd, he shook his head trying to get the idea out of his mind.

"What about these?" He questioned coming out of the changing room stall wearing the last pair of black jeans in his size. "How do I look?"

"Delicious, absolutely scrumptious," the words seemed to rush out of her mouth, and she clapped her hand over her mouth, obviously embarrassed. He laughed at her outburst.

"I'm glad you think so," he chuckled, feeling proud. "I'll take them."

He paid for the items and obediently followed her to their next stop. Unlike him, Meara looked business-like, but charming in a gray pinstripe pencil skirt, red sheer blouse, and red strappy wedge sandals. Her face was free of makeup and her hair was up in a tight bun reminding him of a naughty librarian. All she needed was a pair of dark-rimmed glasses, a ruler, and a stern look on her face to complete the look.

They visited several different department stores and ended up with three full bags of clothes. He didn't mind though. He hated shopping. In truth, he hadn't bought new clothes in a couple of years, and he enjoyed having the beguiling Scot to guide him.

Along the way, the pair conversed, laughed, and made fun of each other. It was like being with someone he'd known for decades rather than a few measly months.

"Are we done yet?" he consulted, hoping to spend a little more time with her.

"I wanted to get you some new shoes, but if you're tired, we can call it a day—"

"It's fine," Paul cheerfully interrupted. "I'm enjoying myself. Usually, I avoid the mall like the plague, but with you it's kinda fun."

It wasn't a lie.

"Thanks." She blushed. "I'm having fun too."

"Paul!" A high feminine voice with a strong Hawaiian lilt called out. "Meara!"

"Damn it!" He winced.

His stunning shopping buddy glanced over her shoulder to see her best friend and business partner running toward them holding a piece of paper in her hand.

"It's only Noelani," she stated the obvious, unclear of his worried expression.

"I don't want people, especially my family members, to know about our arrangement."

"Gotcha," she acknowledged with a stoic face.

"I've been trying to find you two all afternoon," her best friend announced rather loudly.

"And found us you have," Meara greeted sweetly, glancing over at him. "What's up?"

Noelani did a double take before squealing, "Freaking hell! Paul?! You look *hot*!"

"Thanks." He blushed at his cousin's shocked declaration.

"What did you do to yourself?" His cousin circled him as she took in his new and improved look.

"Nothing much, just a haircut—"

"Did you get your eyebrows shaped?" Noelani cut him off in mid-explanation.

"What if I did?" He scowled, ready to deflect any negative comments.

"It wasn't a jibe. It looks really... *hot*!" She swallowed, hard. "If we weren't related—"

He winced like she had physically struck him.

"Gross!" Paul grimaced and pretended to gag. "I think I just threw up in my mouth. Don't finish that sentence."

"We got it! We got the contract!" Noelani squealed again as she turned back to Meara with a flourish of hands and arms,

"Are you joking?" Meara squealed as well. "You better not be joking! If you are, I'll give you a good thrashing."

"I'm not!" the other woman promised. "We just got a fax saying British Vogue Magazine wants to feature our designs in next month's special edition. *Gal Gadot*, *Chrissy Teigen* and *Beyonce* will be modeling our creations! Can you believe it?!"

"No, I can't believe it!"

In the middle of the crowded mall, Meara and his cousin were jumping up and down like they were on an invisible trampoline. Just like a dude, his eyes automatically shifted to Meara's breasts which made his cock immediately harden. As discreetly as possible, he situated the shopping bags in front of his misbehaving member.

"This will put us on the fashion map, but we'll be busy. Really busy." Noelani gave them a brief rundown on the specifications for the magazine spread. "So, they want the preliminary sketches and pictures scanned and emailed back to them by Monday evening. We'll also have to FedEx the clothes they selected early Monday as well."

"Wait, but it's Friday." The woman that he lusted after groaned. "We'll have to work the entire weekend to get everything ready for Monday."

Paul saw her glance over at him longingly but brushed it away as wishful thinking.

"I'm sorry, Paul. We'll have to reschedule our... *lesson* for another time."

"Yeah, the *lesson*. Damn! I was really, *really* looking forward to it." He smirked at the things he wanted her to teach him. "But this is more important. You two go ahead. I'll buy some shoes or something."

"What lesson?" Noelani leered at the two, who both ignored her question.

Meara chuckled at his covertly worded message.

"I'll send a text... to my brother... he'll have to look out for it." She winked, not paying attention to Noelani, who was staring at them both with a weird look on her face.

"The two of you are acting strangely," his cousin stated warily.

"Are we? I didn't notice," Meara lied shamelessly.

"Me either," he agreed.

"Uh, huh." Noelani frowned and shook her head.

Weirdos!

Paul had not seen Meara all weekend. Finally, at the end of the day on Monday, unable to function properly, he made his way to her unit and gently knocked on the front door. Several agonizingly long minutes later, she answered the door wearing only a white, body-hugging, almost see-through tank top, and incredibly short, ridiculously tempting, black and white polka-dot boy-shorts. The sight of her standing in the doorway, looking like she'd just awoken made his cock harden uncomfortably.

"I'm sorry. I didn't mean to wake you," he apologized, backing away.

"It's alright." She yawned and stretched her toned arms above her head, the movement calling attention to her tightly beaded nipples. The sheerness of the well-worn garment allowing him to see the outline of her dark areolas through the thin material, he couldn't help but groan at the sight.

Meara must have realized what he was staring at and quickly covered herself by folding her arms across her chest.

"I'll go grab a robe. Come inside, close the door behind you, please," she added as she jogged down the darkened hallway.

A couple minutes later she reappeared wearing a midthigh, blue terrycloth robe. Unfortunately, the shortness of the robe did nothing to alleviate his arousal. Unsure of what to do or what to say, he stood there looking uncomfortable and guilty.

"How are you?" Meara questioned as she sat down on the sleek black leather sofa and patted the cushion next to her for him to sit. "Sorry I haven't contacted you, but your cousin and I have been swamped."

"No, worries," he mumbled, before glancing around the room at her neatly organized space.

Their units were identical, but Meara's place looked as if an interior designer put it together. Her taste was clearly contemporary, yet comfortable with neutral pieces and colorful accessories. Unlike his place which screamed fraternity house reject with mismatched furniture from his dad and flea market finds.

"I figured you would be busy getting ready for the British Vogue article."

"We got everything done this afternoon and were finally able to come home. I've been sleeping at the boutique for the last few nights." She yawned again. *"Am pure done in."*

"Does that mean 'you're tired'?" Paul smirked, and she nodded.

He couldn't help laughing at her strengthening brogue. Then he held up a generic take-out bag.

"I come bearing dinner," he announced. "If you're too tired to eat, I can leave it and you can have it in the morning for breakfast."

"Mmm," she moaned taking the bag from him. "I'm famished. I'll get us some plates and utensils. Could you get us drinks?"

Eagerly, he walked over to the fridge trying not to look at her ass swaying beneath the robe.

"What would you like? Water, juice, or soda?" he asked, clearing his throat.

"I'll have water, please."

"One water coming up," he repeated, returning with a bottled water and a diet soda.

"Is this from Keanu's restaurant?"

"Yup, I picked-up our usual—"

"Moo goo gai pan, teriyaki beef, and spicy fried shrimp," Meara moaned with delight, the sound making his balls tighten in his khakis.

"Of course." He smiled; their light-hearted banter lessened the ache in his groin.

All through dinner, they chatted incessantly about events during their time apart. He had to concentrate harder than usual to keep his eyes on hers when all he wanted to do was stare at her chest. Meara didn't notice as she told him about the upcoming interview with the world-famous magazine. She was deliriously thrilled, and he was thrilled for her.

"I've missed you," she stated matter-of-factly, the words rushing out of her mouth in a rush.

"I'm glad I'm not the only one going through withdrawal," he teased mischievously.

She laughed then rested her hand on his. The errant appendage in his pants woke up instantly from her gentle touch.

Damn it! Why did she just want to be friends?

After dinner, he helped her clean-up and then curled up on the couch beside her, watching a rerun of *True Blood* on *HBO*.

"This is one of my favorite episodes," he said to himself.

She agreed and then the volume on the television was muted. A bit confused, he glanced up to see her watching him, a wicked gleam in her hypnotic, toffee-colored eyes.

"What happened to the volume?"

"I muted it," Meara purred. The sound catching him off guard.

"Why?" He arched both brows at her declaration.

"I owe you a lesson," she whispered.

He swallowed hard, his hands began to shake, and his mouth suddenly lost all of its moisture.

"Right... the lesson," he practically choked on the words. "Which one are you planning on giving me?"

Please say the lovemaking one. Please say the lovemaking one.

"Let's see," she hummed while moving closer to him. "I think tonight we'll do... *touching*."

Dear father almighty!

The thought of touching her made him nervous and... *well*... anxious.

"Touching, are you sure you're up for it? I mean, you've been working really long hours, and you look really tired."

"*Shh.*" She pressed her finger against his lips. "I'm ready. Are you?"

He took a deep, cleansing breath.

"Please, go easy on me."

Boldly, she crooked a finger at him.

"Come closer."

Holy! Shit!

"I want you to touch me, Paul."

"Consider me your love slave," he whispered, moving closer until their knees touched. The scent of vanilla filling his lungs and making him crazy with desire, and suddenly, he felt lightheaded.

"Pretend I'm someone you're attracted to."

"I think I can manage that." He sighed yearningly.

"A female's body is full of erogenous zones," she informed as she took his right hand in hers and placed it on her ear. "Ears are usually quite sensitive. Sucking on earlobes and nipping the area right below the lobe can be extremely pleasurable."

"That's good to know." His voice was raspier than normal. "What else?"

Next, she put his hand on her neck and using his fingers, traced a line down to her collarbone.

"This area along the slope of the neck, down to the collarbone is also a great place to kiss and lick and nip. It usually drives women crazy."

"Where else... drives you... I mean *women* crazy?"

She smiled before answering.

"Between the breasts... this valley right along the breastbone... is another erogenous area." She took his other hand now and rested both of his hands palm-side down on her firm, full breasts. "These are sensitive too."

His breathing was quickening, and he was about to yell, *'Screw this!'* and just jump her bones, but instead he stayed as still as possible soaking in her words, watching her watching him.

"How do you like them touched?" he asked, trying not to sound like the imbecile he was.

"It depends on my mood actually."

"Can you give me an example?"

Meara giggled and began rubbing her breasts lightly with his hands.

"Sometimes, I like it when they're touched and squeezed gently, licking, and sucking on each nipple. Other times, I like it when they're nipped gently, and then licked to ease the sting away."

"Huh," he gulped down the lump in his throat.

"Other times, I like it a little bit rougher," Meara confessed much to his surprise.

"What do you like then?"

"During those times I enjoy when they get tweaked or pinched, not too hard, but not too soft. It has to be the perfect amount of pressure. Some women can even orgasm just by having their nipples played with."

"Are you one of those women?" He really wanted to know.

"Maybe," she chuckled playfully.

"Tell me more," he begged, watching her guide his hands over her rock-hard nipples. The urge to lean forward and suck the teasing little buds into his mouth, tank-top and all was almost too much to fight. "Your breasts are beautiful. You're beautiful."

He looked into her darkening eyes.

"But I'm sure men tell you that all of the time, don't they?"

The saucy little minx avoided the question, smiling seductively.

"Here," she explained as she slid his hands away from her breasts, heading south over her torso and stomach. "Is another sensitive area."

He gulped.

"Abdomens can be an excellent area to focus on, but just be careful not to tickle; some women don't like being tickled."

"Do you like being tickled?"

She nodded yes before sliding his hands further down, past her cotton-covered mound. He groaned at the thought of what was hiding underneath. Was she shaved completely, or did she have it neatly trimmed? He couldn't wait to find out which.

Finally, she stopped at her inner thighs completely bypassing the area he wanted to learn more about.

"Inner thighs, calves, the soles of her feet, especially the toes, are also areas that can make her go wild. It's a good idea to touch these parts, caress the soft skin there, and run your tongue against the smooth surface."

"I've got it." He inhaled deeply, his senses bombarded with her vanilla scented body lotion and her unique fragrance.

"Next, are the most important areas," she educated, her words sounding slurred with need. Then Meara took his hands and put them on top of her mound over her boy-shorts, moving them in slow, steady circles. "The vagina and the buttocks; stimulate these areas properly and you'll have her like putty in your hands."

"How do I do that?" His eyesight was beginning to blur from his need for release, but he didn't want to stop caressing her.

She smiled before replying.

"You can stimulate these areas with your hands, fingers, mouth, lips, tongue, toys if your lady likes that sort of thing—"

"Do *you* like that sort of thing?" He swallowed, hard.

"Sometimes," she teased wickedly, licking her lips in that all too sensuous way. His already hard cock grew another inch, and he couldn't hold back the groan that escaped his lips.

"Continue," he commanded.

She smiled again.

"Teasing it with the tip of your cock is also a wonderful way to stimulate the vagina."

"How do you mean?" Of course, he had an idea, but he still wanted to hear her say the words.

"Sometimes you can slide the tip against the clit or between the folds." Her eyes closed in a slow blink. "I like that a lot."

"I got it," he panted, feeling tiny sweat beads appear on his upper lip.

"Bottoms," she blushed.

"What about bottoms?"

"I like it when a guy licks me there or fucks me with his tongue."

"Really?"

"Yes, really." She blushed again, and quickly glanced away.

He had to ask, "Has anyone ever fucked your ass, Meara?"

Please say no. The idea of some other guy having that honor made him murderous.

"No." She adamantly shook her head. "I've never had the nerve to try that."

"I see." He studied her expression. "Would you ever try it?"

She shrugged her shoulders.

"I don't know," she awkwardly admitted. "I guess it would depend on how I felt about the guy if I trusted him not to hurt me. You know what I mean?"

"Yeah, trust is a big deal."

"That's everything I can think of," she finished the lesson and released his hands. "Do you have any questions or comments?"

It was now or never.

"I have one important one."

"What's the question?"

"I'm a hands-on type of learner," he began boldly, so unlike himself. "I think I need a practice session. Are you willing to let me practice on you?"

"Umm, I don't... I don't know if that's a good idea." She sat up suddenly, pushing his hands away from her covered mound.

"Do you trust me?" He arched both eyebrows.

"*Aye*, I trust you," she said without hesitation.

"Then let me practice on you" Paul urged. "I promise to stop if you're uneasy with anything I do. Teach me. Tell me what to do. I'm yours to command."

They sat in tension-filled silence as she mulled over his proposal. When he thought she would never answer, a jumble of words rushed past her lips.

"It has to be *over* the clothes," Meara insisted forcefully. "No hands, fingers, tongue, or anything else for that matter, *accidentally* pushing or prodding into any hidden crevices. *Capisce?*"

"I promise," he announced in shock that she was going to let him *'practice'* on *her*. "I'll stay above the clothes... Scout's honor. Unless you beg, then I'm absolved for anything I might push or prod. Deal?"

"Alright, it's a deal." She giggled, the sound going straight to his groin. "Now, let us begin."

CHAPTER SIX

What the hell was she thinking? Better still... what the hell was she doing?

She blamed it on the hot Hawaiian nights, and definitely the hot Hawaiian men. Yeah, that was it. Not to mention all of those scantily clad, hard, fully packed beachgoers she saw everywhere she went, all slick with tanning oils and coconut-scented suntan lotion.

Why didn't the state of Hawai'i have a disclaimer at all of its ports of entry stating: *Hot Hawaiians Here: Guard your personal belongings, valuables, and your private parts with care!*

She'd never... ever... never ever... done anything like this before.

My god, sex lessons!

What crazy island aphrodisiac had they slipped into the Hawaiian water supply? She had half a mind to call *60 Minutes* and ask them to do an in-depth investigation into the problem. Unfortunately, the other half of her mind was currently letting one of the native hotties position her on her brand-new Italian leather couch in order to *practice* his seduction skills on her.

"Where should I start?" Paul queried.

"Start from the head and work your way down," was the only instruction that made sense.

"As you wish," he stated enthusiastically, hands rubbing together like a crazed villain in a silent movie. "Then let the love lessons begin."

Again! What the hell was she thinking?

"Meara," he spoke her name with that mind controlling island lilt. For some reason, the unique accent wreaked havoc on her self-control and her sex, which was currently soaking her boy-shorts.

"Hmm," was the only sound she could muster, considering her first bachelor's degree was in English, it explained a lot about her current state of mind.

"Is this position comfortable?"

She wanted to tell him that he could fold her body in two and wrap her in cling film and she'd still be comfortable, but again all she could do was nod yes.

"Good."

"Paul?" she finally managed a coherent word.

"Yeah?"

"I'm... I'm having second thoughts about this."

"No worries. I'll stop if you want me to," he reassured as he leaned down and placed a chaste kiss on her forehead. The innocent gesture fueled her desire once again.

"Please, could you do it quickly, so I won't have a chance to think about it?" she whispered uneasily.

"Okay," he agreed. "But I want to kiss you first."

She nodded again, her heart threatening to pound straight through her chest.

Without hesitation, Paul bent over and secured their mouths together. The kiss started light. Just an undemanding brush of mouths. She felt him exhale. His warm breath scented by the soda he drank at dinner tickled her cheek and caused heat to stir low in her belly.

"Are you alright?"

She nodded, and released the breath she didn't know she was holding, surprised she hadn't passed out from lack of oxygen. She licked along the seam of his firm lips needing to taste more of him. He gasped and she used it to slip past his lips and into his hot, wet mouth. A strong hand behind the nape of her neck held her firmly against him, their chests crushed together like they had been bonded by *Superglue*.

"I'm not hurting you, am I?" His words escaped like air suddenly spilling out of a deflating balloon.

"No," she managed to say before returning to his mouth.

The moment they were pressed together again, his tongue pushed past her lips, the pink muscles meeting in a slow, wet glide, tasting and stroking and sliding against each other, making her toes curl in response. She moaned into his mouth, the vibration exciting them both, but it was Paul sucking on the tip of her tongue, as if it were the tip of a candy cane, that truly sent her sex into full throttle.

"I can't believe those women told you that you couldn't kiss." Her voice sounded nothing like it usually did. This new voice was much lower and needier than anything she had ever heard.

There must be something in the water.

Paul covered her mouth again, and then pulled away suddenly.

"What should I do next? Do you have a preference?"

"Go... lower," she demanded pushing his rock-hard shoulders farther down her overheated body. "Use your instincts. Do what feels right."

That did it. One minute the man was nervous and wanting directions, the next he was licking, sucking, and nipping a trail from below her ear, down the slope of her neck, over her collarbone until he hovered over her cotton-covered, pebbled nipple.

"May I take this off?" His voice was low, predatory, and laced with lust, and it made her shiver with anticipation.

With that said, her eyes widened as the meaning of what was said sunk into her lust-filled stupor.

"Over the clothes, remember?"

"I need to touch you, skin to skin." Paul took a deep steadying breath before he added. "Please."

She couldn't miss the sound of desperation in his voice or the look of it in his eyes.

"Yes," rushed past her lips before she could stop it.

Quickly, and without indecision, he moved a few inches away from her and pulled the annoying garment up and off, throwing it over his shoulder. Her breasts bounced free, and he groaned, muttering something in Hawaiian, before saying in English, "Holy shit! You're so *fucking* beautiful."

Before she had time to change her mind, he gave the attention-hogging peak a long, moist glide with his wet tongue before sucking it into his humid mouth and laving it with more zeal than it had ever had before. She gasped, unable to stop from arching her body up and grinding her sex against the crotch of Paul's khaki uniform trousers. The hard-as-steel erection she encountered was the size of an over-sized zucchini.

Holy! Moly! Whoever he gave his virginity to, would be more than satisfied. However, the thought of another woman receiving his gigantic *man-part* caused a flashflood of anger to wash over her.

When she moaned her approval, he released the well-sucked peak with a loud, wet pop before attending to its twin with just as much vigor, his free hand pinching and rolling the neglected nipple between his thumb and forefinger. The pull on her nipple shot a current downward to her abdomen and lower to her aching pussy.

"Stop," she gasped, trying to halt the build-up in her sex that was morphing into a familiar sensation that was sure to end in a mind-blowing release. "Stop... you're going to make me come!"

Paul stopped briefly only to say, "That's the whole point, princess. Come for me. Now."

His forceful command pushed her over the edge of the invisible cliff she was teetering on and into one of the most incredible orgasms she had ever experienced. Her sex throbbed, the inner walls of her empty channel clenching and pulsing as if it were expecting to find a cock, but saddened when it didn't.

"*Holy! Mother!*" Her breath left her in short bursts. "That was the best orgasm I've ever had and all you did was play with my nipples."

"So, I get an A," he blushed, smoothing the slopes of her breasts with his palms. The tender act making another rush of liquid desire pool in her sex.

"Mm-hmm," she whimpered against the smooth, tanned flesh of his shoulder. "You get an A plus."

She couldn't hold back the giggle that escaped her throat.

"If there was a higher grade, you'd get that too."

Sitting up, he handed back the discarded tank top laying on the floor beside the couch. She held it against her chest covering herself as best as possible without actually putting it on.

"I better go," he announced his intentions, but hadn't yet moved toward the door.

"Don't go," she pleaded, her voice sounding needier than she liked. "We can finish watching the show."

"If I stay here any longer, I'll want to have my *'love making'* lesson, and I won't want just a pretend session." The man pouted. "I'll want the real thing."

"Certainly, I understand," she whispered, glancing around the room uncomfortably. "I guess you better go then."

He chuckled at her disappointed tone.

"I'll see you tomorrow?" he asked with a grin. "Dinner, maybe?"

"Noelani and I have a dinner meeting with Carlos Santos, the guy who supplies most of the fabrics for our designs," she answered while nodding her head. "He's got some older samples from India he's trying to get rid of before his new stock comes in. He might be willing to give it to us at a real discount."

"I understand completely." It was his turn to look disappointed.

Sadly, she watched as he stood, adjusted his still hard erection before she informed, "I'll be free this Friday. I'll make you dinner."

"You can cook?" His eyes widened.

"Why do you sound so surprised?" She pouted playfully, the action causing him to laugh.

He held up his hands in a sign of surrender, big brown eyes twinkled even in the dim light of her apartment.

"Sorry." He chuckled. "I should have known better. After all, you're good at everything you do."

The compliment warmed her from the inside out and before she knew what she was doing, she had wrapped her arms around his neck and pulled his lips down to hers for a slow, tender kiss. She moaned into his mouth and was surprised when he pulled away.

"If I don't go now, you'll be naked and horizontal before you can say no. Do you understand, Meara?"

She swallowed, hard. The lust in his eyes almost frightened her, even though she had no doubt he would never hurt her.

"*Aye,*" she sighed, placing one final chaste kiss on his stubbly chin. "Good night, Paul."

"Good night, *Sensei*," he replied, giving her backside a playful pat, but lingering a little too long. She smiled again at his lack of movement toward the front door.

"I thought you were going?"

"I am." He blushed. "It's just my cock's so damn hard I don't think I can walk to my apartment."

She giggled, his frown warning her that it wasn't funny, but he smiled at her anyway.

"Do you want me to alleviate that *problem*, for you?" The question was out of her mouth before she could stop it.

Paul's eyes shot open, wide like saucers, and he choked on his spit before whispering, "Are you serious? Or are you just trying to tease me, because right now I'm on the edge and won't need much to push me right over. If you're kidding just say so."

She nodded no.

"I'm not kidding." She dropped her tank top back onto the ground and took both of his hands in hers. "I figure one good turn deserves another."

Impishly, she watched Paul's Adam's apple bobbing nervously, the motion arousing her even more.

"After all, you gave me a mind-blowing orgasm," she purred her appreciation. "You should get the same treatment."

Obediently, Paul followed behind her like a stray puppy.

"*Yes!*"

Damn!

He couldn't believe this was happening. The temptress of his wet dreams was about to give him a tongue bath and he was ready, willing, and able.

"Are you sure you want to do this?" the lieutenant asked hoping she wouldn't change her mind, but needing to give her an out if she wanted one.

"I'm sure." Meara grinned.

His mouth went dry, his heart began to race as Meara held his hands and led him back to the couch. That couch was certainly seeing a lot of action tonight and it wasn't even ten o'clock yet.

"Sit down," she requested. "Good. Now lean back and get comfortable... that's it. Are you ready?"

"More than you'll ever know." The words sounded as if they were some garbled messages on an old-fashioned answering machine. "Meara—"

"Shh. Just sit back and enjoy," she requested. "Leave everything to me. Are you alright?"

The view of her kneeling between the vee of his thighs, breasts swaying with each movement, almost made him come from the sight alone. Trying not to hyperventilate, he took a deep breath in then slowly released it.

Still in shock, he nodded, unable to speak through the large lump in his throat.

His speechlessness made her chuckle, and she giggled while at the same time unbuckling his belt and unzipping his fly, the sound of it being lowered, almost too loud in the eerily quiet room. With much urgency, Meara parted the flap of his pants, reached inside his boxer-briefs, and tugged out his heavy shaft.

"*Oy!* That's quite a *package* you have there, Lieutenant."

He blushed as his hands came up to massage her shoulders, the low moan she gifted him made his balls tighten up painfully.

"I hope you have a permit for that," Meara joked.

He laughed on a groan.

"Hurry, woman! I'm about to explode."

The next thing he knew, she grabbed the base of his shaft with both hands and licked across the plum-sized head and down along a grooved vein.

"Bloody hell!" Her native twang became more pronounced with arousal. "You're a massive lad."

A shiny drop of liquid arousal graced the tip of his cock, and she enthusiastically sucked the bead into her mouth, shivering at the salty-sweet taste of his juices.

"Delicious."

Paul's breath hissed out through clenched teeth, and his hips bucked with a mind of their own. "Please, Meara. I need *more*."

She nodded her understanding, his throbbing member still inside her hot, wet mouth. The increasing pleasure building even more until he thought he might pass out from it. Despite his need to fuck her mouth like an animal, he held back. His shaky hands tangled in her soft locks, holding her in place while he slipped his cock between her parted lips.

"Shit," he hissed on a moan. His eyes squeezing shut unable to bear much more. "I never imagined it would feel so good."

Meara moaned at the feel of his thickly veined shaft sliding along her tongue. His skin felt stretched tight over the pulsing hardness below like steel under velvet. She lightly cupped his balls, kneading and caressing gently, the ministrations urging him to thrust deeper into her warm, wet mouth. She hollowed her cheeks and began to truly suck as he pushed slowly through the tight circle of her saliva-glistening lips in a steady, but shallow pace. The action accompanied by guttural cries from his almost hoarse throat.

"Deeper," he growled, his fingers tugging at her hair. "A little harder. *Shit!* Like that, Meara."

Tightening her lips around his rock-hard shaft, she hollowed her cheeks again, gripping his thighs for extra leverage. Up, down, up, down, over and over again her head bobbed over his throbbing member.

He tensed, his breath escaping in choppy pants and then his entire body stiffened as his cock jerked against her tongue, spurting his seed down her throat. To his surprise, the minx drank every last drop still continuing the heavenly suctioning action of her mouth.

"Damn! Damn! *Damn!*" he whispered, trying to regain his composure as she licked the head of his cock one last time before slipping it back inside his boxer-briefs and re-zipping his khakis. The wicked grin on her gorgeous face made his chest tighten in that now familiar way it did whenever she was near.

He pulled her up off the floor, dragging her across his body as they collapsed lengthwise across the couch. Seemingly content, she folded her arms over his heaving chest and placed her chin on top of them, carefully studying him with those endearing toffee-colored eyes he loved so much.

"Did you like that?" she asked with trembling lips.

"Mmm, no," he stated flatly. Her mouth opened in surprise, as he chuckled playfully. "I loved it! Every single minute of it."

"You brute! I should give you a good thrashing."

"Not right now." He shook his head. "I'm still recuperating."

"Spend the night, Paul." It wasn't a request.

His eyebrows immediately hitched to under his hairline at her unexpected words.

"You wanna have *sex*?" he asked wistfully.

"No," she replied in a hushed voice. "I just want you to cuddle with me. Those crank calls have me on edge. Is that alright?"

"I have to be at work early tomorrow, by seven for the latest."

"I'll set the alarm clock to wake us around five. Please, stay with me."

Unable to tear himself away, he smoothed the stray hairs away from her flushed cheeks and placed a soft kiss to the tip of her nose.

"Not a problem."

Meara quickly found the remote in between the cushions, set the timer on the unit, and then switched the television off.

"I'm too tired to move."

"No worries," he stated as he ran his palms over her naked back, her breasts smashed against his chest. "Wait a minute."

He gently pushed her away and quickly unbuttoned his work shirt before throwing it along with his plain white undershirt on the floor.

"Come back here, beautiful," he commanded, thrilled when she did as she was told.

"Goodnight, Paul." Her voice sounded weak and raspy as she closed her eyes and fell asleep while he lay there enjoying her bare flesh pressed to his.

Finally, he closed his eyes, unable to fight off sleep any longer.

"Goodnight, Meara, sweet dreams."

And he fell asleep too, but this time he didn't dream because he had the girl of his dreams in his arms. It was a good day to be him.

CHAPTER SEVEN

"Good morning, sleepyhead." Meara's sing-song lilt woke him, her luscious breasts covered once again by the white tank top.

Sleepily, he glanced at the digital display on the DVR which informed it was only five-thirty in the morning. He still had thirty minutes before he had to get ready for work.

"Good morning to you too," he beseeched, yawned, and then stretched his arms lazily above his head. "Come back here. I'm cold."

"Nuh uh! There's no way in hell." The chastising tone was given without heat. "If I come back, we'll end up doing something naughty."

He gave her a come-hither look hoping to lure her back to the couch, his semi-erect member greeting her good morning.

"That's why I want you to come back."

Not falling for his scheme, she rolled her eyes and snorted at his suggestion.

"Get up, sailor. I made you breakfast."

"Let me use the bathroom first," he told as he headed toward the washroom. "I'll be right back."

Quickly, he found the restroom. It was modern and fashionable just like her with everything neatly organized and tidy. He relieved himself, washed his hands, and then found an unopened toothbrush under the sink. In a few minutes, his teeth were brushed, his face washed, and his hair finger combed. He had inadvertently slept in his contacts, but the ones he bought were special breathable lenses that could be slept in if so desired.

Leaving the bathroom, Paul went back to the kitchen in search of his woman. *His woman.* The title sounded like music to his ears. Unfortunately, Paul had to acknowledge Meara wasn't his, at least not yet.

Upon his return, he found her bent over, peering into the refrigerator. He couldn't help licking his lips at the sight of her boy-shorts covered ass, the edges of her firm cheeks peeking out from under the material in the position she was in. When she straightened and turned, he noticed the pink tint on her cheeks.

"Stop ogling my arse," she insisted, snickering at his mock indignation. "You Americans have no manners."

"But your ass is so tempting. You shouldn't be carting it around like that if you don't want people drooling over it," he stated rationally.

"You're a right *bawbag*," she said, low and challenging.

He shook his head with confusion.

"What in the world is a *bawbag*?"

"*Bawbag... bollocks... balls... scrotum... sack... man parts.* However, in your case, it means *'an ignorant, obnoxious, or otherwise debatable person'*" She laughed at the indignant look he gave her.

"I got it." He grinned.

"Sit, eat," she commanded in that way of hers. "Before it gets cold."

"You Scottish females are so bossy," he teased, sitting down directly across from her.

"Would you care for a *tassie*?

He frowned.

"Sorry... *a cuppa*."

"What in the world is *'a cuppa'*?" His left eyebrow hitched. "Or *'a tassie'* for that matter?"

"A tassie or a cuppa... ya know... a cup of tea or coffee," she scoffed. "Well?"

He chuckled before he answered.

"No thanks."

As he sat, Meara filled two plates with egg white omelets stuffed with onions, bell peppers, and diced ham, whole wheat toast, and a couple of orange wedges. Finally, she prepared two glasses of freshly squeezed pineapple juice. His eyes narrowed, watching her in amazement.

"What?" she inquired, taking a bite of her lightly buttered toast. "Why are you staring at me like that?"

"This is what I'd normally fix myself for breakfast." Paul's words were filled with surprise and amusement.

"It's quite a coincidence," she acknowledged with a blush. "When I was a child, I was chubby. As an adult, I try to eat healthy most of the time, so I can splurge every once in a while."

"That's interesting," he stated, taking a sip of his juice.

"What?"

"I was also a chunky kid." He frowned but shook off the memory. "Got teased all through middle school, but in high school I shot up, started working out with Koa and I suddenly got too thin. I got teased about that too. At least until I started learning self-defense then the bullies left me alone. It's funny. We've got so much in common."

"I didn't get bullied," she educated with a cheeky grin. "My older brothers threatened to kick anyone's arse that even looked at me meanly, but I took self-defense classes to keep the weight off."

"We've got a lot in common, Miss McBride," he repeated with a chuckle, taking another bite of his tasty breakfast.

"Yeah," she snorted. "I guess great minds think alike."

"I guess so."

Meara couldn't stop smiling. Not even when a bastard of a man cut her off on Wai Nani Way and shot her the bird like it was her fault, he couldn't drive a manual. *The wanker!* She still couldn't stop smiling when she pulled in front of her boutique and found a delivery truck illegally parked in her parking spot.

"Good morning, my best friend in the whole wide wonderful world!" She kissed Noelani on both cheeks as was her custom. "Isn't it a glorious day? The birds are singing, the sun is shining, and the weather is glorious."

Noelani placed her palm against her forehead feeling for a temperature.

"Are you coming down with something?" her business partner responded with all seriousness. "It better not be the flu. The reporter from British Vogue is going to be here in less than an hour. Do you need some vitamins? I've got some chewable vitamin C tablets in my purse... *somewhere.*"

"Gonnae no' dae that!" Meara admonished as she set her purse down on her drawing desk and sat in her soft leather office chair with a built-in massager. "I'm not getting sick. *Jeez!* Can't a girl just be happy?"

She swung around her chair like a child spinning on a merry-go-round.

"Okay, Meara doppelganger," Noelani poked fun. "I don't know what you've done to my brooding, sulking, forlorn best friend, but I want her back, right the hell now."

"Stropping cow," she hissed playfully.

"Tell me," the lovely Hawaiian pleaded. "What's got you so Mary Poppins-*ish*?"

"No one—I mean nothing," Meara quickly corrected herself.

"No one?" Her best friend's eyes narrowed suspiciously. "Could it possibly be a tall, dark, and handsome Navy Lieutenant who goes by the name, Paul Alexander Choy?"

"Did Paul say something to you?" she interrogated; hands planted defiantly on her hips.

"Ah! Ha!" Noelani pointed at her like a schoolyard stool pigeon. "I knew it! I knew it! You two have been acting so weird lately... always going out together... making googly eyes at each other when you think no one is watching. I should be a detective."

"But—"

"Nope! Don't even try to deny it, missy."

"I wasn't going to deny it," the declaration took her by surprise. "I like Paul. He's sweet and kind and thoughtful. Why wouldn't I like him?"

"Is it serious?" Noelani beamed.

"No." She sighed. "We have fun together and we have a lot in common."

"Does Paul know it's not serious?"

"I'm sure he does. Doesn't he?"

"I've seen the way he looks at you, Meara. I don't think *he* thinks you two are just having fun. Don't hurt him." It wasn't a request.

"I won't, but after the fiasco with Roger, I'm not ready for another serious relationship yet."

"Then you better tell my cousin that before he gets his heart crushed." Paul's cousin looked sad.

Meara nodded her agreement, suddenly wanting to toss her cookies at the idea of hurting Paul.

"Hang on." Noelani remembered something. "Before I forget, this was left on the doorstep for you."

"Cheers." Meara took the small rectangular shaped gift box from Noelani's hand, watching her intently. Finally, she got the wrapping paper off and pried open the lid then screamed and dropped the box into the trashcan.

"Damn it!" Noelani yelled with surprise. "What's the matter? What's in the box?"

She felt bile rise in her throat before she stuttered weakly, "I-I... it's a... f-finger! It's a fucking finger!"

"What the hell?" Noelani looked into the trashcan with her; the need to vomit really did take over then. "Did it have a note, or anything attached?"

She shook her head no.

"Call the police. Right now, Meara"

"What did you say?" she questioned, not fully understanding the instructions through the haze of disgust and mind-blowing fear. "Dear father, who would do this?"

She tried to steady her breathing, but it was becoming harder with each passing moment.

"I'm going to call the police and report it." Noelani's level-headedness took over.

"Of course," she stated in a defeated tone.

Now she really did feel like tossing her cookies.

"Aloha, beautiful," Paul whispered into her ear when she finally opened the door. "I'm here and I'm starving."

"You're always starving," she mumbled flatly, looking past his shoulder.

"Mmm," he agreed, grabbing her around the waist and hauling her against his chest. Her soft curves molding to fit his body perfectly. Wasting no time, he buried his nose in her hair, inhaling deeply. "God, you smell tasty."

"Stop that," her voice sounded strangely distant, and his gut tightened at the gruffness of her voice.

"What's wrong?"

"Nothing." She stiffened when he kissed the side of her mouth. "Dinner is getting cold that's all."

The coldness radiating off of her was making him nervous.

"Whatever you say," he murmured as he followed her to the eat-in kitchen.

Looking around the apartment's open floor plan, he noticed the area had a few new items including new potted orchids in a variety of colors and sizes, a small Ficus tree in the far corner near the sliding glass doors leading out onto the balcony, and a couple of succulents on the breakfast bar.

"The place looks homey now." He chuckled. "It definitely represents you."

"Thanks," she replied without emotion. "I've had a lot of sleepless nights this week, so I've taken advantage of it."

"Why haven't you been sleeping?" The man was getting worried. "Are you still getting those stupid calls? Or did you just miss me?"

He bent to kiss her, but she stopped him.

"Gonnae no' dae that," she sighed then clarified. "I mean, don't do that."

"Damn it, Meara!" He lost his cool. "What's going on? And don't tell me nothing because obviously something is."

"What are we?" Her words were strained.

"What do you mean what are we?" he countered, his temper rising along with his voice.

"I mean, what do you think we are?"

"We're friends hopefully leading to being more than just friends."

"If you were to introduce me to one of your Navy blokes, what title would you assign me?"

"I'd like to call you my *girlfriend*, if that's alright with you?"

"No. No. It's not alright with me," she chastised bluntly. "We're not dating, Paul. We're just good friends who enjoy each other's company. That's it."

"So, you usually kiss and give blow-jobs to your friends?" he retaliated, sarcasm seeping into his words without thought. "Because I've never had a *friend*, do that to me."

"I'm not ready for another serious relationship yet. After Roger, I promised myself time to heal."

"Well then what was all this shit about love lessons and what not? Something to pass the time until you didn't feel so lonely because I was a harmless inexperienced guy who was too nervous to hit on you?"

"No, that's not it." Meara ran her hands up and down her jean-covered thighs, the motion making him hard even though he was angry with her. "I like you a lot, but I just want to continue being good friends: going to the movies, having dinner, talking about life and stuff. I want it to go back to the way it was before I messed it up."

"I got it. Just friends. Are you still going to mentor me?" His words came out caustic and harsh even to him.

"You don't need any more mentoring." She shook her head. "You're amazing just the way you are. Any *hen* would be thrilled to land you."

"I see." He stood ramrod straight at her contradicting comment. "You don't want me, so that's it."

"Please, let's just eat."

He shook his head, his stomach tangled up in knots.

"I'm not hungry anymore. I think I'll head back to my place."

"Wait, Paul. Don't go away angry," her words a breathless plea. "I don't want to lose you as a—"

"... a friend. I know." He glared at her for a tension filled moment before saying, "I need a little space to get my head on straight."

"Sure, whatever you need," she agreed immediately, and he wished he could take back the whole conversation.

"I'll see you around, Meara."

"When?" she blurted as her eyes began to fill with unshed tears.

The sudden need to grab her and kiss some sense into her took over his brain, but he didn't.

"I'm not sure. I'll call you," he answered truthfully, not wanting to lead her on the way she had led him on.

"I understand." Meara sniffled. "Take all of the time you need."

Without another word, he turned and left her apartment, the sight of her now making his heart ache.

How did such a perfect day turn out to be so shitty?

CHAPTER EIGHT

"*Aloha, brah!*" Koa yelled across the base common area, his bright, toothy smile making Paul cringe. "Haven't seen you in a while. Where have you been hiding?"

"I haven't been hiding, *brah*," he lied.

"Bullshit," his older cousin returned his ire.

"Excuse me, dickhead?"

"You heard me, son." Koa planted himself between him and his car, the damn mountain of a man blocking out everything behind him.

"Get out of the way and don't call me *son*, asshole."

"Okay... no worries, *Lieutenant Choy*. Now, you can talk to me cousin-to-cousin, or you can talk to me as your commanding officer, you choose."

Defiantly, he rolled his eyes at the arrogant SEAL. All he wanted to do was go home and watch TV. He didn't even care that his fridge was empty, and his dirty laundry was scattered all over his bedroom floor.

"Technically, you are not my C-O," Paul reminded then tried to go around him. "So, get out of my way."

Koa's features darkened as he stared him down. Honestly, we was waiting for the Thor-sized warrior to smash him into the pavement, but instead he took a deep breath.

"Technically, I out rank you, so therefore I am your C-O just by my superior rank."

"Whatever." Paul dared roll his eyes.

"Not, *whatever*, brah," the other man continued. "The family hasn't seen you for over a month and they're starting to get worried. Now, you want to talk to me or to your father, because either way... you're gonna talk to someone."

Feeling defeated, he snarled, "Fine, but not here."

"We'll round up the fellas and go shoot some hoops." Koa's demeanor softened, but not by much.

"Whatever."

Within an hour he, Koa, Aiden, and Marcus, Aiden's best friend who was in town for two weeks on a special military assignment, were on the basketball court in Aiden's subdivision.

"What's the problem, cousin?" Aiden asked as the ball swished into the net. "In your face girls!"

"Who are you calling girls, pansy-ass?" Marcus chuckled. "Koa and I are leading eight to six. We only need two more points to win, Kaplan."

"That's only because I'm stuck with Mister Mopey here." Aiden motioned to Paul. "And I'm the only one with his head out of his ass."

"Hell!" Paul admonished. "I'm being forced to play, remember?"

Abruptly, he stole the ball from Koa and dunked it into the basket, holding on to the rim briefly before releasing it then drifted back down to the court.

Aiden grabbed the ball as it bounced toward him, calling time-out.

"We're all worried about you, so just spill it already."

"I was seeing someone—" He sighed loudly.

"You mean Meara," Marcus interrupted waggling his brows humorously, but Paul didn't find it funny.

"How the hell do you know about Meara?!"

"She stopped coming to Sunday brunch the same time you did," Koa explained. "It doesn't take an MIT graduate to figure out something was going on between the two of you."

"Also," Aiden added. "The way you both look at each other... I looked at Kai like that for four years. Hell, I still look at her that way."

"I was introduced to her last week at Aiden's place when she and Noelani visited." Marcus chuckled, the sound grinding his nerves. "If I wasn't married, I'd tap that."

Paul punched the 6'4", African American, Naval Engineer on the arm... hard, the force of the blow making the man flinch.

"*Shit!* What was that for?"

"Don't talk about her like that." He stepped up to the much larger, much stronger man and challenged him to say something else.

"Why not?" Aiden's smug glare made him violent.

"It's disrespectful, that's why." He reached down to grab his duffle bag.

"What guy in his right mind wouldn't jump on that ass if it were being offered up like an all-you-can-eat pancake breakfast?" Marcus chuckled again, the indecent innuendo fueling his rage.

"I don't know, son, I certainly would." Aiden laughed while pumping his hips suggestively.

"Shut up, you *sonofabitch*!" Paul's fist hit Aiden's jaw with a loud crack sending the other man sprawling onto the ground. Before he could get another punch in, Koa had his arms pinned behind his head and Marcus had stepped in front of his would be target. "Get off me, Koa!"

"I'm sorry, dude," Aiden sputtered holding his jaw, a purplish bruise forming where Paul's fist made contact. "I was just trying to make a point."

"What point is that?" Paul snarled. "That you're a low-life pervert who doesn't know when to keep his damn mouth shut?"

"Nah," Aiden replied, letting Marcus pull him to a standing position. "That you're in love with her."

Paul shook his head.

"No... no... you're wrong. I don't feel that way about Meara. We're just friends."

"That's horseshit and you know it," Koa reasoned, finally releasing him from the lock he held him in. "Any other chick and you'd just laugh it off. You might even join in the fun, but not with her. And do you know why?"

"No, but I'm sure you're going to tell me," he growled sarcastically.

"Because you're head over heels in love with her, jackass, that's why."

"No, way," Paul denied, shaking his head to cement his point. "I'm not in love with her."

"Brah, you've hardly left your house." Koa frowned. "You weren't even around for the holidays."

"I came to Thanksgiving dinner at your parents' house and Christmas at Aiden's," he huffed.

Koa shook his head as he stated, "Shoveling food into your face and then disappearing into thin air doesn't count as time spent with the family and you know it. And Meara... Noelani invited her for Christmas, but she made up some pathetic excuse not to come. Her reason for missing Thanksgiving was they don't celebrate it in Scotland."

"Sounds like a good excuse to me," he agreed.

"C'mon, brah, admit it." Koa smirked. "You're pining away for her. Believe me, I know what you're going through. Remember when Adrienne and I went through that rough patch when she wanted to be *friends*?"

"It's not the same." Standing straighter, Paul defended himself. "That had nothing to do with her."

His temper flared.

"And... I'm not in love with her," he repeated through clenched teeth.

"Good for you! Then back off, let her date someone else, possibly get serious about him, even marry, and have kids with him, how would that make you feel?" Koa demanded.

The question caused bile to rise in his throat.

"Like I'd want to commit *hari-kari* or pull the guy's spleen out and make him eat it."

"There you go," Koa said, pulling out a five-dollar bill from his basketball shorts and handing it to Aiden.

"Why are you giving him money?"

"Aiden bet me five dollars you were in love with her. I thought it was just a crush."

"I thought you just wanted to get laid," Marcus added his commentary.

"Great! Freaking great, you guys!" Paul groaned in distress. "My life is shit and you all are placing bets on it. Fuck this shit! I'm leaving. Later bitches."

"Paul, come back," Marcus pleaded. "What happened?"

Reluctantly, Paul told them the whole sordid story leaving out all of the steamy parts as well as the fact that he was still a virgin.

"She likes you more than a friend, brah," Koa stated with finality. "That's obvious to everyone except her and apparently you.

"I tell ya, for two geniuses, you two are really stupid."

The four of them arrived at Aiden and Kai's house just in time for dinner.

"Aloha, guys! How was the—Oh my god! What happened to your face?" Kai blustered frantically, scanning the room for the guilty party. The traitors all pointed to him. "Why did you hit my husband, Paul?"

"I insulted the woman he loves," Aiden chimed in.

"Why would you insult Meara?" his wife grumbled, examining his black-and-blue bruise. "You like her."

"*Really?* Does everyone know?" Paul's exasperation filled his words. When everyone in the room, including A.J. shook their heads yes, he wanted to crawl into a corner and die. "Great!"

"Do you need to talk?" his cousin Kai asked, concern filling her eyes.

"Kai, I need advice. How do I make her mine?"

"Tell me what's going on." Kai wiped her wet hands on a dishcloth and sat on a barstool at the breakfast bar.

"In private," he mumbled as he nodded to the eavesdroppers.

"If you don't have boobs, please leave." Kai glanced around the room.

"But, baby," Aiden pleaded.

She pointed to the backyard and the four others, including A.J., left the kitchen without a word. He smirked at the idea that three rather large Navy men could be intimidated by a woman as nurturing as Kai.

"Go ahead," she encouraged, leaning against the cool granite surface of the breakfast bar. "Start from the beginning and don't leave out any details."

Taking in a deep breath, Paul told his older cousin everything that happened between him and Meara, even how much he craved her. Needed her. Every amazing inch of her.

"... And then I left her apartment," he finished with a huff, watching Kai's reaction.

"*Wow!*" she whispered. "I can't believe you are still a virgin. I think it's sweet."

"No, it's really not."

"If it makes you feel better, Aiden was my first and only."

"Seriously?" He couldn't hide the shock in his voice.

"Yes," she stated confidently. "If I hadn't met him, I think I might still be. No one ever made me feel the way he does... cherished, beautiful, and sexy. If you feel anything close to that for Meara, you better grab her up before someone else does."

"How do I know it's love and not lust?" It was a valid concern.

"How do you feel about her?"

"I love the way she looks, she's gorgeous," he said, unable to hold back a feral smile at Kai's agreeing nod.

"That's not enough to love someone," she added. "Continue."

"I love the way she tilts her head to the side before she gives me a chastising look and she gives me those often," he stated wryly. "I also love when her accent gets so thick that I can barely understand her, and she has to explain all of her strange words to me."

"Strange words like what?" The woman grinned.

"*Wanker, thrashing, bampot, cuppa, quine, bawbag, messages...* the list is too long to repeat, but it's so adorable when she says them."

"Is there anything else?"

Paul winced as he continued.

"I find her fascinating and a bit intimidating. I think it's great that she knows about everything from the ingredients in Crepes Suzette to the chemical makeup of Tanzanite."

"Are you finished?"

He shook his head no.

"I enjoy being with her, even when neither one of us speaks. And we like the same foods and music... and movies... most of time."

He closed his eyes and pictured her making funny faces at him when he tried to be serious about what he couldn't remember. His rambling list of things he loved about the exasperating fashion designer took him by surprise.

"I'm no expert," Kai's words soothed the chaos he had felt in his soul for almost a month. "But it sounds like love to me."

"I do... I... I think I love her." The realization hit him like a ton of bricks. "No. I know I love her. Damn it!"

"Finally," Kai huffed out. "I thought you'd never figure it out. You know, for a smart guy—"

"I know. I know. I'm really stupid."

"Kinda." Her words sounded surprisingly sympathetic to him. "But that doesn't surprise me."

"How do I make her realize that she feels the same way about me, if she even does?" Paul begged, needing all the help he could get.

Kai thought about his situation for several long, drawn out minutes before saying:

"Here's what you're gonna do, cuz..."

Knock! Knock! Knock!

Meara glanced over at the DVRs digital display, rolling her eyes in agitation. It was only a few minutes past eight o'clock in the evening. She snuggled back under the Egyptian cotton comforter ignoring the sound. Maybe if she stayed extremely quiet, whoever was doing the banging would go away.

Knock! Knock! Knock!

"*Blimey!*" She yanked the comforter off and stumbled out of bed wearing only her over-sized, blue, and white *Oxford University* t-shirt that reached mid-thigh and nothing else, her long hair resembling *The Bride of Frankenstein* or another similar looking nightmare.

"Ugg! For the love of all that's decent in this bloody freaking world—" She jerked open the door ready to attack, her eyes widened at the sight of the gorgeous Paul Choy standing in her doorway, dressed in his new black, denim jeans, a pale blue, button-down dress shirt and black loafers. His hair subtly spiked in the front and looking even better than she remembered.

His chocolate brown gaze raked her from head to toe.

"Wow!" Paul sputtered, unable to hide his surprise. "You're a hot mess."

"Hello to you too." She leaned against the foyer wall, head tilted to one side, giving him her best *F-off* look. "We haven't seen each other in a month, and this is how you greet me?"

"It's been a month already?" Meara responded, trying to seem unaffected by the sight of him.

Had it been a month since their falling-out, she had lost count, the days blurring into one another.

"W-what are you d-doing here, Lieutenant?" She stumbled over her words as he gazed at her through hooded eyes, the deep chocolate pools shining with some unknown emotion.

"I've heard from reliable sources that you've hardly left this apartment in almost twenty days, not counting work or the supermarket. And F-Y-I, it is *Lieutenant Commander* now."

He smiled that sweet boyish smile she had come to love; her heart did that happy flipping motion.

"I've heard the same of you," she stated with more confidence than she actually felt. "Except, you haven't left your abode in nearly thirty days," her tone was cocky and a tad bit flippant. "Also, congratulations on the promotion. You've been working really hard lately. It's good that it paid off. I'm proud of you, Lieutenant Commander Choy."

She smiled as he blushed reminding her of a small child.

With newfound confidence, he laughed before pushing past her into her incredibly messy apartment.

"Get ready," Paul informed matter-of-factly. "We're going out."

"I can't," she declined. "I'm watching a Buffy the Vampire Slayer marathon, and I'm up to the episode where Spike and Buffy shag."

"C'mon, Meara. We both need to get over... whatever this is," he said, motioning his hands wildly between them. "It's not healthy to be locked in our apartments like veal."

"Where are we going?" she questioned after a few moments.

"Club Red," he notified proudly.

One of her brows rose.

"That's the most exclusive club in Oahu," Meara gasped. "The waiting list to get in is weeks long. How did you manage this?"

He laughed.

"My old friend, J.T. owns it," he politely explained. "He's an ex-chess club geek I went to high school with. He wanted to do me a solid since I debugged his computer network last year at his nightclub in Maui."

Dramatically, she cleared her throat before saying, "*Jeremy Takiyama...* is an old friend... *of yours?*"

"Yep," he chuckled. "It's like I always say, geeks rule the world."

"I guess you're right." She giggled, feeling better just because he was with her.

"Get ready."

She tilted her head, contemplating her options, before saying, "It might take a while. I haven't showered today."

Quietly, he chuckled.

"I wondered what that smell was."

"Brut!" Meara felt her cheeks flooding with heat. "That's not funny, not at all. I certainly do not smell."

He tapped the tip of her nose playfully before settling onto the couch.

"Ah," he lamented. "I've had many a dream about what we've done on this couch." The heated look he gave made the inner muscles of her sex clench with need. "But it's over now and I want my friend back in my life. I miss her."

"Are you certain being friends is truly alright?" Hope filled her heart and her loneliness.

He nodded.

"I miss you, my Scottish princess and, if friendship is the only thing, I can have from you then so be it."

"Great!" She tried to sit on his lap, but he stopped her and patted the cushion next to him. "What's the matter?"

He smiled, watching her intently as if he were memorizing the aspects of her face.

"None of that," he firmly instructed, even though he wanted to touch her more than he wanted to take his next breath.

"None of what, may I ask?" she pouted.

"I don't want to misunderstand our relationship or lack thereof," he stated in his most military sounding tone. "Therefore, there has to be rules."

"Rules?" Meara repeated. The word felt like gravel over her tongue. "What type of rules?"

"For one thing," he stressed. "No more inappropriate touching, groping, kissing, etc."

"Sure," she stated flatly. "Of course. I'm sorry. It won't happen again."

"Also, when we go out, we go *Dutch*, that way it doesn't feel like a date."

"Fine," she replied, her answer sounding weak even to her own ears.

"And definitely, no more sex lessons," he concluded, giving her a toothy smile.

"What about your virginity problem? You still are one... right?" Her voice suddenly sounded panic-filled, and she cleared her throat to hide it.

He shook his head.

"I'm still a virgin, but I'm not worried about it anymore," Paul explained coolly. "When I find the right lady, it'll happen."

She narrowed her eyes at those last words, longing rushing into her core.

"Certainly, we'll go back to how things were before when we were mates."

"*Mates?*" His almond-shaped eyes narrowed to almost slits.

"*Mate* is another word for friend." She rolled her eyes at his lack of knowledge of British slang. "Jeez!"

Smiling, she leaned in to kiss his cheek, but he placed his large, capable hands on her shoulders to hold her at bay.

"I don't think that falls under the stated rules, Meara." The bluntness of his words, as well as his stern gaze, surprised her.

"Sorry," she apologized uncomfortably, slowly backing away. "I'm going to get ready now. Please, make yourself at home. The remote is on the coffee table, look at whatever you like. I'll hurry."

Following her instructions, Paul sat and waited. Did he care that he couldn't show her any type of affection? Of course, he did, but according to Kai this new plan would work. She would want him as much as he wanted and needed her.

Meara on the other hand, was baffled that the dreamy Lieutenant Commander was back in her life, but only wanted to be platonic chums. Did she care that the insufferable man wouldn't hold her, touch her, or kiss her in any way, shape, or fashion? She definitely did, but for right now, she was glad to have him in her apartment, on her couch, watching her *Telly*.

Bloody! Hell! Why didn't she keep her big mouth shut?

On pins and needles, Paul waited until she disappeared into the bathroom before calling Kai. Thankfully, she answered on the third ring.

"Aloha."

"I don't know if I can do this?" he whispered, staring at the closed bathroom door. "Even unkempt she's drop-dead gorgeous."

"Be strong," his cousin pleaded. "Do you want her?"

"Yes," he stated without any thought.

"Then you must stick with the plan," his faceless cousin reminded. "Remember, no physical contact whatsoever."

"Damn it!" he swore. "That's going to be hard."

"Think positively," the wife and mother of two encouraged. "It will all work out. I promise."

"You sound more and more like your mom every day." He smiled even though she couldn't see his expression.

"That's what everyone tells me." Kai giggled. "I accept the compliment. Now, go woo your dream girl."

"Mahalo, Kai."

"No worries. Good luck, Paul."

Then the other end went dead, and he sat back on the couch and found a basketball game on one of the sports channels to watch while he waited.

Thirty minutes later, Meara emerged in a glorious gold and black halter top, a form-hugging, mid-calf black, denim skirt with black wedge strappy sandals, large gold hoop earrings and her makeup simple, eyeliner and lip gloss. Her long locks straightened and pulled back into a casual chignon, the hair-style bringing attention to her smooth, flawless exposed back.

Upon seeing her, he gulped, loudly.

"Holy! Cow!" he whispered under his breath, the sight of her making his heart pound so quickly he thought he might pass out.

"Do I look presentable?" she asked coyly, already knowing the answer by the way he was staring at her, mouth slightly ajar, eyes wide, cheeks flushed. It took a few seconds for his mouth to catch up with his brain.

"As usual," he replied sincerely, his voice low and raspy as if he'd just stumbled out of bed. "You look absolutely stunning."

It was Meara's turn to blush which made him feel better.

"Thank you. I'm ready if you are." It wasn't a question.

Paul motioned for her to lead the way, and gladly ogled her softly swaying hips whose power mesmerized him like a hypnotist's watch. Against his will, his member sprung to life... literally, and he to adjust himself as discreetly as possible while he waited for her to lock the door. Then, as was their custom, they made their way to the elevator in comfortable silence.

"I'm so glad you came over," Meara stated sweetly, the corners of her perfectly sculpted mouth curling into a wicked smile.

"Me too," he agreed. "I hope the place isn't too crowded."

She shook her head.

"I wouldn't hold my breath."

It took almost fifteen minutes to drive from their condominium on Wai Nani Way to the new dance club near the Pearl Harbor-Hickam base, the traffic not unusual for a Friday night. To his surprise, he quickly found a parking space toward the far corner of the club's parking lot. He and Meara chatted about work and television while they waited in the rather long VIP line to get in.

After ten minutes or so, they finally made it to the front of the line where an extremely large, extremely intimidating, Samoan-looking bouncer stood carding and stamping people's wrists, a dangerous sneer across his features.

"Name," the bouncer prodded, ogling Meara from head to toe then back again before staring at him.

Paul cleared his throat to get the man's attention.

"Lieutenant Commander Paul Choy," he replied, looking the other man dead in the face. "And guest."

Paul watched Meara watching him, an unfamiliar emotion on her unworried face. The man must have gotten the unspoken message because he smiled uneasily before checking their ID's and stamping both their wrists with a special neon green stamp in the shape of a shell.

"You and your lady have a good time, Sir," the gorilla sized bouncer wished the pair. "The VIP section is on the second level, just show the attendant your stamp. He'll take care of anything you need. Have a good time."

"Mahalo, we will," Paul responded, ushering Meara inside; his hand placed on the small of her back, not-so subtly touching her bare skin.

"Must I remind the Lieutenant Commander of his own rule of no inappropriate touching?" She snorted.

He laughed shaking his head at her cocky tone.

"Sorry, I must have lost my head. Do you want a drink?"

She nodded and he guided her over to the bar area.

They paused for a brief moment to admire the space. Even he had to admit it was breathtaking. Jeremy Takiyama, Hawai'i's most sought-after nightclub designer and a personal friend, purchased the club for a steal of four million dollars and redesigned the building with dramatic features inspired by the grand Hollywood gentlemen's clubs of the late 1920's early 1930's.

Club Red featured a luxurious mix of imported lead crystal chandeliers, plush, jewel-toned fabrics hand-woven in India, faux crocodile and Italian leather seating, a four-sided futuristic glass fireplace, glass elevators providing 360-degree views, eclectic Tinsel

Town era memorabilia and rich mahogany wood, creating a vibe that gave a modern South Pacific nod to old Hollywood glamour.

Created with both the jet-set elite as well as the everyday person in mind, the multi-level Great Room was designed to provide privacy to guests who wanted to party in the utmost luxury while still enveloped in *Club Red's* festive vibe. The Great Room was inspired by what a 1940's Hollywood mogul's private library may have looked like, featuring plush leather chairs, trophies, awards and artifacts, and a dramatic lighted bar featuring hand-blown Austrian crystal decanters. Celebrities had all taken refuge in The Great Room where they could watch the action below via a window facing the dance floor without being harassed.

"Incredible!"

He heard her mutter as they both stood gaping at the luxurious surroundings.

Paul let out a low whistle.

"J.T. really out-did himself with this place."

"I'm glad you like it, *kolohe*." A deep male voice came from beside him.

Swiftly, he turned to find J.T. smiling at him.

"And who's this lovely lady accompanying you tonight?" Meara blushed but didn't look away.

"This is my friend, Meara McBride," he made the introductions. "Meara this is Jeremy Takiyama, he's a *kolohe* as well, so be careful."

Jeremy Takiyama was an inch shorter than him with exotic Asian features, flawless olive complexion, dark brown almost black, almond-shaped eyes, and thick ebony locks. The nightclub owner wore a simple dark gray *Armani* suit and loafers, and looked nothing like the nerd he once was.

Meara's head tilted in that way she often did before asking, "A what?"

"*Kolohe* is a Hawaiian word that means rascal." Paul chuckled at their reversed positions. "Now you know how I feel when you use those Scottish words on me."

Meara stuck her tongue out at him playfully making him laugh.

"Don't tempt me with that tongue, young lady" Paul mischievously warned. "You know the rules."

J.T. watched them both questioningly.

"Come on you two." The club owner grinned. "We can get some drinks and appetizers upstairs. I'll give you the grand tour."

J.T. was charming as usual, showing them around the nightclub before sitting with them at a private table on the second floor. Meara sipped on a Mai Tai while he had a *Corona* and J.T. nursed a diet soda with lemon.

"My gosh!" Meara snorted as J.T. told her about the time in high school when they filled the football team's helmets with shaving cream before a big game. "Did they ever find out it was the two of you?"

Paul grimaced.

"Koa did. He was a tight-end—"

"*Aye*, he's definitely got a *tight-end*." Her sudden peal of laughter made him, and his friend laugh as well.

"Be careful," J.T. teased. "You don't want Adrienne knowing you've been checking out her husband's *tight-end*."

"That's true." Meara chuckled. "She'd kick my *arse*."

"And what an ass it is," J.T. replied under his breath, so only Paul could hear.

"Well, pardon me gents, while I visit the *loo*. I mean the lavatory," Meara clarified. "Be back in a moment."

Both men stood as she left the table, both watching her slightly swaying arse... ass as she walked away.

When she was out of hearing distance, J.T. punched him on the shoulder.

"How in the world did you end up with a woman like that?"

"She's not mine." Paul rolled his eyes at the other man's comment.

"My ass!"

He shook his head again trying to reemphasize his previous comment.

"We're just friends. At least that's what she claims."

His long-time buddy rubbed the back of his neck in confusion.

"I don't know, brah. She looks at you like you're more than *just friends*."

"I don't think so," he complained then took another pull on his beer. "I wish it were true though. I… I love her."

J.T. frowned.

"Man, it sucks to be you." His friend hesitated for a beat before adding, "Since you two are just friends, do you mind if I ask her out?"

Paul shot his soon-to-be-ex-friend an angry look.

"I'll break every single bone in your body if you so much as look at her funny."

"Okay." J.T. held up his hands in mock surrender. "No asking her out. I got it. There's no need to get violent."

Several minutes later, Meara returned followed closely by a guy wearing faded jeans, a black t-shirt, and Timberland boots. The other man looked as if he could have been a model too with shaggy, well-coiffed sandy brown hair and bright blue eyes and at the moment the man was watching Meara like she was the last rib-eye steak on the grill, and he hadn't eaten in days.

"Is there a problem, brah?" Paul confronted, staring at the man, wanting to cause him bodily injury.

"No problem, dude." The male reminded him of Aiden. "I didn't know she was taken. My mistake."

Meara's brow furrowed at their conversation but kept quiet.

His friend sat with them until one of his assistants needed him to take care of a situation downstairs.

"You two enjoy yourself. It's on me. Paul, I'll talk to you soon. Maybe I'll stop by one of those famous Kapahu volleyball matches," he said before turning to Meara.

Paul nodded his approval and gave a quick *shaka*.

"Meara, you are truly one of the most gorgeous, fascinating creatures I've ever set eyes on. And if my best friend wasn't so lovesick over you, I'd ask you out myself, but I don't want any computer viruses *'accidentally'* infesting my network, so I'll just have to admire you from afar."

Then J.T. bent, took her hand in his, and placed several tiny kisses on her wrist and palm before Paul pushed him away.

"Get outta here, you letch," Paul insulted with amusement.

The other man laughed.

"It was a pleasure meeting you, Meara. If I don't see you before you leave, have a good night," J.T. said before walking away, his female assistant talking with him as they walked downstairs.

"He's quite a character." Meara giggled unable to look him in the eyes.

"Yup, that he is," Paul agreed with a smile.

"Well," she licked her full lips nervously then educated, "J.T. thinks you're in love with me. Is that true?"

"Yes, it is," he stated straightforwardly, his words making her gasp in surprise. "But I know you don't feel the same, so I've decided to move on."

One perfectly shaped brow shot up in disbelief.

"Really? You're just going to... *move on.*"

"I'm not going to lose sleep over you anymore, Meara." Paul nodded. "I've accepted it."

"What if I said I don't believe you?"

He scoffed at her as he swept the room. His gaze landed on an attractive blonde wearing a dress that barely covered her ass or her breasts, the plump mounds peeking over her plunging neckline. With all of the courage he could muster, he stood.

"I'm going to prove it to you." He winked. "I'll see you in a while."

On shaky legs, he made his way toward the blonde, his breath coming in harsh pants before he took a calming breath. It was true. He had to do this to show the stubborn woman that she wanted him as much as he wanted her, and not for a few minutes or hours or days, but for as long as they both lived.

"Where are you going?" He heard Meara call from behind him, her tone sounding raspy and harsh. "Paul, what the hell are you doing?"

"I'm practicing my seduction skills on a real life target."

He straightened and didn't stop until he was standing in front of the busty, blonde bombshell who really wasn't his type at all, but the wench he was in love with didn't know that.

"Hello, beautiful. I'm Lieutenant Commander Paul Choy with the U.S. Navy, and who might you be?"

Meara felt her heart come to a complete stop as Paul made his way over to the blond bimbette who was currently trying to cover her bottom, unsuccessfully, with a dress that was at least one size too small.

Appalled, she watched as he smiled and chatted up the hen, all the while devouring the hen's obviously plastic bosom. Thank goodness she had only eaten a couple of egg rolls because right now she felt as if she would lose everything in her stomach.

"What's he doing?" J.T.'s voice broke her stupor.

Frazzled, Meara turned to see J.T. over her shoulder watching the same scene she was. She shook her head, but didn't say anything, *couldn't* say anything, and her lungs felt as if they were on fire.

The blonde kept touching Paul's ripped biceps, drawing flirtatious circles with her *Lee Press-on Nails*. The sight of the blatant foreplay with *her man* made her feel somewhat violent.

Shite! she thought to herself. *Her man. Paul wasn't her man. And whose fault was that anyway, you big wanker!*

Then, from across the room, she heard him ask the tramp to dance, who quickly took his hand and followed him to the nearest dance floor. The upbeat song from *Pitbull* was pumping and so was the blonde... all over her man's thighs, which so happened to be between her indecently spread legs.

"Bloody! Fucking! Hell!" The string of swear words left her mouth before she could stop them.

"Meara, I know this doesn't look good, but I'm sure that—" J.T.'s eyes narrowed as he tried to convince her not to make a scene.

"I told him I wanted to be friends," she admitted, inhaling deeply to keep from having a meltdown in front of J.T.

"Ah ha!" J.T. whisper exclaimed.

"But I didn't think—" she stopped in midsentence when Paul took his prey by the hand and led her over to the table where she and J.T. sat staring.

"J.T., could you take Meara home for me?" Paul smirked. "Erika invited me back to her place for a nightcap."

The giant ass-wipe of a *sonofabitch* actually had the nerve to waggle his newly threaded eyebrows at them. She immediately became rigid. Her stomach roiled like she was on a tiny ship in the middle of the Pacific Ocean during a monsoon.

"What are you doing, brah?" J.T. glared at him with disgust.

"Yeah," she added. "What exactly are you doing?"

"Following your advice and getting a girlfriend." He winked at her for the second time, and it only made her want to gouge his eyes out with her nails.

J.T. watched her watching him, an angry scowl marring his handsome face.

"This isn't smart, Paul. Not smart at all."

"You owe me, brah."

"Cool." J.T. frowned and shook his head. "I'll take Meara home, you big idiot."

Frantically, she shook her head at both of them, unwilling to be taken care of like some sort of child.

"I can find my way back home, *Mister Wonderful*," she hissed sarcastically at her 'date' through gritted teeth.

"I thought you said your name is Paul Choy?" The blonde's eyebrows hitched in confusion.

Meara chuckled maniacally, the sound actually scaring her a bit.

"You're perfect for him," she teased. "I see you both share the same IQ."

Then she quickly turned to J.T. and gave him a chaste kiss on the cheek before saying, "It was a pleasure meeting you, J.T. I hope to see you soon. As for you." She spun around to face Paul who was looking at her questioningly. "Stay away from me if you have any commonsense at all or you'll be sorry and so will your *bawbag*."

With those words fueling her on, she raced downstairs to get an *Uber* home. The unwanted vision of Paul and the *Marilyn Monroe* look-alike writhing and sweating all over each other kept playing over and over in her mind.

That was it! No more fucking men! She would rather be gay.

"I think I messed up." Paul stood outside the nightclub alone, his cell phone practically glued to his ear, worrying about Meara as Kai tried to assess the situation.

"Slow down, Paul. What did you do now?"

"I did what you told me to do," he spoke in a hushed whisper trying not to be overheard by passersby. "I spoke with someone else, flirted with her, danced with her, and then I asked J.T. to take Meara home so I could have some quality time alone with Erika."

"Wait!" Kai blustered, her voice turning into a high-pitched shriek that only a dog could hear. "That's not what I told you to do!"

"It's not... yes, it is." He tried without success to defend his actions but knew deep down that he had fucked up royally.

"I said find someone, flirt with her, dance with her, not abandon Meara and pretend you were going to have sex with a stranger you just picked up at a nightclub."

"I'm confused," he confessed. "I thought that's what I did."

"No, idiot. You just wanted Meara to feel jealous not to make her hate you for the rest of her life." Kai was muttering some Hawaiian chant over the phone, and he hoped it wasn't some sort of curse. When she finished, she asked, "How did Meara get home?"

He sighed.

"I think she took an Uber."

"You think!" He moved the cell phone away from his ear to save his eardrum from bursting. "Where's the blonde you picked up?"

"I apologized after Meara left and told her what my real intentions were."

"How did she take the news?" Kai groaned; the exasperation clear in her voice.

"I have a large, red handprint on my face for my honesty."

"Good! You deserved it," Kai snarled.

"What should I do?"

"Go find Meara," his cousin ordered. "Cry, whimper, and beg for her forgiveness. Do whatever it takes to explain yourself and hope she believes you."

"And if she won't listen to me?" He gulped.

"Well, let's just say you might really die a virgin."

CHAPTER NINE

Meara had never been so livid in her entire twenty-five years of life. The insufferable Hawaiian had left her stranded at the nightclub so he could stick his deliciously shaped zucchini in some blonde bimbo.

What a right bastard!

She had gotten home over an hour ago, called Noelani to vent her anger, then called Paul and left a rather nasty, extremely vivid, heated message in his voicemail. If she thought she could get away with it, she'd break into his apartment and cut out all of the crotches out of his pants. Maybe she could use a bobby pin to pick the lock like they did in the movies.

"Arrrggg!" She growled at the top of her lungs, kicked her beloved couch that held so many memories of them, then walked briskly back to her bedroom.

Without thought, she tore off her clothes, almost ripping her halter-top in two in her rage, leaving only her black lace panties on, before sitting on her mattress and staring at the walls, practically naked and extremely angry.

Why did she let things get so out of control?

She liked him. Really and truly liked him. Perhaps, even loved him. She sat in the dark room and mentally listed all of the things she liked about Paul: his Adonis-like body, his *GQ* model face, his over-the-top sense of humor, his brilliant mind, his genuine protective nature. He was everything she wanted in her dream man all wrapped-up in a Paul-sized package.

Shite!

She had caused this fiasco by telling him they should be just friends when in actuality she wanted... *more*. More hugging. More kissing. More of everything, and she wanted more with him. Only him. She was in love with the guy.

But it was too late. The blasted IT geek was probably dick-deep in that female's yoo-hoo by now, his prized virginity burned to a cinder. Great! *Freaking great!*

Knock! Knock! Knock!

"Who the hell could that be?" she asked herself.

Haphazardly, she threw on her blue robe and ran to the front door before the person could wake the neighbors. As she opened the barrier, Paul grabbed her around the waist, hauled her against his muscled chest, and sealed his mouth over hers. Instinctively, she bit his bottom lip... *hard*.

"*Shit!* What did you do that for?" he bellowed when she narrowed her eyes, hands on hips, a scowl of epic proportion on her mouth. "Okay, I know why you did it. Let me explain—"

Pushing him away with a strength she didn't know she possessed, she snarled, "*Haud yer wheesht!* Get out! Get out right now! Or... or I'll get the cleaver."

"You wouldn't."

"Is that what you think?" she hissed through clenched teeth and ran to the kitchen, pulling open the utensil drawer and removing a huge stainless steel meat cleaver.

His eyes widened.

"Meara, put that damn thing down before you hurt someone... namely me!" he commanded.

"I said, get your arse outta my flat... you philandering prick!"

She couldn't find the words to describe how upset and betrayed she felt. So instead, she sat on the couch, covered her face with both hands, and did what she wanted to do since seeing Paul and the blonde on the dance floor at *Club Red*.

She cried, and not the soft, gentile cry of a proper lady, but the loud, unattractive wail of a woman scorned.

She felt Paul take the meat cleaver out of her hand, placing it on the coffee table, before sitting beside her and wrapping those strong arms around her shoulders, pulling her against him as she poured out every last tear she possessed.

"I'm sorry," he whispered against her hair. "I didn't sleep with her. I just wanted to make you jealous."

"What?" She looked up, certain her eyeliner had run, and she probably looked like a rabid raccoon.

"I didn't even leave the club with her," he rapidly explained. "In fact, she slapped me pretty damn hard when I told her I was only using her to make you jealous."

"How hard did she hit you?" She used the sleeve of her robe to wipe her nose.

He turned his head to show her the handprint that was still decorating his cheek.

"I'd say extremely hard." He winced when she touched the enflamed area.

She couldn't help the giggle that escaped her throat at his puppy-dog pout.

"I love you," the nervous, yet determined guy confessed. "And I only want to be with you, but for some reason you want to pretend we're just friends, but were not—"

"I love you too." She pulled him down to her, holding onto his broad shoulders for support and kissed him gently, his body immediately tensed. "Relax. I won't bite. Not if you don't want me to."

"Meara," he moaned against her lips. The sound sending an electric current from their lips, down her torso, along her abdomen, and into her now dripping, wet sex. "What do I do?"

"Just do what comes naturally," she encouraged, feeling his shoulders relax as he pushed his tongue against the seam of her lips demanding entry into her mouth; both of his large hands cupping her face while his slightly calloused thumbs stroked her cheeks.

She gasped at his silent request.

Her lips parting as he took the opportunity to slip past into her awaiting mouth. Their tongues danced together, writhing like sinewy serpents sliding along and over each other, the sensation overwhelming her senses.

"Paul," she moaned into his mouth unable to think coherently.

His hands left her cheeks, gliding over her neck and then her shoulders, past her arms and hips then back up again. The unhurried exploratory motion made her toes curl. "That feels so good," she whimpered.

"Mmm," he growled low and needy. "*You* feel so good."

Both hands ventured away from their path along her body to find her aching breasts, her nipples already tightly beaded peaks as they awaited his touch. He palmed both mounds through her robe, gently rolling and tugging and pinching the raised points.

"That feels amazing." Her breath leaving her lungs in heavy gusts, she squeezed her thighs together trying to relieve the pressure building at the apex of her sex.

He pulled away suddenly and yanked the two sides of her robe apart exposing her breasts to his gaze. "I love your breasts, Meara."

He leaned down, gifting her right nipple with a long swipe before sucking in her entire areola into the hot cavern of his mouth.

"Mmm," he moaned against the sensitive peak, the vibration on her skin shooting down to her sex.

"Paul."

She gripped his thick black locks with both hands, the strands reminding her of raw silk.

"Move lower," she commanded.

"So bossy," he chuckled.

Instead of following her instruction, the stubborn man released her nipple and latched onto its twin.

"Heaven help me!" she whimpered when he lavished the other one in a similar fashion but added circular swipes around the needy nipple with the entire length of his talented tongue. She squealed with pleasure. "If you're really a virgin, how do you know how to do that?"

"I've been watching a lot of porn lately," he confessed with a smirk, the sound doing strange things to her nether regions.

Her right eyebrow automatically hitched.

"Are you serious?"

"Extremely serious," he said playfully against the nipple still inside his mouth.

Without wasting any more time, Paul gave her raised peak a final kiss before laying her down on the cushions, removing her unwanted panties, and spreading her thighs wide open to his curious eyes. Using the tip of his middle finger, he traced the seam of her pussy from her slit to her clit, giving the little bud a gentle flick. Her body bowed in reaction.

"Please," she begged needing more.

Paul positioned himself between the vee of her thighs, licking and nipping the inside of her inner thighs like she'd taught him before placing his mouth over her labia and sucking one side into his mouth. The man suckled it until she thought she'd pass out from the pleasure, then released it and did the same to the other side.

"You taste like honey. So sweet."

She tried to comment, but no thought formed in her mind as Paul continued exploring her sex, nipping, and licking her clit, studying the effects each of his movements had on her body. When he was satisfied, he moved on to her slick entrance spearing his tongue and fucking into her core like a man possessed while gently rubbing her clit with his fingertips.

"Holy... hell!" she practically screamed as she felt the tingling in her core. "I'm going to come soon."

With that declaration, Paul removed his tongue and plunged two thick digits inside her creamy channel continuing the circling over her pulsing clit, and then speared his tongue once again and slipped it inside her entrance along with his still pumping fingers. It was the final catalyst that she needed.

"Holy mother of the universe!" she yelled, her whole-body stiffening, legs locking his head in place as her orgasm hit with the force of a tractor trailer. She trembled as Paul kept licking and pumping through her release, slowly bringing her back down to earth. *"Wow!"*

He chuckled low in his throat. The sound reminded her he hadn't lost his virginity yet. Meara sat up, pulling him up to her lips and kissed him hard. The taste of her juices glistening on his swollen lips, but she didn't care, all she wanted was more of him.

"Come here, Lieutenant Commander," she practically purred with anticipation. "I'm going to claim my prize."

CHAPTER TEN

It was really happening... with *Meara*.

Paul thought he had died and gone to heaven. He even said a silent prayer to make him last long enough to satisfy her and not embarrass himself.

"Sit back," she commanded. "Yeah! Just like that. We don't need all of these clothes, do we?"

Slowly, she unbuttoned his shirt, pushing the garment off of his shoulders, his sculpted chest gloriously naked and ripe for the picking. He caressed her arms and chest with his palms enjoying the smooth, café-au-lait skin beneath his hands.

Next, she unbuckled his belt, making quick work of his button and zipper before saying, "Lift your hips... there we go."

The little minx pulled off his boxer-briefs and his jeans in one fell swoop. Stopping briefly to place a wet kiss to the tip of his cock; the action made him bow off of the couch.

"Please hurry, princess," he begged.

"Be patient." She giggled.

"I've been patient for over twenty-seven years," he groaned. "I've been patient long enough. *Hurry!*"

Meara leaned forward and swiped her tongue teasingly over his nipple, the tiny bud peaked instantly and so did his cock.

"This is how good it feels when you do it to me." She did the same to the other one.

"Stop playing, *wench*," he implored, voice strained with need.

Without further ado, she went lower down his body and sucked the entire head of his member into her hot, wet mouth, licking and sucking like it was a delicious treat.

"Mmm," she hummed on a moan. "So tasty."

Then she stood suddenly and straddled his legs, her breasts now at eye level, the dark chocolate nipples taunting him. Paul took the opportunity to reach between her beautifully toned legs, parting her delicate folds with eager fingers, finding her slick and ready.

Immediately, her body stiffened as he found her slit and worked two fingers inside her drenched core. She widened her legs, allowing him to push inside her up to the third knuckle. Her cream dripped down his digits, her inner muscles clenched greedily as he fucked her at his leisure. The sweet scent of honey suffocated him as she bucked her hips against his thrusting hand.

Teetering on that invisible cliff where orgasm was imminent, he bit his bottom lip to keep from blowing his load, slowly exhaling when he felt her tremble beneath his stroking fingertips. Ever so gently, he continued circling the tiny nubbin, licking his lips at the sight of his woman lost in his ministrations. A low whimper escaped her as her nipples pebbled further, directly in front of his curious gaze. Glancing down at her neatly trimmed pubic hair, he noticed how soft the strands were. Afterward, maybe he'd run his fingers through it and nuzzle it with his nose.

Unable to fight his instincts any longer, he leaned forward, and sucked her nipple into his open mouth while using his free hand to gently squeeze and knead the other heavy mound. Intuitively, he hollowed his cheeks, pressing the dark, chocolate-colored nipple to the roof of his mouth and then ran his tongue back and forth along the underside of the heavy swell.

He felt a sharp pinching sensation as her nails dug into the bare skin of his shoulders, but he didn't care. She could chop off his right arm as long as she stayed like this forever. Completely lost in the moment, he pumped her pussy with a steady rhythm, in and out, over and over, working her sex until she begged for his cock.

"Paul, for heaven's sake. Just do it," she pleaded, her inflection heavy with desire.

"*Mmm*," he purred. "You are so bossy, princess, but luckily tonight I'm taking requests."

He waggled both brows at her when she rolled her eyes in response.

Reaching for her hips, he adjusted her as he slung her leg over his, so her knees were resting on either side of his, the evidence of her arousal leaving a slippery trail of moisture behind.

Before he went any further the little commonsense, he still retained reminded him to ask, "What about protection?"

"I'm on the pill and I'm clean if you want you can go bareback. I know *you're* clean," her whispered words were music to his ears. She giggled. "I've never popped someone's cherry before."

"I want to be inside you, Meara."

The emotion in his voice affected her as much as it affected him. Then slowly, she nodded her reply and reached between their bodies, wrapped her hands around his cock and positioned him at her dripping entrance.

"Hurry!" he groaned as his cock pulsed with the need for release.

Needing to be joined, she pumped her body over his, wriggling and circling her full hips over the head of his member. The movement allowed her to sheath only half of him before she pronounced, "Your package is so incredibly... *Huge!*"

"Do you want to stop?" He almost choked on the words but didn't want to hurt her.

Meara nodded her head vehemently.

"Hell no! Let me try something," she announced reaching between them with her hand and slowly began to rub gentle circles over her engorged nubbin at the apex of her sex.

A flood of cream rushed over his hard-as-nails cock, allowing her to sheath the rest of him with a deft, hard thrust of her hips that made him purr like a contented cat.

"Ah... that's it... so good... so damn good."

"Holy shit!" He pulled her against his chest, her breasts smashed against him, his member buried to the hilt in her tight channel.

"Why don't you do the honors?" she whispered, her voice raspy and dripping with desire for him.

"Excuse me?" he asked, his confusion evident as he watched her through hooded eyes.

"Take me from the top," she commanded helping him maneuver their bodies, so that she was resting on the couch with him on top, his lean hips nestled between her athletic legs. "Take me, Paul. Make me yours."

Without hesitation, he kneed her thighs as wide as possible, withdrawing from her clinging depths with exquisite leisure, torturing them both. Then driven totally by instinct, he plunged into her with a quick, hard thrust, the action making her cry out with pleasure.

Paul smiled as he withdrew, so only the head of his cock was lodged at the entrance of her sex before he plunged back inside, burying himself balls deep.

"*Mine*," he growled, unable to stop the possessiveness he had always felt for Meara suddenly increased one hundred-fold. "You. Are. Mine." He emphasized each word with a hard, deep thrust of his cock.

"*Aye,*" she whimpered as he made love to her as he'd always wanted. "I love you, Paul. I love you so much. I can't breathe without you. Only you."

"I love you too, princess." He kissed her soft, full lips, the overwhelming need to mark her as his drumming through his body.

Driven by the feel of her beneath him, joined so intimately, he drove into her depths with strong lunges. Her breasts bouncing with each movement turning him on even more and causing his member to lengthen painfully.

"Mine," he stated again as she arched into his invading movements, pounding her hips in an unrelenting rhythm.

Pulling back to her opening one last time, he reached up and pinched both nipples then lunged deep again, it was the only stimuli Meara needed to find her release.

"*What... the... fu—*" Meara's stuttered words morphed into a breathless squeak as her head thrashed wildly from side to side. She screamed her pleasure, her body trembling, her channel pulsing and clamping onto his cock. The sensation making his balls tighten up as a painful burst of seed was wrenched from the depths of his soul.

"*Fuck!*" He rammed into her as he found his pleasure.

The power of it buckling his legs and he had to use his elbows to hold up his much larger body so not to suffocate her.

"Meara, Meara, Meara," he whispered her name like a prayer. "I love you."

He didn't know how long they both lay on the couch, panting until their breathing returned to normal. Meara's lovely face smiling in a way he'd seen once before... the first time he'd made her climax.

"How was it?" he asked, hoping he had done well or at least not terribly. The idea of making love to her once was similar to the idea of drinking battery acid. It was disturbing and unacceptable.

"*Goodgraciousmeohmyoh...* my!" Meara proclaimed loudly in an almost incoherent rushed jumble of words. "Those pornographic videos were really great study-aids," she stated, her breasts heaving in time to her panting, her Scottish brogue sounding thick and sultry.

He laughed, stroking her bare back and shoulders as she lay against him, cheek pressed to his chest, a sated smile gracing her luscious lips. "I have to agree with you one hundred and fifty percent, princess."

"Paul?"

"Yeah?"

"Do you think we'll ever make it off of this bloody couch?"

He laughed, stood up and adjusted her body over his shoulder in a fireman's hold.

"We can take care of that right now."

And he carried her down the hallway to her bedroom.

Meara awoke to a strange sensation between her legs. Slowly opening her eyes, she spied Paul's head bobbing over her sex. His wicked tongue licking along the seam then moving up to her aching clit.

"Good morning to you too," she whispered huskily.

He chuckled as his mouth clamped onto her tiny nubbin and sucked it into his mouth. His massive hands reaching up to gently roll and pinch her hard nipples. The added stimulation wreaking havoc on her senses.

"You are gonna kill me with sex, beast," she whispered on a breathless sigh.

Ignoring her, he adjusted her legs over his broad, muscular shoulders opening her wide to his plundering tongue. The muscle speared her opening like a miniature cock, thrusting in and out, in and out, over, and over and over again, until she was going out of her mind with the need for release.

"You like that, don't you?" It wasn't a question, but an accurate observation on his part. "Now that I've tasted you, I can't seem to get enough."

He flattened his tongue then and gave her inside folds a long, wet swipe, making her cry out with the first ripples of her impending release.

The Hawaiian sex-god must have recognized the signs leading up to her quickly building orgasm and suddenly released her legs, kneeling between them and lining up the head of his member at her slippery slit, using the tip to stimulate the tiny bundle of nerves at the apex of her sex.

"*Bloody hell!*" she groaned as he held the bottom of his long, thick shaft and drove inside her sopping wet channel, but the damn thing only lodged inside a few inches.

"*Jeez!*" he hissed through clenched teeth. "Your pussy is so *tight*."

She shook her head no.

"I'm tight, but not that tight," she grunted uncomfortably. "You're massive."

Her entire body tensed as he slowly began to work his huge organ inside her core.

An arrogant snort escaped before he spoke.

"That's one of the best things you can tell your guy."

Pushing in a bit further, she tensed practically locking him into her heat.

"Damn it!" she swore.

"Am I hurting you?" concern filled his question.

"Yes, damn it," she groaned. "You are. You are really huge."

He looked frazzled.

"What should I do?" His eyes widened.

She took his right hand and reached between their bodies, positioning his finger over her nubbin again.

"Make little circles," she commanded, voice laced with lust. "Ah... a little harder... yeah, just like that."

A whimper escaped her throat before she could subdue it.

"Now, suck my nipples... *freaking hell*... yes, like that... that feels so good."

The man truly had a talented tongue.

A gush of cream flooded her sex, dripping down her inner core and along his wide shaft.

"You're soaking me, princess," he exclaimed against her nipple as he slowly pushed into the clenching depths of her body.

The feeling so exquisite she thought she'd die from it. She hissed with pleasure when he filled her to the hilt, his heavy balls slapping against the seam of her backside.

"My gracious! You are so deep. Make love to me, Paul. Right the hell now!"

That was all the encouragement he needed as he slowly retreated from her then worked his way back inside, rocking his hips, his long, thick appendage thrusting deeper, the wide girth stretching her to the limits of sanity. Her whole body was suddenly on high alert, begging for a mind-shattering orgasm.

Once again, Paul's head descended claiming her mouth in a toe-curling kiss. He plunged inside the last couple inches, bottoming out when he bumped her cervix.

"Holy mother of the universe! You're so bloody deep."

He chuckled.

"I love it when you get all proper and Scottish on me. It makes me hot."

"Insipid man," she hissed, clenching her teeth to prolong the onslaught of her quickly building orgasm, her eyes squeezed closed. "Stop playing around. I need to come."

Straightening, Paul hooked his arms underneath her legs and lifted her hips from the mattress. In her raised position, he stroked deeper, his heavy balls slapping rhythmically against the curve of her arse, the wet noise like an erotic tune wafting through the room. It was like a dream... a beautiful pornographic dream.

She glanced up at him, his eyes watching her watching him, dark and heavy-lidded, jaw clenched tightly, and she worried about his teeth. His whole body was a wet dream come to life with his highly defined biceps and pectorals, an abdomen that could have been used as the muse for *Michel Angelo's David* that flexed as he drove inside her, a backside you could eat breakfast on, and his flawless olive skin glistening with sweat as he moved sinuously against her, driving her toward the edge of reason.

"You are breathtaking," she whispered, cupping his cheek in one hand, and tracing his lips with the fingers of the other. "Even before the makeover, I thought you were gorgeous."

He smiled, continuing his steady pace; bending his head he gave her nipple several long-wet glides with his tongue, pushing her over that invisible cliff. Her entire body stiffened as she gasped for air, the climax hitting her with a powerful force that made her dizzy.

Paul continued his movements, groaning and grunting and swearing as he fucked through her spasms, his balls slapping against her ass in that delightful way.

"You're gonna kill me," she moaned, as he suddenly increased his pace until she thought she might pass out from the pleasure.

She felt him grow impossibly harder, plunging to the hilt and growled, "Meara!"

Finally, he came... *hard*; muttering praises and loving words as he emptied into her, grinding the root of his cock hard against her pelvis. The first stream of hot seed blasting inside her still pulsating channel, jerking deep. His fine body shaky with completion, chocolate irises locked with her toffee-colored ones, a hint of a boyish smile on his beautifully sculpted mouth.

"Princess," he stated fondly, the endearment for her tugging at her heart. "You. Are. Amazing."

Meara's body slumped against him. The man was a Hawaiian sex-deity. In the encyclopedia along with the definition should be a picture of him with a disclaimer reading: *Paul Choy, Hawaiian sex-god... picture is not actual size... please see the following three pages.*

Paul reached for her, tucked her head under his stubbled chin, and positioned her limp, sated body over his much larger one. He closed his eyes, a broad arrogant grin gracing his face.

Leaning up, she licked his Adam's apple enjoying the bobbing motion it made when he swallowed, the taste of his salty essence arousing her even more.

"No, you are amazing, Paul Choy... utterly, unrequitedly, without-a-doubt, amazing."

A couple hours later, they made breakfast together in comfortable silence, each preparing a traditional food from their culture. Paul made coconut-macadamia nut pancakes while she made Welch Rarebits, or what her mum would call a posh cheese-on-toast since she was English, but it was basically thickly sliced toasted bread with a creamy cheese sauce poured over it. It was delicious.

"How's the Welch Rarebit?" she asked nervously.

"Simply scrumptious, just like you," he stated sincerely. "How are the pancakes?"

"*Blimey*," she purred as she took another bite of Paul's pancakes, the light buttery morsel better than any pancake she'd ever eaten. "Who taught you to cook?"

"My dad," he boasted watching her reaction as she chewed. "He's a professional baker by trade, but he actually went to culinary school before I was born."

"Amazing," she replied, trying not to lick the sweet coconut syrup he also made from scratch from the tines of her fork, but in the end, she licked them anyway. "What does your mum do as a career?"

His body stiffened and she knew she had said something wrong.

"She was a seamstress. She taught Noelani how to cut patterns, hem clothing, and make simple repairs." He cleared his throat before continuing. "She would have loved to see Noelani graduate from the Fashion Institute and then have both of you all's designs featured in British Vogue."

He reached across the table and rested his hand over hers, its warmth heating not only her body, but her heart as well.

"I take it your mum isn't with you anymore." He shook his head no and she squeezed his hand in an attempt to comfort him. "How did she—"

"Cancer," he responded emotionlessly, but his expressive, brown eyes said so much more than he ever would.

"When did she pass away?" she prodded gently, wanting to know more about the man she loved.

"The year I entered the Naval Academy at Annapolis after M-I-T, about seven years ago," he replied in a low raspy voice, the sound making her heart tighten.

"Do you think she'd approve of me?"

He leaned over the small dining table and brushed his lips against hers.

"She would have loved you, probably as much as I do."

Her phone rang as she stood to sit on his lap. The man looked tempting wearing only his black jeans from the previous night, his sculpted abdomen sporting a six-pack, actually it was more of an eight-pack, truth be told.

Paul's body was a masterpiece, and she couldn't wait to trace all of those ridges and valleys with her tongue.

"Good morning," she answered, voice thick with desire as Paul encircled her from behind, nuzzling the nape of her neck with the tip of his nose as his persistent hands cupped her breasts from behind and rubbed his rock-hard erection against the seam of her behind.

"Miss McBride?" The official-sounding question brought her back to reality.

"This is she," she said curtly. "To whom am I speaking?"

She swatted Paul's head to make him stop.

"What's going on?" he mouthed.

"I'm not sure," she mouthed back.

"This is Gregory Larkin with the Department of Immigration and Naturalization. Sorry to contact you on the weekend, but there seems to be a problem with your work visa."

"What's wrong with it?" Meara sat straight in her chair.

"It appears you didn't report a criminal misdemeanor on your paperwork, so you'll be removed from the country as soon as possible."

"Wait... wait!" she practically yelled into the receiver; her legs began to shake until Paul held her against his chest listening to the one-sided conversation. "I've never been arrested for anything. I've never even had a speeding ticket. Who reported this blatant lie?"

"According to our records, a Mister Roger McVicor of the Harris and Harris Law Firm reported the discrepancy over a month ago. There's been a backlog of cases, that's why it's taken this long to contact you. Are you familiar with Mister McVicor?"

"He's my ex-boyfriend," she muttered as panic began to assault her brain. "He's just trying to get back at me for breaking up with him that's it."

"Perhaps, but we still have to investigate it."

Her cheeks filled with heat and her lips started trembling with rage.

"When did he contact your office?"

She heard papers being shuffled around before the other man replied. "Before the holidays."

"Did he do it by phone?" she questioned, trying to process what was being said.

"No, ma'am," Mr. Larkin replied in a clear tone. "It was in person. He said he had just transferred to his firm's sister law office in Oahu."

"Good to know," she huffed, feeling the bile rising in her throat.

"We'll need to see you immediately, Miss McBride, first thing Monday morning."

"Yes, Sir."

"And Miss McBride?"

"Yes?" Meara held her breath.

"If we can't get this situation cleared-up, we will administratively remove you from the country."

"You mean deport me." She flinched.

"No, not exactly. For deportation we'd need a judge to file a court order, but just removing you is within the Department of Immigration's authority. If you get things straightened out, you may reapply in a year."

"I understand, Mister Larkin," she responded with a hushed tone.

"See you Monday," he said stiffly then gave her the building's address, directions, and the office number.

After she hung up the call, she quickly phoned her mum's cell, who picked up on the second ring.

"Meara?"

"Hi, Mum," she greeted as calmly as possible. "Did you know about it?"

"Know about what, sweetheart?"

"Did you have any knowledge of Roger reporting that I failed to file a criminal misdemeanor on my work visa paperwork?"

Her mum gasped, her voice immediately sounded shaky, and she knew she was innocent.

"No, of course not!" Mrs. McBride blurted with sincerity. "I'll call your dad; he's at the office and I need to speak with him. What did the immigration agent tell you?"

"He said that if I can't clear this up, they'll be removing me from the island right away."

Her mother quickly shifted into attorney-mode as she relayed the phone call.

"I'll contact Immigration Services first thing Monday morning, and sweetheart?"

"Aye, Mum?"

"I know your father and I haven't been supportive about your fashion design career, but I just wanted you to know, I would never, ever sabotage your dreams... *never*. We just miss you so much."

"Dad said he'd disown me if I left Edinburgh, remember?" Meara stiffened at the memory. "And he hasn't contacted me since."

"Your father is a *thrawn* man, but he's been miserable since you've been away," her mother explained, her English accent strengthening. "He even mentioned coming down for a vacation."

"Dad never goes on vacation," Meara gasped her surprise.

"Well, that's how much he misses his *quine*."

"I'm not a young girl anymore, but thanks, Mum. I appreciate it."

"By the way," her parent said enthusiastically. "My assistant showed me the article in British Vogue about the boutique and you and Noelani's online store. You are the talk of the town. Everyone from your old headmaster at your secondary school to Sister Agnes who spanked you in primary school for sticking your tongue out at her is raving about you.

"I'm so *bloody* proud of you, honey!" Her mum's Cockney accent bubbled to the surface with her excitement. "Daddy is too."

She couldn't help the muffled choke that slipped out.

"Mum, I can't get removed from Hawai'i," she rambled and cried at the same time. "I've met someone. His name is Paul Choy, he's a Lieutenant Commander in the Navy and he's fantastic. Mum... I love him."

Her mum gasped in surprise.

"I wasn't expecting to hear that sort of news," Mrs. McBride informed, and then paused dramatically. "Then I guess we'll have to fix this quickly then."

Paul was livid. It was Sunday morning, and they had spent all Saturday trying to reach upper management employees at the state department in order to file a temporary injunction to prevent Meara from being sent back to Scotland, but nothing was working out.

He was on the verge of having a meltdown.

"Fucking shit of an asshole motherfucker!" he growled, slamming the cordless phone back into its cradle, the plastic casing almost cracking with the force of impact.

"Paul," his dad stated firmly, the other man's gentle voice soothing his frayed nerves. "Getting angry isn't going to solve anything."

Meara placed a slender hand on his shoulder, and he pulled her against him burying his nose in her vanilla-scented locks.

"If things don't work out, I'll just go back to Scotland, file the proper paperwork and reapply for another visa," she stated trying to reassure him, but failing miserably.

"How long will that be?" Kai and Aiden asked in unison.

"Probably a year," she stated without heat.

He shook his head adamantly.

"No. No way am I going to be without you for a year. I'll go crazy."

"I don't think we have a choice," his girlfriend stated, biting her bottom lip nervously.

"I'll get a transfer," Paul declared with all seriousness. "No problem. Should only take a couple of months. I know a guy in—"

It was Adrienne's turn to cut him off.

"The closest Navy base in that area is in Italy," Koa's better half informed. "I know because that was the base where I was born."

"Damn it," Paul huffed, not knowing what to do next. "Then I'll quit the Navy and move with you."

"No," Meara asserted firmly. "I won't let you do it, not for me, not under these circumstances."

"Why?" he asked, looking at her determined face.

"If you quit because of me, down the road, you'd resent me and that would be worse. I won't let you leave the Navy and that's final."

"I wish I knew what to do," Joseph Kapahu, Kai, and Koa's father, chimed in. The goliath-sized man's voice was calm and kind, in contrast to his intimidating size. Koa was his exact replica.

"There's got to be something," Leilani Kapahu, Joseph's wife, looked as worried as she felt.

"There is," Paul proclaimed, turning to Meara suddenly. "We can get married."

She choked on her saliva as soon as the words left his mouth.

"What?"

"You heard me," he stated, eyes filled with sincerity. "I think we should get married. Today."

She stared at him, but wouldn't say anything, couldn't say anything.

"We barely know one another... *you mad, mad man*," she said finally.

"That's not true," he adamantly disagreed. "I think you're the *only* person who's ever really known me."

She shook her head as tears welled up in her expressive, toffee-hued eyes. "Paul—"

"Listen, you know all of those *lessons* you gave me?"

"Aye?" Meara glanced around at the other family members who were all looking at each other in confusion, all except for Kai, who grinned knowingly at them.

"I figured out why I did so *well* with them... with you."

"Really." It wasn't a question.

"I've always been nervous around women, except ones who are related to me," the determined lieutenant revealed. "Talking to the opposite sex rarely happens and on the occasions that it did, I always managed to stick my foot in my mouth or insult them or just plain embarrass myself."

"I don't understand."

"And didn't you once tell me that sometimes you get so nervous you actually can cause bodily harm to yourself and others? Like that incident at the fashion show you modeled at in Milan. The one where you fell off the catwalk and into the lap of Vera Wang?"

"So...?"

"So, have you ever been nervous around me?"

"No," she said without hesitation.

"That's how I feel when I'm around you: calm, centered, self-confident," he poured out his soul. "I've never felt that way about anyone... except with you, Meara. It's only ever been you."

Suddenly, Paul sat down on the nearby dining chair and tugged her onto his lap. The feel of her ass against his groin causing his cock to flex and grow and he had to silently remind the appendage that family was present.

"I've never been tense around you. I can be myself no matter how geeky and know that you'll accept it, because even though you're *hot,* you are just as geeky as I am."

"That's true," Noelani spoke out. "He's comfortable around you. In fact, he's so comfortable that he had the nerve to be mean to you at the beach that first Sunday you came to brunch. He's never insulted anyone like that except family."

"*See?* That has to count for something." He smiled at her contorted facial expression. "But most importantly, I love you, so much it hurts when I look at you, when I think of you. You are the first person I want to see in the morning and the last person I want to see at night. You are everything I ever wanted, but never believed I could have.

"Please, Meara, make me complete and marry me."

She tried to think but was having difficulties.

"What if we get married and there was no need to? How will you feel then... like I used you, that's how you'll feel."

Tears started to roll down her cheeks and she swiped angrily at them.

Paul shook his head no.

"I'll be happy that we started our future together *now* instead of later."

He smiled as he took her shaking hands in his. Meara sat speechless for a few tense moments, all eyes staring anxiously at her beautiful face.

"I love you so much!" she finally exclaimed, tears streaming even harder down her face. "I would love to marry you, Lieutenant Commander Paul Choy, more than I could ever tell you."

"Then I guess you'll just have to show me." And in front of his entire family, his amazing Scottish princess, who was smarter than he, kissed him sweetly until his body relaxed.

His!

And she would be *his*, very soon.

CHAPTER ELEVEN

After she and Paul called her parents in Edinburgh to get their blessing and to promise to keep in touch on a regular basis, Kai, Adrienne, and she went to her apartment to get ready. Noelani, on the other hand, ran to the boutique to pick up a dress they had designed for a famous singer's nuptials, but decided it would look better on her instead.

Kai styled her hair into an elegant half-up-half-down hairdo with a few soft curls framing her face while Adrienne applied some neutral smoky eye shadow, eyeliner, and lip gloss with a hint of color to emphasize her full lips.

"Here it is!" Noelani raced into the bedroom carrying a garment bag which she knew held her dream wedding dress. "I lowered the hem by a couple of inches, so it should be the correct length. I can't believe we're going to be related!"

She giggled before insisting, "We've always been family, this will just make it official."

"One more thing," Noelani added playfully, her dark brown eyes gleaming. "I stopped by my house to pick this up."

Her best friend placed an antique sterling silver and topaz butterfly hair clip in her right palm.

"It's gorgeous," Meara gasped. "But I can't accept it... this is your mother's... isn't it?"

The tears began to well in her eyes as she remembered the day her friend received a phone call that both her parents had been killed in a car accident when she was away at the *Fashion Institute*.

"I couldn't possibly." She tried to hand it back. "This was meant for your big day, not mine."

"It's only for today." Noelani took the clip from her and arranged it in her hair. "We are practically sisters, Meara McBride. Your dress will be your something new, and *this* will be your something old, something borrowed, and something blue."

Noelani looked at her through their reflection in the vanity mirror.

"There." Her fiancé's cousin beamed. "Now you look like part of the family."

Paul was a man on a mission as he drove through the bustling streets of East Waikiki trying to find a jewelry store open at nine o'clock on a Sunday morning.

"Damn it!" he swore at the colorful sign adorning the front door of the tiny jewelry store on Kapahulu Avenue that was turned to the closed side. According to the hours of operations, the damn place wouldn't be open until noon.

Fuck a duck! He snarled. How could he get married without a ring? Meara deserved a ring... an amazing-take-her-breath-away ring. He ran both hands through his hair in frustration.

What to do now?

As if by divine intervention, his cell phone rang showing his father's face on the screen.

"Aloha, Pop," he answered, trying to sound chipper, but failing miserably. "What's going on? I thought you were going straight to Koa and Adrienne's place to help set-up?"

"I had to stop at home for something. Are you already dressed?" His father and voice of reason, Alexander Paul Choy, came over the speaker. "Where are you?"

"I'm looking for a damn jewelry store. I need a wedding ring for Meara, and nothing is open this early. I've already been to five different places." He looked down at his formal Navy dress whites. "I'm ready, but I can't get married without a proper ring."

"Don't worry about a ring, just get your butt over to Koa's place before you're late for your own wedding," his father teased. "And Meara comes to her senses and changes her mind."

"She deserves a ring, Pop," he sounded defeated even to his own ears.

"She'll have one," Mr. Choy promised. "Just get to the ceremony on time. It will all work out for the best, I promise."

"What about a ring for Paul? Heaven preserve us! He needs a ring. He can't get married without one," Meara whined from the backseat of Adrienne's *Toyota Camry*. "We need to stop at the boutique."

"Now?" Adrienne watched her from the rearview mirror, an unhappy frown marring her otherwise lovely exotic features.

The bride shook her head.

"I have something that will work," Meara hastily explained. "A project I've been working on for our new fall jewelry collection."

"But we'll be late," Kai chimed in.

"It'll only take ten minutes. Please." Meara folded her hands together as if she were praying.

"Ok, ok," Adrienne relented, her French accent more pronounced. "You Scots are always causing problems." Her soon-to-be cousin-in-law badgered her affectionately making her feel like a member of the family already.

She laughed.

"Hey *Frenchy*, that's the pot calling the kettle black."

The entire family drove to Lanikai Beach, a lesser-known beach on the windward side of the island where Koa and Adrienne's bungalow was located, nestled in a residential neighborhood of Kailua.

The beach was absolutely stunning with sparkling white sand, calm waters, and towering palms. The *Mokuluas or Moks* that served as a bird safe haven stood proudly against the azure background. She could imagine her and Paul, laying on the soft Hawaiian sand, soaking up the temperate sunshine, and listening to quarreling gulls overhead. She couldn't have imagined a more romantic setting to get married than the one in front of her.

There was no arguing, mid-January in Hawai'i was sheer perfection. Above, the serene azure sky was dotted with billowy clouds drifting on the coconut-scented breeze, while distant sailboats caressed the Polynesian horizon. It was a scene right out of the pages of a fairytale and similar to a fairytale, her prince would be waiting for her.

"Are you ready?" Noelani asked as she adjusted her hairclip one last time and looked her up and down, a sigh of approval slipping past her lips.

"I am," she stated confidently, wondering why she wasn't having second thoughts over their rushed nuptials, but somehow it all felt right. "But I miss my mum and dad and brothers—"

Noelani must have sensed her worry.

"Don't worry about your family not being here to see you tie the knot," the woman consoled empathetically. "My Uncle Joseph is video recording the entire ceremony and reception as a wedding present for you."

"Thank you," Meara said with sincerity. "How did I manage to find a friend like you?"

Her best friend shrugged her shoulders.

"I guess you're just lucky," Noelani jibed, lightening the mood.

Meara stuck her tongue out at her, and they both giggled.

Noelani led her down a short wooden boardwalk lined with tall cattails and saw grass to the sandy area below. Their arms hooked together at the elbow. Her best friend's turquoise sundress blended perfectly into the surrounding vista. As they reached the steps leading down to the beach area, she saw Paul waiting at the bottom dressed in his service whites and looking much too sophisticated for his own good. The man stole her senses.

The sight before her made her gasp and Noelani automatically tightened her grip on her arm. When they arrived, the beach overlooking the *Moks* was already set with a large white pavilion.

There were white folding chairs draped in white muslin chair covers on each side of the aisle with a special azure fabric runner made specifically for beach weddings sprinkled with pink and white orchid petals separating the groom's side from the bride's sides. Even though all of the guests in attendance were related to Paul, it was perfectly staged. Someone had thoughtfully set several meticulously placed lit bamboo tiki-torches to keep the sand flies at bay, their fragrant citronella oil perfuming the air.

With all her entire being, she wished her family could be there with her. The idea saddened her, and she felt tears brimming in her eyes again. But she shook her head, pushing the unwanted thought out of her head and focused instead on the small white pavilion and her soon-to-be husband.

Respectfully, the crowd stood as she and Noelani walked down the wooden steps.

All smiled simultaneously at her except for Paul who mouthed, *"You look beautiful."*

Just as she had hoped, the simple white dress, inspired by a vintage find at a local *Goodwill* store, combined the romance of a *Provence* eyelet with a flattering, feminine halter shape. The fully lined, cotton material with an empire waist and well-placed eyelet overlay at the waist and hem had a fitted bodice, full skirt that fell to mid-calf, and tied at the back of the neck. The heated look he gave made her satisfied with her choice.

As though no one else was in attendance, their gazes locked, and she swore she saw him rub his hand over his heart muttering something. The pounding in her chest suddenly flooded her ears as she walked toward her future. When they finally reached the groom, Noelani placed Meara's hand in his before kissing her on both cheeks, then turned and did the same to Paul, who smiled, turned, and led her to the pavilion where Mr. Choy waited for them both.

Carefully, Mr. Choy put the traditional leis on both of their necks, a ti leaf lei around Paul's neck and a white ginger lei around hers. The lovely fragrance of the beautiful lei almost overwhelmed her senses. They in turn did the same to him as was the ancient custom Noelani had educated her about during the ride over. Then the ceremony began.

Meara felt the air rush out of her lungs as her groom took her hand in his; everything seemed to be moving in slow motion. Her eyes welled-up, dark curls ruffling softly in the early morning breeze, and the man who had captured her heart only a few months before was going to be her husband. *Mine.*

The *kahu*, or Hawaiian holy man, performed a customary Polynesian chant and with the song *Waiting for Thee* playing softly on the ukulele in the background, they began their vow recital.

"Meara," Paul looked at her, chocolate-brown to toffee eyes. "Never in my imaginings did I think I'd be getting married and never in my imaginings did I think I'd end up with a person like you.

"You are intellectual... stunning... and the most fascinating, unpredictable, ambitious person I've ever known, and I wouldn't change anything about you. Even before we became... more," the embarrassing man stated teasingly, "It has only been you... will always be you.

"You are my heart and my spirit and my better half and from this moment forward, I promise to love, honor, and cherish you forever."

Paul gently squeezed her hands and she had to slowly inhale and exhale to compose herself. Clearing her throat, she began.

"Paul." She smiled up into those chocolate-brown irises and felt her heart lurch inside her chest. "The first time we met you wouldn't speak to me. The second time we met you insulted me, and the third time we met I knew that we would become great friends. Imagine my surprise when I realized we would also become lovers and soul mates.

"Today I accept all of you... the sexy, playful, intelligent, insufferable man that I love. You are the other half of my soul and I promise to love, honor, and cherish you for the rest of our lives."

"Paul, do you take this woman to be your lawfully wedded wife?" the kahu queried, already knowing the answer.

"I do." He grinned.

"And Meara, do you take this man to be your lawfully wedded husband?" The holy man gave her a small approving nod.

"I do." She beamed.

"Now you may present the rings," the wedding official instructed.

She heard Paul whisper, "I don't have a ring. The jewelry stores were still closed."

Disappointment filled his words, and she knew she was making the right choice to marry the wonderful man standing beside her.

"It's alright," she whispered back. "All I need is you."

Paul released a breath which made her giggle.

"Pardon me, you two."

They both turned to the deep baritone voice of Mr. Choy.

"Sorry to interrupt the ceremony," Alexander apologized to the holy man. "But we do have a ring."

"Pop, I didn't get one, remember?"

Mr. Choy walked over and placed a small, gold velvet bag with a drawstring tie in his palm. Paul quickly undid the tie and looked inside, his eyes tearing and a flush of pink appearing on his cheeks.

"Mom's ring?" he gasped, the emotion on his face making her tear up as well. "Are you sure you want to do this?"

The incredibly handsome, older version of Paul nodded his head before turning to her.

"My wife, Alana, and I always wanted a houseful of children," Alexander began. "But God blessed us with only a son. This boy filled our hearts as if he were many children. Alana and I always wanted a daughter and now we have one."

Then he placed a chaste kiss on both her cheeks, gently wiped away the tear that was rolling down her face, and then returned to his seat.

Meara reached into a hidden pocket sewn into the dress and pulled out a gold and silver ring, both metals swirled together, but remained separate in a unique undulating pattern.

"Where did you get this?" His big smile warmed her heart.

"I made it." She gave him a saucy wink. "I've been learning to make jewelry and thought I'd make custom bands for the online store. Do you like it?"

"No," he stated flatly.

Her eyes narrowed at his tone.

"I love it, almost as much as I love you," the officer stated.

"May I have both rings?" the official requested with a grin on his round face.

Then the *kahu* took both rings and dipped a *ti* leaf into a small bowl of sea water and sprinkled both rings with the water three times chanting in Hawaiian. While the priest completed his blessing over the bands, A.J. and Aria placed colorful tropical flowers in a circle around Meara and Paul. Next, the couple poured two different colored sand into a container, symbolizing their unbreakable bond.

Meara grinned when Paul mouthed, "Sorry, Hawaiians have a lot of traditions."

"I think it's wonderful," she mouthed back.

Finally, a lava rock was wrapped in a *ti* leaf and placed on the sand behind the pavilion commiserating their union.

"Paul," the *kahu* instructed. "Place the ring on Meara's finger and repeat after me."

Obediently, Paul took her left hand, listening carefully to the *kahu*, then placed a simple white gold band with a brilliant two carat, oval faceted, Tanzanite stone onto her slightly shaking finger. The ring was hand-crafted and looked extremely expensive and must have been a family heirloom.

"Meara Elizabeth McBride, with this ring I thee wed," Paul repeated confidently, smiling the entire time.

"Ah dinnae ken what to say," her voice was almost too low to be heard.

"Say, *'thank you,'* said the wedding official smiling at both of them.

She suddenly felt overwhelmed at the amount of love and acceptance she already felt from Paul's family, and she struggled to hold back tears of happiness.

"It's gorgeous, thank you," she mouthed to Mr. Choy, who gave her a thumbs-up.

"Meara, please do the same and repeat after me," the *kahu* requested.

Listening carefully, she repeated.

"Paul Alexander Choy, with this ring I thee wed," her voice was low and shaky with emotion.

When she was ready, the holy man repeated the phrase that would legally bind them.

"With the power vested in me by the great state of Hawai'i, I now pronounce you man and wife." The man made a puckering motion making the audience laugh. "Now, you may kiss your bride."

Without further ado, Paul took her around the waist, pulled her into his arms and kissed her until her toes curled and all sensation in her lips disappeared. When he finally released her, she had to lean against him to regain her equilibrium.

"I love you," she said as her husband gazed into her weepy eyes.

"I love you more." Then kissed her on the lips briefly.

Then, in a loud, strong voice the wedding official announced, "It is my great honor to introduce, Lieutenant Commander Paul Choy and his lovely wife, Meara McBride-Choy!"

CHAPTER TWELVE

The reception was an intimate affair with only family members and close friends. Besides his father, Noelani, the Kaplan's, and both sets of the Kapahu's, a variety of aunts, uncles, and cousins, and of course J.T., it was a fairly small party. About eighty people were in attendance in total.

However, brunch was a bit more sophisticated with Cousin Keanu manning the grill along with several uncles as line cooks. The menu of grilled, marinated rib-eye steaks, freshly caught spiny lobster tails, corn on the cob with a spicy kimchi butter, and baked potatoes wrapped in aluminum foil and cooked on two professional, stainless steel gas grills sounded more like a meal served at a fancy four-star restaurant instead of a casual beach reception. It was no wonder, the delicious aroma filling the air made his stomach growl as he and Meara danced their first dance, barefoot in the soft, white sand, as a married couple to the ukulele version of *I'll Melt with You* by *Modern English*.

"How does it feel being married?" Paul asked his beautiful new bride.

"Actually," she confessed playfully. "*Ah dinnae ken*. It's only been two hours. Ask me again after the honeymoon."

Meara arched a perfectly shaped brow, her whimsical ebony curls brushing against her smooth skin.

"So cheeky," he leaned close, whispering other naughty things into her ear, smiling to himself when he heard her breath catch. Her reaction made him chuckle like a villain in an old western.

"*Cheeky?* You're starting to sound like me."

His bride swatted him playfully on the ass making his cock instantly hard. Assertively, he rubbed the eager appendage against her hip and laughed when she swatted him again, but this time harder. Although, her hand did linger a little longer than it had to.

"Hey, you two, come and eat before it gets cold!" Uncle Joseph yelled motioning them toward Koa's beach bungalow.

Obediently, he took his wife's hand—wow, *his wife*—and led her up the stairs to Koa's backdoor.

Koa and Adrienne's beachfront bungalow was incredible with modern, comfortable furnishings and unique pieces Koa had built himself. The space always felt inviting and one day he hoped to live somewhere just as beautiful with his... wife. His wife, he smiled to himself at the thought he'd married the girl of his dreams.

"What's the matter?" She looked a little worried.

Affectionately, he raised her hand to his lips then kissed the back of it, enjoying the sound of Meara's low, aroused groan.

"Nothing's the matter," he said sincerely. "Everything is as it should be."

In the kitchen, the small dinette was covered by a white linen tablecloth under a beautiful bronze, silk organza overlay with Wedgewood China, crystal stemware and sterling silver utensils. Several votive candles were lit surrounding a twelve-inch, teardrop-shaped, glass vase filled with two dozen long stemmed, lavender roses. Heavy blackout drapes were pulled closed for privacy as romantic Hawaiian love songs played softly in the background.

"Have a seat, my princess. Or should I say Missus Choy or Missus McBride-Choy or Missus McBride. It doesn't matter to me as long as we're together," he declared before giving her a quick chaste kiss on the forehead.

Gallantly, he pulled out her chair and waited for her to be seated before moving to his seat across from her. Like a well-trained waiter, he lifted the silver domes covering the plates to reveal a dinner fit for the President and first lady.

Famished from the morning's events, they ate with gusto. The tenderness of the grilled steak melting like butter over his tongue, he'd never tasted a better steak. Next, he took a bite of succulent lobster. The rich, savory flavor paired with the warm drawn butter and the sweetness of the corn was too delicious for words.

"How's the food?" Paul studied her intently, his eyes ogling her lips every time she licked them.

"Perfect." Her normally toffee-colored eyes were now almost black with lust.

"Just like you," he complimented, wanting to lean across the table and lick the butter from her delicate fingertips, so he did.

"Behave," Meara reprimanded as his tongue encircled her index finger. "You're gonna make me come like this."

Turned on by her statement, his eyes widened, and his cock grew to an impossibly painful length.

"We can sneak off to the guestroom." He grinned enjoying the slow smile that spread over her flushed face.

"Don't do it," Koa warned playfully from behind him, a sympathetic look on his face. "None of that *business*, in my guestroom. Adrienne just bought a new comforter set for that room and she'd kill you for christening it before we can."

They all chuckled at his words.

"Plus, you have to come and cut the wedding cake."

"What wedding cake?" both he and his bride spoke in unison.

"It's on the lanai along with the rest of the family." Koa motioned them outside.

Somewhat confused, they followed his cousin to the large screened-in lanai overlooking the *Moks* and the calm Pacific. The serene scene was awe inspiring.

"*Surprise!*" The entire group yelled and parted to reveal an exquisite two-tiered wedding cake decorated with edible seashells, pearls, and a variety of sea creatures. It was a work of art.

"Pop!" he gushed, engulfing the man in a tight bear hug, "When did you do this?"

Gleefully, he watched as Meara took-in the cake from every angle, ooh-ing and ahh-ing in surprised delight.

"It was meant to be a sample cake for a cake tasting," his smiling father admitted. "But with a few embellishments it got transformed into a beach-themed wedding cake."

Meara hugged her new father-in-law hard, tears streaming down her face.

"I love it," she whispered, so only he and his father could hear. "Thank you, Pop. May I call you, Pop?"

"You're my daughter now." The older man smiled. "I *expect* you to call me Pop."

Paul picked up the already filled Champagne flute and waited for his wife to do the same.

"A toast," he announced lightheartedly. "To spending the rest of my life with the woman I love most in the world."

He raised his glass dramatically watching Meara blush.

"Thank you for marrying me, princess."

"And to the handsome man of my dreams," she said with a big grin, "I can't wait for the honeymoon."

"What's taking so long?" Paul knocked gently on the closed bathroom door.

Not surprised at his impatience, Meara rolled her eyes at her reflection in the mirror.

"Be patient," she reprimanded loud enough for him to hear. "Jeez!"

True to form, he laughed before saying, "Hurry up! I can't wait any longer. You've been in there for over fifteen minutes."

"Don't you want me to look sexy for you?"

"Meara," he said, frustration coating his words. "You would look sexy wearing a burlap sack and dead fish on your feet as slippers. Now, hurry up before I self-combust."

Taking one last look at her reflection in the full-length mirror of the honeymoon suite at the *Outrigger Resort and Spa* on Waikiki Beach, she pulled open the door.

"Well," she purred, spinning around slowly to make sure her husband could admire the new negligee given to her as a wedding present from Kai and Aiden. "What do you think? Do you approve?"

"Holy shit!" he gasped, mouth open, tongue peeking out between his teeth, brown eyes dark with arousal and she had to stifle a chuckle.

"I guess, I'll take that as a yes," she said confidently, walking toward him swaying her hips a little more suggestively than usual. The sight of him in black, silk boxers and nothing else made her mouth water.

"Wow!" he whispered as she looped her arms around his neck and smashed her breasts against his heaving chest. The choppy movements made her nipples pebble. "You look beautiful."

His hands immediately drifted down over her torso, waist, hips, then around to her backside where he gently squeezed the full, firm exposed globes not covered by the matching red, silk thong with his large palms, all the while grinding his erection over her silk-covered mound.

"I can't wait to bury my cock inside this sweet, tight, little pussy of yours, Meara. Feeling all of those inner muscles squeezing my dick is unbelievable."

Her sex dampened and her clit began to throb painfully at his words. She pressed her thighs together to ease the pressure building in her core, but it didn't help. In fact, it seemed to make it worse.

"Who gave this to you?" His hands moved up her back and around to fondle her heavy breasts through the sheer, red, baby-doll negligee. The feel of the material on her adding to the ache between her legs.

"Kai... Aiden," she answered on a whisper. "Do you like it?"

Overwhelmed by his proximity, she closed her eyes as he took one nipple into his mouth along with the fabric.

"More than life itself," he groaned, bending his knees to line up their pelvises as she pushed her sex against his groin, loving the massive erection rubbing her clit through the sleepwear.

His wife blushed.

"I can see everything," he whispered before pulling away and scooping her up in his arms like she weighed nothing at all. "It's absolutely perfect. I couldn't have asked for a better wedding present."

She giggled then added, "Wait there's more."

"More?" He slowed his step.

"We haven't opened Noelani's gifts yet."

"Gifts?" he gulped. "As in multiple?"

"I knew you were a genius," she teased, running her fingers over his slightly, stubbled chin, then over soft, kissable lips. The difference in textures made her even wetter. "It's on the nightstand next to the bed."

"Good."

"Why is that good?" She smiled.

"Because that's where we are going. To the bed," he informed, the feral smirk on his face not easing her desire at all. "I'm going to have my wicked way with you."

"Is that so?" she snickered, licking her lips seductively.

"Yup!"

"Goodie for me," she paused then added. "Open your cousin's gift first."

"Whatever you want."

With a few long strides, he reached the large king-sized bed and deposited her gently on the edge of the mattress. Then Paul grabbed the expertly wrapped, shoebox-sized gift from the nightstand. The silver and black designs were elegant even to her well-trained eyes.

"Hurry, Paul!" she scolded her husband. "Just rip the bloody thing open. I'm about to start without you."

And from the raspy tone of her voice, she hoped he knew she was serious.

Doing as he was told, he ripped the wrapping off, tore the cardboard open, and stood staring at what was hidden inside. He looked as if a sudden wave of heat washed over his body, and she wasn't surprised when his upper lip began to sweat.

"What is it?" she inquired, propping up on her elbows to watch him.

Without explanation, he handed her the box, eyes dilated to the point of being completely black with lust. Carefully, she poured the contents onto the comforter to get a better look. A Cheshire cat grin suddenly came upon her lips.

"Are those what I think they are?" Paul nodded at the spilt items, mocking, and teasing where they lay.

"You've got a one-forty-two IQ; what do you think they are?"

It took a minute for him to utter the words.

"Handcuffs and lube..." he gulped, hard. "And a v-vibrator?"

"Houston, we have liftoff." She winked at her still gawking husband. "I'll have to get them all thank-you cards and Noelani. I'll have to do the same for her when she gets married."

"Forget *'thank you'* cards. Remind me to buy them a bottle of their favorite Champagne," Paul hissed with unbridled need.

Meara sat on her haunches watching him, watching her before asking, "How do you want me?"

"Get on your hands and knees, princess, near the headboard. I'm gonna fuck you from behind."

She did exactly what she was told, anticipation thrumming through her veins. When she got into position near the head of the bed, Paul took the fuzzy, pink handcuffs, secured them to her right wrist, looped it through the wooden slats of the headboard then attached the empty cuff to her left wrist.

"Have you ever been restrained before?"

She wasn't sure he wanted to know the answer.

"Only once," she replied on a breathy moan, but felt sad when a look of disappointment appeared on his devilishly, handsome face.

Trying to lighten the mood, she wiggled her bottom teasingly and gasped when she felt his hand swat her ass cheek hard, yet not painful. Totally turned-on, she gasped when he did it again then rubbed his palm over the area to ease the sting.

"What was that for?" She looked at him over her shoulder, the desire in his eyes dark and hypnotic.

"I saw it in one of those movies and I wanted to test it out, but if you don't like it, I'll stop."

"It's alright." She smiled at his sweetness. "I like it, but don't do it too hard."

"I'd never do anything to hurt you," Paul promised, smiling that lop-sided grin of his that made her heart clench before dropping to his knees behind her, making him eye level with her wide-opened sex, glistening with her arousal.

Meara nodded her approval.

"I'm gonna kiss you here," her husband's hoarse voice stated as he pulled the thin strip of material to the side and then traced her wet opening with the tip of a finger. "Then I'm gonna take you."

She nodded her head in agreement at the same time he leaned forward and gave her opening a long, wet, leisurely swipe with his tongue.

"Paul..."

His splayed hand caressed the length of her back, and then traced the seam of her backside making her jump nervously.

"Bend over a little. Put that ass in the air for me. Yeah... like that... you're stunning, Meara."

Large capable hands cupped the back of her thighs at the crease right below the curve of her ass. His thumbs rubbing gently over her lower lips, parting her like the Red Sea. Warm breath fanned her sensitive folds; making her wilder and needier than she thought possible.

"I'm gonna taste this prize of mine," he informed a second before he slowly licked across her swollen labia.

She bit her bottom lip to muffle the moan that escaped.

"You are so responsive."

His tongue swiped over her sensitive tissue once again.

"Paul," she whimpered as he continued.

The next glide of his talented pink muscle teased her slick opening, rimming it slowly as if he had an eternity to enjoy her taste. She pushed back, but he kept her in place with an easy grip.

"Delicious," he stated before he nudged her swollen clit with the tip of his tongue, circling the tiny nubbin until she was panting and wheezing for breath.

"If you don't stop, I'm going to come in your mouth," she warned, hoping he'd take her out of her misery and slip his hard member inside of her.

"Princess," he whimpered against the nubbin he suckled. "Tell me what you need."

"I need you," she stated matter-of-factly, grinding her flesh into his open mouth.

"You need me to... *what?*"

She rolled her eyes.

"I need you to... *you know*."

"No," he said. "I don't know. I need you to say it."

Frustration built with every lash of his demanding tongue, stubbornly she refused to beg.

"Come on, my sexy minx," he urged sweetly, too sweetly for her liking. The man was becoming a dominant presence in the bedroom, and God help her... she liked it! No. She loved it.

"Tell me what you want me to do to this sexy body of yours and I'll take you out of your misery."

She tried to straighten, but the bastard of a brute held her in place with a hand at the small of her back.

"Come on, princess. Make me a happy man and tell me what to do with this soft pussy."

"I... " his wife of only a few hours spoke then trailed off.

"Yes?" Paul grinned, knowing he was the cause of her distraction.

"Want..."

"Uh huh?" he continued to press for a response.

"You to..."

"Out with it, Meara. I'm going to come before I ever get inside of you at this rate."

Those whispered words fueled her passion. She certainly wasn't going to miss having his cock inside of her.

Looking at him over her shoulder, his ruggedly handsome face strained with emotions and love, and she couldn't hold the words back any more.

"I want you to fuck my pussy with your tongue until I come all over your face and then I want you to fuck me with your cock until I come... *again*. Is that clear enough?" she added defiantly.

"Crystal," he said, smiling before leaning forward again and spearing his tongue into her slick opening.

"Paul!" she gasped, holding the wooden slats in her tightly clenched fists.

Thank goodness she was already on the bed because his first deep lick would have made her legs give way. The overly zealous lieutenant used his mouth like a master violinist uses a bow. His teasing tongue tasted every nook and crevice, licking and nipping and stroking. Instinctively, she pressed back moving her hips in circular motions until the first sensations of her impending release announced itself.

Loudly, she whimpered as he massaged her nubbin with the length of his tongue before rubbing two fingers through her cream, coating his thick digits, and then plunging them inside her, pumping a few times while giving her clit a quick suck. It was all she needed to find her own pleasure. Wildly, her hips bucked like a bronco against his still suckling mouth and pumping fingers as she trembled and moaned her release.

The feel of him against her as he stood behind her widening her legs with one of his muscular thighs reignited her need.

"Spread these lovely legs of yours... perfect."

Her breath quickened as he positioned the wide crest of his member against her and pushed inside, reaching around between her legs to gently rub her clit with a calloused finger.

"Bloody... hell!" she moaned, as he stretched her to fit his unrelenting cock, the pleasurable pain flooding her sex with another surge of liquid desire. It was incredible.

"*Fuck,*" he hissed through gritted teeth. "In this position you're even tighter."

"Then I guess you better work for it, Lieutenant Commander," she teased, pushing against him. His low groan of pleasure almost made her climax again.

Moving his hand from between her legs, he held her hips, controlling the speed of his thrusts and the angle of his entrance, filling her to the hilt before pulling out until only the tip of his plum-shaped cockhead was lodged in her opening.

"You feel so good... *so good*... I can't stand it."

Enjoying her reaction, Paul reached between her legs again and found her clit peeking out from under its hood and began massaging it with an open palm. She felt another orgasm slam into her, leaving her to hold herself up with shaking arms and legs.

"*Shite!*" she whimpered with a soft cry.

"I can feel your pussy clenching my dick," he announced, continuing to pump leisurely inside of her. "It gets even tighter... even better after your climax."

He kissed her shoulder blade and then the nape of her neck.

"Do you want to come again?" he asked wickedly.

She shook her head no.

"I don't think I can."

"Let's find out, shall we."

Ignoring her, he pulled her to a kneeling position. His hips pumping into her with delicious slow stokes as he palmed one heavy breast while his empty hand continued to draw invisible circles over her overly sensitized nubbin.

"Feel me, princess?"

"Aye," she groaned as he quickened his pace, slamming inside her again and again.

She succumbed to his unrelenting speed. The almost desperate in-and-out glide of his pumping hips, the rushed whispers of love and devotion emptying from his mouth as his body stiffened as an intense orgasm tore through him.

It slammed into him hard, breath heaving from overworked lungs as he shot hot cum into her already soaked channel, the intensity of the release leaving him tired and sated. It was all she needed to find her pleasure... for the third time, as the orgasm rippled through her body like a slow wave washing over her limbs.

When she thought he would pull out, he started again. She gasped at the thought he still had the strength or the stamina to continue.

"I'm not finished with you yet."

"You can't be serious," his wife wheezed.

It wasn't a question. He only chuckled.

"Wait," he stopped, removing his cock from her clenching depths, the emptiness filled her immediately. "I almost forgot about our *other* presents."

Her eyes widened in shock.

"You're gonna kill me with sex," she accused with a pout.

"But what a way to go," her husband chuckled low, his muscular torso covered with a thin layer of sweat. "I want to be your first, Meara."

Then he ran his middle finger along the seam of her ass, stopping over her tight rosette. She whimpered as he drew invisible circles over her virgin entrance.

"You are my first for everything and I know I'm not yours," he pleaded. "It doesn't bother me, but I want to be your first... and only... for this. What do you think?"

His sincere expression warmed her heart and her soul. Paul Choy was the perfect man or as close to perfect as a man could get. Slowly, she nodded her consent. Happiness overwhelmed her when he graced her with a mischievous grin.

"I promise, I'll go slowly. We can stop at any time if it's too much."

He kissed her shoulder, then her spine, finally the curve of her bum. From her peripheral vision, she saw as he reached for the hot pink vibrator that happened to match the fuzzy handcuffs and the bottle of lube.

A dollop of the cold, thick substance smeared across her back entrance startled her. A second later her husband began that mind-blowing, slow circular pattern with his finger on her rosette, the steady motion made her squirm. When she thought she'd die from the pleasure, he began working that long, thick digit into the entrance, she stiffened at the unfamiliar sensation and true to his word Paul stopped immediately.

"Did I hurt you?"

"No, it feels strange," she moaned. "Give me a moment to adjust to it. I'm alright, don't stop."

And he didn't. He started the motion again, waiting for her to relax; when she did, he added a second finger, never ceasing the slow pumping action. As she opened further, he added a third finger to his ministrations, the sensation making her desperate to be filled.

"I'm ready," she informed, glancing over her shoulder at him. His features tense with his own need for release; she remembered he had just come a few minutes before.

Quickly, Paul grabbed the tube of lube again and slathered his massive cock generously; moving behind her he held his rock-hard appendage firmly at the base and lined up the wide cockhead to the entrance of her backside. Holding her breath, she braced for the pain... surprised when none came... only the pressure as he entered only an inch inside of her tight hole.

He stopped, letting her adjust to his size, which was impressive in her pussy... suddenly became overwhelming inside her arse.

"Paul, please move."

Slowly, and with extra care he worked his length inside another inch, withdrew, and then continued the ritual until half of his cock was inside of her tight space.

"Fuck!" he practically growled. "You're so tight."

He began a steady advance and retreat, never going any deeper. The pleasure grew to the point of being painful.

"I need to come," she begged, her eyes beginning to tear from the intensity.

Paul quickened his pace, working himself in and out... in and out, stroking her with smooth, steady glides. Before she could request him to move faster, she heard a buzzing sound through the haze of lust surrounding her.

Glancing back at her husband, she noticed he held the vibrator in his right hand, covering the penis-shaped device with more lube.

He grinned, the sort of grin that could make her do almost anything he wanted her to do. And she realized life with him would never be boring.

"Are you ready?"

"Please," her voice strained with need.

Reaching between her spread legs once again, he placed the vibrating tip of the toy directly on top of her swollen nub. Meara couldn't stop the scream that tore from her. He continued to make those small circles over her bud, the motion causing her to see nonexistent stars. Increasing the pace of his cock in her back entrance, using the dildo to make her crazy with lust.

Another orgasm started to grow low in her belly, building slowly... steadily. The sensation strengthened by leaps and bounds when Paul moved the vibrator from her clit to the entrance of her soaked pussy, pushing it inside the tight channel a few inches.

The orgasm hit her so hard she lunged forward against the headboard, hands clenching the wooden slats to the point she swore she heard wood creak. The motion allowed her right wrist to escape the loosely secured, handcuffs.

"Fuuuuuck!" he snarled, the sound harsh and animalistic. However, the Hawaiian sex god continued pumping her from behind, breath hot against her shoulder blade as he draped over her back, whispering dirty nothings in her ear.

The continual motion created another weaker orgasm that rolled through her in a gentle caress.

Unable to handle another mind-blowing release, she reached between her parted legs and massaged his tight balls with her freed hand. Paul's body stiffened, hands pulling her against his still pumping hips while hot jets of cum flooded her still clutching inner muscles.

"I love you so damn much, Meara," he moaned, his body trembling as he emptied into her.

A few minutes passed as they caught their breaths, then he found the release button and freed her other wrist from the handcuffs, gently rubbing both.

"*Wow!*" He kissed the side of her neck before slowly pulling out of his wife's tight channel and maneuvering their bodies onto the mattress.

"I concur," she hissed through gritted teeth, her fingers drawing invisible circles over his heaving chest.

"Thank you," he whispered at the room in general. "This was the best present ever."

Meara turned onto her side; her full, rounded breasts exposed to his greedy gaze. Automatically, his cock began hardening again until it brushed against her abdomen.

Her eyes widened and she laughed whole-heartedly.

"You're so naughty, Lieutenant Commander Choy. It's a wonder how you lasted all these years with your virtue intact."

"It's simple." He turned to face her, touching her collarbone before leaning over and giving it a playful nip. "My virtue was waiting for you, my dear."

"Seriously?" she smirked.

"Absolutely," he said, hooking her toned leg over his hip and pushed forward until he was as deep inside her pussy as he could get in their current position. The low growl that reached the surface encouraged him as he began a fast, but steady thrusting motion.

"Paul!" she cried out, meeting his motion with the same ferociousness he felt.

"That's it, princess," his words a garbled rush, "fuck me like you can't get enough." He'd make it his life's mission to make certain she wouldn't, no, couldn't get enough.

"*Holy cow!*" The words slammed out of her at the same time he felt her pussy tighten around his cock, her muscles so snug they wrenched the seed right out of him... again.

"Damn! Damn! Damn!" he hissed as his third orgasm exploded into her sex, his vision blurring before he could steady himself causing him to lean against her heaving breasts. She clung to his shoulders whispering nonsensical phrases he couldn't understand, but the sound of her voice surrounded him with contentment.

After several long minutes, he pulled out and left for the bathroom returning with a warm, wet washcloth. He cleaned her sex then wiped off his cock before returning to the bathroom to dispose of the item in the clothes hamper.

Quietly, he turned off the bedside lamp and arranged her against his side then covered them both with the plush, down-filled comforter.

"Have I told you how much I love being married to you?"

His new bride giggled.

"Not in the last ten minutes." She snorted, a rather undignified sound, but it was like music to his ears.

"I guess, I'll have to fix that," he whispered against her temple. "I love you, princess. Always and forever."

And with that being said they held each other and fell fast asleep as husband and wife.

CHAPTER THIRTEEN

"That was an incredible couple of days." Paul nuzzled his new bride's nape as she tried to unlock the door to her condominium unit. "Hurry! What's taking you so long, Missus McBride-Choy?"

He chuckled under his breath at the satisfaction he felt over her recent name change.

Meara growled playfully.

"If my husband would stop groping me long enough for me to unlock the door, we'd be inside right now."

"So feisty." He grabbed her ass and squeezed roughly. "I wish I was inside this sweet pussy right now."

"Stop," she chastised. "Someone will hear you."

"The entire twentieth floor is gonna hear you screaming my name, in less than five minutes, if you would just hurry."

He slapped her luscious bottom impishly; her breath caught in her throat as she pushed back against his groin, his cock was ready to jump out of his pants.

Finally, Meara opened the door, allowing him to follow her inside. The apartment looked the same as it had a few days ago.

"We can't fool around right now," she chastised with a grin. "I have to meet a potential client at the boutique in forty-five minutes."

Enthusiastically, he grabbed her by the wrist and pulled her against his body. They fit together like two halves of a whole, and the realization made his chest tighten.

"I guess I can move a few of my things over here," he stated. "Unless you want to move your things to my place."

She laughed then, leaning her head to the side.

"I refuse to live in that bachelor pad with those bobble-head dolls and those sports collectibles."

Her teasing tone made him grab both of her firm butt cheeks.

"First of all, they're not dolls," he reminded with a pout. "They're action figures."

"Whatever," she scoffed.

"Fine," he said while kissing the side of her neck right below the left ear. "I guess we'll live here until we find a place. Koa was telling me yesterday there's a foreclosed beach bungalow for sale a few houses down the street from him and Adrienne. It only went on the market this past weekend."

Her eyes widened with excitement.

"I would love to live on the beach," she squealed with excitement. "Please, honey. We should at least check it out."

"I thought you'd say that, so I made an appointment with the realtor for this Saturday. I hope that's alright. I didn't want it to get taken."

"I agree," she said, nodding and grinning. "I want to see it as soon as possible."

"Great, our appointment is at noon," he told. "Add it to your calendar."

"Perfect," she said, trying to get access to her cell's voice message. "I have a few messages. Hold on."

The first message was from Mr. Larkin at the Immigration office. They had met with him on Monday morning as instructed for their interview, but after a brief investigation into Roger's accusation they immediately withdrew the order to revoke her work visa. In addition, when they told Mr. Larkin they were married, he wished them good luck and offered his blessings. He also stated that charges would be filed against her accuser for blatantly reporting false information to a government entity.

Roger McVicor III might even be deported himself. Ha! Ha! That would suit him just fine.

Meara played the message while trying to fend off his wandering hands that had somehow found their way under the hem of her sundress and inside her thong.

"Behave!" she disciplined before placing the message on speaker.

"Hello Mister and Missus Choy. This is Mister Larkin. Your paperwork is in order as I stated at our last meeting, but Mister McVicor resigned from his law firm and hasn't been seen for several months. There are also no records of him leaving the island. I'll let you know if we get in contact with him. Aloha."

"That's strange," she said, looking at her phone. "Roger loves being a *solicitor*; it's another word for lawyer. He wouldn't have just quit."

Paul shrugged his shoulders. Another message came up; all that could be heard was a low hum in the background. She deleted it. An exact message with that same rushing air and low hum played, but in this one a muffled voice could be heard. Three more of the same types of messages followed, but this time she didn't erase them. With an annoyed huff she ended the call.

She smiled before crooking her finger at him.

"Now... come here. You've got just ten minutes to have your way with me."

Meara's meeting went well. Mrs. Anna Devlin, owner of the Waikiki Women and Children Center wanted her and Noelani to help put on a charity fashion show and auction where a few of their designs would be auctioned to help raise funds. It was a worthy cause and all of the island's wealthy well-to-doers would be attending. Allowing their work to be showcased meant more people coming through the doors of their boutique. Business was definitely picking up, but they couldn't become complacent if they wanted to truly make their mark in the fashion world.

Arming the security system, she quickly shut and locked the boutique door. The sun had already set over an hour ago giving long, creepy shadows dominance over the dimly lit parking lot behind the store. She was meant to hire someone to install more floodlights but hadn't gotten around to it yet.

Quickly, she retrieved her car keys from her purse, pressing the open button on the fob, before finding her cell phone which was currently ringing.

"Hey, honey," she answered, knowing who was calling without looking at her screen.

"I've missed you, Meara," an unfamiliar voice stated on the other end.

"Paul?" She stopped in her tracks.

"No, wrong guess," the man corrected. "Would you like to try again?"

A chill went up her spine as she looked at the caller ID that only said blocked caller, info not available.

"Who is this?"

"An acquaintance or a former friend perhaps." His words were manipulated by a voice modulator making it practically unrecognizable.

"Who is this?" she asked again as she reached her white *Toyota 4-Runner*. "How did you get this number?"

The faceless voice chuckled.

"How are you getting home, Meara? It's not safe at night standing in an empty parking lot all by yourself. You never know what might happen."

Terrified, Meara hit the end button with shaky fingers before getting into the car, locking the doors, and turning the key in the ignition. Nothing happened.

"Shite!" she whispered, tears welling in her eyes as she turned the key again, waiting anxiously for the damn SUV to start, but it didn't. "Please, no!"

Scared, she looked up as a dark shadow passed behind her vehicle. Immediately, she reached for the can of mace hidden in the glove compartment while she steadied herself. Her breath now heaved out of her chest like bellows, and a thin layer of perspiration formed on her upper lip as she called Paul's cell, but it went straight to voicemail.

"Paul, call me back! I'm stuck at work. My car won't start—" Then her cell lost signal, unnerving her even more. "Damn unreliable network!"

By this time, the adrenaline was pumping through her veins like a drug, and she was starting to feel a little lightheaded and nauseous. Without warning her cell rang again and she picked it up.

"Paul! Thank goodness you called."

"Sorry, Meara, still not him. Do you need some help starting your SUV? I'm close by if you need some help."

"Haud yer wheesht!" she yelled into the line; her palms sweaty. "Stop calling me!"

Frantic, she hung up again.

A hard knock on the driver's side window startled her causing a high-pitched scream to tear from her lungs in response.

"Meara!" Her husband's handsome face came into focus.

Throwing open the driver's door she hopped out, almost knocking over her spouse as she smashed her body against him.

"Thank God it's you!" She was crying now, soft whimpering sobs that racked her frame.

"I tried calling you, but it went to voicemail." Paul embraced her tightly, smoothing her hair with comfortable strokes.

"My phone died earlier, so I left it charging at home." He held her as she whimpered and shook like a leaf in a windstorm. "I must have forgotten it. What's wrong? What has you so jumpy?"

"My car won't start, and a strange man has been calling me... he asked me how I was getting home, and he said he was looking at me... that he was close by! Paul, I'm about to lose my mind!"

"Don't worry. I'm here now," he spoke, calmly looking around the parking lot, but seeing no one. "Lemme take a look at the engine."

The engineer took a look under the hood and then announced.

"Someone unhooked one of the battery cables. That's why your car won't start. Damn it!" He reattached the equipment before turning back to her. "I'm going to take a look around the building."

"No," she stated firmly, shaking her head. "I only want to get out of here."

"Meara, I'll be fine. You're not the only one with mad fighting skills in this family," he said, giving her a reassuring wink.

"No, Paul. I have a bad feeling. We need to go right now."

The worried look she gave did the trick.

"Fine."

"Sweet heaven," she said, clutching her can of mace tightly.

"If it makes you feel better, we can get out of here," he agreed. "I'll feel better once I've gotten you home."

He opened her door and waited for her to start it up; when it did, he kissed her chastely on the forehead before going back to his car and following her home.

When they reached the condo Kai, Aiden and the kids, Koa, and Adrienne, Noelani, Mr. Choy, and Joseph and Leilani were waiting in the front lobby with the on-duty security guard.

"Paul called us. Thank goodness you are alright." Pop hugged her tightly. "What happened?"

"Someone fucked with her engine, that's what happened," Paul hissed through clenched teeth.

"Are you alright?" Adrienne's French accent strengthened with concern.

Meara shook her head no, tears welling again.

"We'll talk more upstairs," Paul stated as he took her trembling hand in his and led the way to the elevators.

Dinner was tense as she and Noelani explained to Paul and his family—their family— about the strange calls she'd been receiving lately and the odd gifts she'd found left on her car and boutique doorstep.

"I can't believe this is happening." Noelani looked at Meara and then at her cousin who looked madder than she'd ever seen him.

"I'm sorry you had to cut your date short with Spencer," his wife apologized. "I know you hardly see him as it is because of his missions. Please apologize for me."

Her cousin-in-law nodded.

"No worries. He had to leave early. Something about a debriefing at the Army base, so I was just sitting at home watching old reruns of Gilligan's Island—"

"Fuck, Spencer!" Paul growled, pushing his chair back in a rage.

"Excuse me?" Meara asked, her eyes wide with surprise.

"I don't care about, Spencer, when my wife's life is in danger," he snarled and suddenly wanted to hit something or someone.

"Honey, calm down," Meara begged. "The kids are playing in our room. They'll hear you."

"Shit!" Paul stood beginning to pace the length of the small kitchen/dining area. "Why didn't you say something before, Meara? Why didn't you mention you're still receiving crank phone calls? As your husband, it would have been an important fact to know."

"I didn't think much of them," she replied, shrugging her shoulders. "It seemed harmless at the time. Anyway, Noelani made me report it to the police after I got a severed finger as a gift—"

"Fuck!" he yelled, his hands suddenly clamping into tight fists at his side. "Why didn't you tell me about all of this shit that's been going on? No wonder you can't sleep."

"I thought it was a prank at first," she gasped through tears. "It wasn't until the finger arrived that I realized the severity of the danger."

Paul closed his eyes trying to reign in his quickly skyrocketing temper.

"Who does the finger belong to?"

"The police don't know who it belongs to," Noelani answered in a hushed tone. "The fingerprint was purposely removed."

She gulped like something was constricting her throat.

"Please, don't make me explain how it was removed."

"What about DNA testing?" he huffed, his headache turning into a migraine.

"They tried that already, but whoever's finger it is, doesn't show up in any of the databases, they've checked," his equally terrified cousin responded.

"Fuck-a-duck!"

"Paul, I thought it was a harmless prankster—" Meara began, unable to control her temper.

"It isn't a harmless prankster if this freak is messing with your car engine now." Paul's voice was laced with rage, but his eyes still comforted her. "Tomorrow, I'm gonna report this latest incident to the police, so they have it on record, and I'll get Uncle Alfred to add better lighting to the boutique parking lot. I'll also set-up some internal and external surveillance cameras."

"I have a friend, ex-SEAL, who does private security now," Koa interjected. "He's a good guy. I'll see if he can keep an eye on the store. See if there's anyone suspicious casing the place. I'll set up a meeting with him tomorrow and introduce you guys."

"Is it Dorian?" Paul asked the worried SEAL.

"Yes."

"Mahalo, brah." Paul smiled, but it didn't reach his eyes. "I'll speak with the condo's management group in the morning and set up a list of people who are allowed into the building that should lessen the threat while she's at home."

"Good thinking," Aiden added. "How's Meara gonna get to and from work, or to the store... to anywhere?"

"I'll drop her to work and pick her up when she has meetings," Paul informed, cracking his knuckles. "I'll even stay during the meetings, just in case. She can work from home until this gets fixed."

"Stop talking about me like I'm not here," his wife stated matter-of-factly, giving him a dirty look like he was the villain.

"I'm sorry," he apologized. "But suppose I hadn't stopped by to check on you. Do you realize what might have happened?"

Her look softened.

"I can still drive myself, Paul. I'm not some helpless *quine*."

"My mind's made up," he said dryly, refusing to back down. "I'll drive you."

"No," Meara refused, her eyes narrowing on him. "You have a job too. You can't hang around all day babysitting me. I won't let you."

"You don't have much of a choice right now."

Stubbornly, he folded his arms over his chest daring her to argue, but she only nodded her head, her entire body stiffening. He knew that look and he knew he'd hear about it after the family left.

"Noelani," Joseph spoke trying to defuse the situation. "Has anything strange happened to you? Anything at all that was out of the ordinary?"

"No, Uncle," Noelani educated calmly. "Meara, I can't believe you were being harassed and you didn't say anything to me."

"I'm sorry." Meara looked tired and overwhelmed. "Don't be angry."

Noelani stood up suddenly and sat beside Meara on the couch, encircling her shoulders in a comforting hug, the action making his wife bury her head in her best friend's neck and cry. He felt as if his heart was being ripped out and a new determination to keep her safe emerged.

"It'll be okay, Meara," Noelani whispered against Meara's hair. "I promise. It will be okay."

The family left around ten o'clock, leaving him and his new bride alone and angry with each other. He for not being told his wife was being stalked, and she for not wanting to be treated like a child. Both of them were too stubborn to apologize.

After he had finished sulking, he found Meara in their bedroom, staring at the wedding album Kai and Adrienne had created for them as a wedding gift.

"Here." He handed her a plate with a grilled ham and cheese sandwich. "Eat."

"Thanks," she said, but rested it on the bed beside her.

"Aren't you going to eat?" her caretaker grilled as he glared at her.

"Will you hand feed me if I don't?" Meara huffed, gaze narrowing with irritation.

"If I have to," he answered his temper waning, but his concern growing.

"I'll eat," his wife replied, taking a large bite of the hot sandwich.

This made him smile.

"Happy?" she asked with her mouth full.

"Very."

He felt his chest tighten and a lump forming in his throat before he dove toward her, hugging her like she'd disappear if he released her.

"Don't be mad, Meara. I keep thinking about what could have happened. You're my wife... *mine*... and I can't stand the thought of something happening to you."

She hugged him back.

"I know, but I feel bad enough about not telling you about it and you're just making me feel guiltier."

"I'm sorry." He pulled back a few inches. "That's not my intention. When my mom died, I couldn't help her, couldn't save her, but you—you I can help, and if that means following you around or getting someone to follow you around... well that's what I'm gonna do."

A light came on in her dark eyes before she graced him with a shy smile.

"We'll figure it out and I'll try not to be so... *difficult*, but you have to include me in the decisions," she implored, gazing into his eyes. "We are married now, a team. I promise to tell you everything from now on, if you agree to treat me like an equal, not an errant child. Deal?"

"Deal," he agreed, while stripping down to his boxer-briefs and sitting beside her as she finished her sandwich. "Is it good?"

"Mmm," she moaned. "It's delicious."

"I added some of that smelly cheese you like so much." He grimaced teasingly.

"It's not smelly."

His eyes narrowed at her comment.

"Ok, maybe it's a little smelly." She shook her head. "But it's *pure dead brilliant*. Here try some."

Reluctantly, he opened his mouth, letting her feed him like a small child. He chewed slowly, and then swallowed, and then his eyes widened.

"It's not bad," he admitted with a smirk.

"Not bad?"

"Fine," he amended. "It's *'pure dead brilliant'*."

"Told ya!" she boasted with her sing-song Scottish lilt, reminding him of a nursery rhyme.

Her nose crinkled making her face beam like it was lit from beneath her skin.

"You look beautiful tonight," Paul blushed as he admired the black cotton, sleeveless sleep shirt that hung to her knees with a low scoop neckline that showed her amazing cleavage. "This isn't new, is it?"

"No, it's not new," she grinned. "I've had it since Edinburgh."

"Meara." He kissed her on the corner of her mouth. "I-I'm sorry I yelled at you this evening. I was just—"

"I know." She interrupted his apology.

Carefully, he took the album from her hands and placed it on the night table before switching off the tableside lamp. Pure done in, Meara allowed him to pull her body against his, her back to his front, his arms hanging possessively around her waist, her head tucked below his chin.

"Did you remember to set the security alarm?" she asked before closing her eyes.

"Yes, princess."

"Paul?" His wife's gaze became clouded with unshed tears.

"Yeah?" the lieutenant whispered hoping to steady his voice.

"I'm so glad you came to check on me." Meara released a held breath.

He tightened his grip on her.

"Me too, princess... me too."

"Thank you for coming down and reporting what happened, Missus McBride-Choy," Sergeant Murphy said as he signed the incident report.

"Certainly." Meara's hands tightened on her husband's.

"You're lucky," the plump man stated, his thick Irish accent sprinkled with a hint of concern.

"What do you mean by lucky?" Paul inquired, holding his wife's hand while they sat warily at the Honolulu police station.

"Well," the man said while leaning back into his chair. "This person has obviously got an agenda. He knows where she lives, where she works and had found out her *unlisted* cell number. And now he's messing with your car. That's not a good sign."

"What should I do?" she asked, her voice sounding raspy.

"Unfortunately, you and your business partner are celebrities," the older man in his late fifties stated.

Meara sighed and glanced at her husband's ticked-off face.

Blushing, he quickly added, "I have teenage daughters still living at home. I've read the article about your designs and boutique."

Her brow furrowed this time, making the detective laugh at her expression before clarifying.

"It was the only magazine in the bathroom."

"Ah-ha," she and Paul both sighed in unison, another blush spread across the man's face making her smile.

"Unfortunately, the media has inadvertently given this guy all of your personal information," the man collaborated what they both already knew. "Including how and where to locate you. He's probably been watching you at work and then followed you home. He probably knows your habits better than you do."

"Damn it!" her husband swore under his breath.

She gave his hand a gentle squeeze as she asked, "How do we catch this bastard?"

"Unfortunately, all we can do is wait until—"

"—until he kills you." Paul ran both hands through his thick black locks, the heavy strands immediately falling back into place, even frustrated the man was stunning.

"Paul," she admonished, watching him watching the detective, the feral look on his face scaring her a bit.

"He's not wrong," Sergent Murphy agreed. "What I mean is, we won't know who it is until we catch him in the act."

"What do you suggest I do?"

"If it happened to one of my own, I would change my cell number, move if possible, or beef up security at your residence, and if you don't own a weapon... I'd get one. There are gun ranges that give lessons, but your husband is a military man, so I'm sure he'd train you."

Paul nodded his head in agreement.

"Is there anyone you can think of who has a grudge against you?"

"Roger McVicor," Paul announced, a streak of malice darkening his usually kind eyes. "He tried to get her deported because she broke up with him, but the Immigration agent, Mister Larkin, said he quit his job at Harris and Harris law firm in Honolulu, and hasn't been seen for a few months."

"He lives here?"

"He moved here from Edinburgh," Meara spoke, willing her knees to stop knocking. "Roger said he relocated so we could be together... to fix our relationship."

"Good, now we're getting somewhere." The police detective wrote a few notes on his notepad before adding, "This is a good lead to follow, Missus McBride-Choy. Don't worry we'll catch this arse."

She smiled. It was good to hear a familiar accent.

"I'll call you as soon as I have anything important to share," the officer informed with a stern expression. "In the meanwhile, remember what I said. Don't go anywhere alone. If you do, make sure you let someone know where you are going and when you'll be heading back. If anything at any time seems weird or out of place to you... especially at home or at the boutique, call nine-one-one immediately. Understand?"

"Aye, Sir," she responded robotically without emotion.

"Thanks, Sergeant." Paul shook the detective's chubby hand.

"Keep an eye on her, lad."

"I fully intend to, Sir... I fully intend to."

CHAPTER FOURTEEN

"My giddy aunt!" Meara mumbled, so only Paul could hear her.

Her husband nodded in agreement.

"This is it," she stated confidently. "This is where we're going to start our family."

"It's got potential." Paul ran a hand through his hair for the third time in two minutes which meant he was feeling a bit out of his element. "It's gonna need a lot of work though, Meara."

She nodded her agreement also.

"A lot of work," he groaned as the realtor took them out of the master bedroom and back downstairs to the large living room.

"Honey!" she gasped. "Look at the view! Isn't it spectacular?"

Paul came up behind her and wrapped his strong, muscular arms around her waist.

"Miss Blackwell, could you give my wife and I a few minutes alone, please?"

"No worries." The pretty strawberry blonde realtor smiled sweetly before turning back to the garage area. "Don't go out onto any of the balconies there are rotten planks on the floors that aren't sturdy at all."

"Mahalo," Paul called to her retreating back as her plump form disappeared around the corner. "I don't know about this. There are a lot of repairs that need to be done. The plumbing needs to be replaced, the flooring needs repair, the roof has got to be changed, and the place hasn't been updated since the late nineteen-sixties. It's got lime-green, Formica countertops for God's sake."

"It also has four bedrooms, two and a half baths, a two-car garage, over three thousand square feet of living space, lots of natural lighting, and a view that I would sell my own mother for..." the seasoned realtor relayed. "You know what I mean."

"It's also expensive," he reminded, glancing at the spec sheet he held tightly in his sweaty palms. "Especially for a foreclosure."

"Noelani and I got an order for twelve custom-made gowns from a well-known department store chain that rhymes with the word Groomingdale's."

She made a funny face which made him laugh.

"It's still a big purchase, princess, and we'll have to make the mortgage payments for thirty years."

He frowned then glanced around.

"Thirty!"

"But its eighty thousand dollars under market value for this area, honey," she made a compelling case. "And I think we can probably talk her down by at least another ten thousand dollars. How can we go wrong?"

"What about the financing?" he whispered, feeling a bit queasy.

"We've already been preapproved for a VA loan since my handsome spouse is in the military." The savvy female reminded with a playful wink.

"What about the closing costs?" he mumbled below his breath.

"I have twenty thousand saved," she confessed proudly. "How much do you have?"

Paul stood looking like he was about to be sick, and then she saw his eyes darken when he calculated the amount that they would need to make the purchase affordable.

"I have about forty thousand in the bank."

"That's a good start." Meara tried to be positive in the face of his valid points.

"The mortgage payment will still be astronomical," Paul announced, kissing behind her ear before pulling away to study the house one more time.

"My parents are gonna give us an additional fifty thousand U.S. towards whatever we buy." His wife beamed.

That made him pause.

"I know they're big-time attorneys, but how can they afford that amount?"

"Simple conversion," Meara explained. "The British pound is worth almost twice as much as the American dollar."

"I didn't realize that." His surprise was evident by his tone.

"And your dad—"

"What did Pop say?"

"I'm not sure," Meara chuckled. "He was kind of cryptic. Something about insurance or some such nonsense he wants to talk with us on Sunday."

"That sounds a bit ominous."

"Paul, I think we should make an offer."

"Who's gonna help us with all this work?" He pointed to the peeling paint, bare drywall, and exposed wiring.

"Our family—that's who," the convincing Scottish babe said enthusiastically. "C'mon, take the plunge with me. Let's buy the bloody house."

"I don't know, Meara."

She turned to face him, toffee eyes to chocolate brown.

"You, sir, are married to a celebrity designer." She beamed. "I can redo this house for shillings and use my many contacts to get the materials we need, *at cost*. How does that sound?"

"I'm still not sold on the idea, princess."

"I'll throw in a blowjob for good measure."

She brushed her hand over his crotch for emphasis.

"Missus Blackwell!" Paul called out.

"Yes, Lieutenant Commander Choy?"

"We'll, take it!"

Paul still couldn't believe he'd let his nymph of a wife talk him into buying the two-story beach bungalow in Kailua down the street from Koa and Adrienne. It had been three weeks since they made their formal offer to purchase the ramshackle edifice; and he still had panic attacks over it.

"Congratulations, Meara, Paul! You are now officially homeowners," Mrs. Blackwell congratulated cheerfully shaking his hand and giving Meara a hug. "I know you were hesitant about making the offer, Paul, but that extra money your father gave you really made it affordable."

He still couldn't believe his dad had invested the one-million-dollar life insurance policy he'd gotten when his mother died, and the damn thing had almost quadrupled in size. Meara and he tried to persuade him to reinvest it, but he said he had already taken a quarter of it for his own retirement and whatever they didn't use as down payment money could be used to bring the house up to code, then reinvested.

It was a dream come true.

His father had also confided in him that his own home had been paid off years ago, and the bakery was doing so well, that he had quite a sizable nest egg himself. Meara had been ecstatic and had already scheduled the first contractor, his Uncle Alfred, to begin demolition tomorrow. Uncle Alfred had inspected the house before they made their offer and determined the structure had a solid foundation.

The thorough businessman had also established the house had a brand-new air-conditioning system, along with double-pane, hurricane-resistant windows updated a few years prior. Another cost-saving surprise was that the Douglas fir hardwood floors only needed to be stripped, sanded, and refinished. The moldings, also original to the dwelling, were hand carved and worth a small fortune themselves only required some light sanding to remove the years of paint build-up and then revarnished.

Everyone was constantly reminding him that it was a piece of Hawaiian history.

"Here is the key," the kind realtor said as she placed the key in his palm. "If you need anything at all, please, don't hesitate to call."

"Thank you so much, Missus Blackwell." Paul gave a tight smile. "We will."

Meara's smile was growing larger.

"When we get this place sorted-out, you'll be coming over for a housewarming barbeque."

Their realtor laughed.

"Of course, I wouldn't miss a famous Kapahu-Choy cookout. Your Aunty Leilani's macaroni and cheese is to die for."

Meara agreed silently before giving her one last hug. They both waved as she left through the squeaky front door.

"Stop looking so worried." Meara squeezed his hips. "In a few months, you'll thank me."

"I'll thank you?" He pulled her against his chest securing her by the waist with both arms. "Is that right?"

She nodded, the motion shook her long hair that hung loose down her back; the gentle sway of it as it moved with every turn or shake of her head mesmerized him.

"Absolutely."

"I guess I'll see in a few months then," he joked and patted her behind.

"Can we spend the night here tonight?" his wife pleaded with a devilish grin, and then leaned forward resting her cheek against his cotton-covered chest.

"No, not until everything is up to code," he answered, shaking his head vehemently. "I'm not gonna have you living in some sort of deathtrap."

"Where's your sense of adventure?" The smile she gave him was brighter than the low-hanging Hawaiian sun outside their newly purchased beach house.

"If you haven't yet realized this, my lovely Scottish nymph, I'm not an adventurous man when it comes to keeping you safe... in every aspect. Do you understand?"

"Aye," Meara purred wickedly then tiptoed and kissed him on the side of his face below his right ear. "You smell sinful."

"Do I?" Paul replied with a thin smile.

Her hands lowered from his waist as she fully cupped his jeans covered ass.

"When can we start christening all of these rooms?" Her voice suddenly turned raspy like she'd just awoken.

He chuckled at her implication of having sex in the almost dilapidated building.

"Are you serious?"

"As a heart attack," she growled, glancing down at his growing member. The traitorous appendage giving him up like a five-dollar snitch. "I want you."

His new bride rubbed her pelvis against his; the seductive slow circles she made wreaked havoc with his nervous system. Without hesitation, he started to slowly inch her sage green, halter sundress up her well-toned thighs. She was practically panting as his fingers found smooth, silky skin.

"Now I know you're insane." His eyes widened.

"Hey you two!" Spencer's voice startled them both.

"Aloha, dude!" Paul responded, trying to get the thought of Meara on all fours waiting for instructions.

"Nice place," Noelani's boyfriend added sarcastically while an amused grin spread across his face.

Paul smoothed the material back into place before the other man could see his wife's upper legs.

"What are you doing here, brah?" Paul released her and shook Spencer's hand.

Spencer spun slowly sweeping the room with an assessing gaze.

"Noelani and I stopped by to see what all of the fuss was about. So, you're moving out of that sports museum you call an apartment with all of those dolls?" the other man teased.

Paul sighed before correcting him.

"They are not *dolls*, they are *action figures*," he spoke slowly like he was talking to someone with a limited IQ.

Spencer chuckled under his breath. "Sure, man, whatever you say."

"Where's my best friend?" Meara asked, giving the other man a quick chaste kiss on the cheek. He thought Spencer stiffened a bit, but he immediately relaxed again. Paul assumed he just felt strange about being kissed by someone who was married.

Nodding his head in disbelief, he answered, "She's outside in the front yard mentally designing your flowerbeds."

Meara's face lit up with excitement.

"I hadn't even thought about that area yet. I'm going to go out and throw some ideas past her. See you boys in a while."

"You know they'll probably be out there for at least an hour, right man?" Paul shook his head in amusement.

"You've got that right."

Then they both laughed at their women.

"Spencer," Paul stated, nodding toward the rest of the house. "You want a tour of the place while the women do their *mental* designing?"

"Sure, why not." The other man turned to follow him out of the room they were currently in. "If you need any help with the demo or the rebuild, I'd be more than happy to help out when I'm not on assignment."

"Thanks, brah. The freer hands on this project the better."

Paul and Meara left the beach house and headed to the boutique where she had a final meeting with Carlos Santos to buy several bolts of fabric for the upcoming charity fashion show and auction. While her husband hid out in the back storeroom, she and Noelani decided on which patterns to buy.

"I love this one," Noelani proclaimed, holding up a silver-blue damask cloth, hand-woven in Sri Lanka. "What do you think of this one for the strapless gown with the bolero jacket? It is unique and elegant with a touch of the exotic."

She agreed then turned her attention to a metallic gold Lamé fabric, holding the delicate cloth over a piece of burnished gold raw silk.

"This combination would be perfect for the vintage empire-waist gown," the Scottish owner told. "I can also make a less expensive pantsuit with it."

"I agree." Noelani grabbed her calculator and began adding the numbers. "We have enough to buy two more bolts."

"You have excellent taste, Meara." Carlos Santos beamed at their choices; the man obviously grateful for the sale. "How's married life treating you?"

"Great!" Her voice was low and needy at the thought of her husband and his newly acquired bedroom skills.

"And the new house, how are the upgrades going?"

She couldn't help the smile that crept onto her face.

"Pretty good, the renovations on the beach house are going to start tomorrow, I hope. Thank goodness we have a large family that can help with all of the restorations. Only a few more details to finish before work can really get started and it will be fabulous."

"Congrats again," the thickly accented man said as he gave her a tight hug. "Your husband is a lucky man."

"Thank you!" Meara blushed like a schoolgirl.

"*Mija*, why did you get married so quickly? You got a bun in the oven or something?" he joked, his arms waving flamboyantly.

She shook her head and laughed when one perfectly threaded brow rose questioningly.

"No, my ex-boyfriend, the one I told you about—"

"Yeah, the cheater, right?" His Spanish accent getting stronger as his emotions got the better of him.

"Correct," she confirmed, her Scottish accent doing the same, "He lied to an immigration officer and tried to get me sent back to Scotland. Isn't that crazy?"

"*Muy loco*," he said cheekily making them both laugh. "It is a marriage of convenience then?"

"No, it was a love match," she grinned, sighing on a whisper. "The threat of being apart made us realize we wanted to be together no matter what, so we tied the knot, sooner rather than later."

Noelani returned holding a check for the material they had just purchased.

"Here you go, Carlos. Thank you so much for the discount. We really appreciate it."

"No problem, *Chica*," he said, gathering up the remaining bolts. "I love you both."

"Goodbye, Carlos. See you next week."

After Carlos left, Meara went back to the storage room to find her husband on the phone, brows furrowed, a scowl on his handsome face. The sight of him that worked up worried her, but for some unknown reason it aroused her as well, over six feet of pure, edible, male-sexiness.

Sinful... he was absolutely sinful.

"What's wrong?" she questioned when the left vein at his temple kept jumping.

He held up a pensive finger, silently asking her to wait.

"Hey, Dorian, can you do me a solid and run a background check on a guy named Carlos Santos?"

Dorian Matthews, Koa's ex-SEAL friend who now owned his own private security company, had been helping them find the bastard who was stalking her. The middle-aged man was a darker version of Koa, 6'7", all-muscle, with a heart of gold under that intimidating physique.

"Sure, do you think this is the guy we're searching for?" Dorian's voice was unnaturally loud over the speaker.

"I don't know, but there's something off with him," Paul huffed and ran his hand through his hair before looking at her with a concerned expression.

"I'll see what I can dig up," Dorian confirmed.

"Mahalo, brah."

"No worries, tell your gorgeous wife I've got it covered."

"I'll tell her," Paul informed his friend then hung up and turned to her with a frown. "Dorian wanted you to know that he's doing everything in his power to find this dickhead."

"I'm sure he'll find him," his lovely spouse smiled, but it didn't reach her eyes.

Slowly, she walked over to him, looped her arms around his neck before pulling him down for a long, wet kiss.

"Hmm," he groaned against her lips, the vibration exciting her further. "What was that for?"

"It was to let you know how much I appreciate you looking after me so well."

She kissed him again, but this time he took control, pushing her against the storeroom wall hiking her denim covered legs around his waist and grinding their sexes against each other.

"Bastard," Meara moaned on a whisper. "Stop. Your cousin is right outside."

"Don't worry she can't hear anything," her extra horny husband sputtered, and then laughed quietly below his breath.

"Yes, I can," Noelani said chuckling and snorting loudly, her voice muffled by the wooden barrier separating them. "I agree with your wife. Stop with that mushiness before my ears burn off. Jeez!"

They both laughed at his cousin's unique way of coining a phrase.

Temptress

The tantalizing new fragrance by Wahine nani

Available Exclusively at
Waikiki Fragrances
1234 Kalākaua Ave, Honolulu, HI

CHAPTER FIFTEEN

Three months later...

The almost-fully restored two-story, four bedroom, two and a half bath, 1930's beachside bungalow was immaculate to say the least; after all, she and her husband were practically OCD when it came to cleanliness. Both she and Paul prided themselves on being neat and organized. The military had drilled it into her husband from the first day of basic training. While she had inherited it from her perfectionist mother, God help them when they had children... they'd go bonkers.

She decorated most of the space herself, with only a few minor suggestions from Paul. And with Noelani's help, she chose a neutral color scheme and an almost Fung Shui furniture placement. According to her husband, he didn't care about how things coordinated or clashed in a space let alone how to achieve a consistent flow from room to room. All he cared about was having a massive HD flat screen, smart television with a *Dolby* surround-sound system to hook up his gaming system.

In the living room, their furnishings were minimal consisting of her full-sized black, Italian leather couch paired with a hand-made, stainless steel and glass coffee table they had purchased cheap at an estate auction. Other than that, the space was empty. They saved quite a bit of money doing most of the renovation projects themselves, but they didn't want to rush to buy furniture until they could build back up their savings.

Everything she couldn't make herself, they purchased on *eBay*, *Craig's List* or wholesale on-line vendors. But their one true indulgence was the humongous eighty-inch, flat-screen television, which Paul loved almost as much as her, and showed his affection by cleaning and dusting it every other morning. For some reason, he felt the need to constantly remind her that it was the only *request* he'd been allowed to have in the entire house.

Paul, Pop, Koa, and Joseph built a low, wrap-around storage / bench seating / shelving unit that ran along most of the back wall of the enormous living room. The stylish, yet practical system housed design books, her husband's *X-Box* games, a variety of networking cables and other IT items, *Blu-rays*, vintage vinyl records including old-school *Gershwin* to new CD releases like *Calvin Harris, Sam Smith, Dua Lipa* and *Ariana Grande* to name a few.

Paul's huge collection of antique Hawaiian artifacts, pottery, and tribal masks along with her assortment of Scottish fabrics, they'd collected during their single lives, were meticulously framed, and incorporated throughout the house as a distinctive, but free design element.

Her favorite aspect of the house, however, was the living room wall. The entire east-facing, back wall was made entirely of typhoon-resistant glass overlooking the Pacific Ocean outback. Paul and Koa had also installed double French doors leading out to the screened in lanai.

After a tough day of IT projects or a long day of clothing design, they could come home and relax in the space while warm tropical trade winds washed over them. The space was perfect for family gatherings or future kids' birthday parties. And every morning since they'd *officially* moved in, she'd greet the new day with a cup of tea and the morning paper while enjoying the sound of the surf along with the 180-degree view of a fiery Hawaiian sunrise of scarlet, bronze, and indigo.

The original Douglas fir flooring, which had to be painstakingly stripped, sanded, and refinished, took a lot of man-hours, late nights, and weekends to finish, but the end result couldn't be debated. It was well worth the calluses and splinters.

Even the 60's-styled kitchen got an overhaul with new granite countertops, polished mahogany cabinets, dual-farmhouse sinks, and all new stainless-steel appliances. They had even expanded the small pantry into a walk-in pantry, at Koa's suggestion, allowing them to buy in bulk and saving them a great deal of money on *'messages'*.

Downstairs, they painted all the interior walls of the bungalow a subdued shade of Tiffany blue and added pops of neutrals with furniture and accessories to add interest and personality to the space. Upstairs was a work in progress, she hoped would be complete before the end of the year. The house was the perfect representation of them both and she loved everything about it. The only repairs left to be done were the master bedroom balcony, laundry room, and ensuite bathroom.

"What are you doing in here, all by yourself?" Paul asked, fresh from a shower and wearing only a loose-fitting pair of gray pajama bottoms. His muscular chest and abs made her mouth go dry.

"I'm contemplating the next project for our new... well, newly renovated home."

Paul grimaced.

"Just kidding," she smirked when her husband sighed with relief.

They had been working a lot of late hours on what Paul affectionately called, 'The money pit.'

"I'm enjoying our new living room on our well-used couch." Meara giggled when he maneuvered his body between her and the arm of the couch, nestling her buttocks in the vee of his powerfully built thighs up against his huge, semi-erect appendage. "The house is coming together nicely, don't you think?"

He swept her curls aside exposing her neck then kissed a trail from her collarbone to her throat before saying, "It's looking like a home instead of a money-pit."

"I love this house," Meara sighed with contentment.

"I love it too, princess," Paul returned the sentiment as he glanced around their place.

"And Brutus loves it too," Meara spoke with a baby voice. "Don't ya, boy?"

The massive Rottweiler raised his large, squared head, cocked his ears, and barked his approval making them both chuckle.

Brutus—the one-year-old Rottweiler puppy, and the newest member of the McBride-Choy household—was another component of their newly added state-of-the-art security monitoring system to their home. Not only was he great to cuddle with, but his bark alone was enough to scare away a prowler.

Paul rubbed his ears playfully then motioned to the dog to lie on the floor. Brutus did as he was told and resettled on the thick, shag rug covering the hardwood floor of the living area.

"Did you lock up and turn on the alarm?" his wife reminded.

"Yes, I did."

"Did you take Brutus for a walk yet?"

"I did that earlier, but I let him out about thirty minutes ago and he did his business," he reassured in a low, hushed whisper as he began to rub and knead her tense shoulders, stopping every few seconds to kiss and nip over the sensitive skin. The feel of his hands making her panties dampen.

"How does this feel?" Paul questioned thoughtfully.

"Good. Maybe you could give me a whole-body massage," she suggested, her words dripping with need.

"I can arrange that." Her spouse began to rub along her spine and lower back.

"Don't stop, that feels wonderful," Meara moaned as she leaned back into the massage, the steady pressure awakening other desires. Without warning, she stood, peeled off her lilac silk nightgown and dropped it to the floor.

"What are you doing young lady?" Paul chuckled huskily; his chocolate-brown eyes almost black with lust.

"I'm going to take advantage of you," she informed, easing her panties down her legs before throwing the cotton material at his flushed face.

Easily, he caught it, lifted it to his nose and inhaled deeply.

"You smell delicious, like honey," Paul complimented, eyes immediately lowering as he studied her from head to toe then back again and she could have sworn he growled.

"Is that right?" She wiggled playfully.

"Uh huh," he answered as she rested her hands on his shoulders and straddled his lap, kissing him on his right earlobe before moving down to his Adam's apple.

"I'm going to fuck you until you can't walk, Lieutenant Commander Choy."

"Really?" He cleared his throat. "That sounds scandalous. Are you trying to scandalize me, Missus McBride-Choy?'

"Yup."

Boldly, she reached into his pajama bottoms and retrieved his long, thick member; the appendage seemed to have a mind of its own as it jutted proudly away from his body. The beauty of it made her mouth water.

"I see you're ready for me," his wife informed and wagged her eyebrows playfully.

"Always," he countered then began fondling her heavy breasts using his thumbs to tease the straining peaks. "I love the way you move... the way you feel against me... you were meant for me, Meara. Did you know that? From the moment we met you were mine."

"Yes," she moaned. *"Yours."*

Her cell phone rang just as her husband was about to do something naughty to her nether regions.

"Don't answer it," he commanded taking her nipple into his moist, warm mouth, his tongue flicked against it driving her crazy.

"If you insist," she agreed on a breathless whimper. The hard length of his cock rested in her palm as she used the tiny bead of pre-cum that appeared to lubricate the wide head. "I'll let it go to voicemail."

"Good idea," Paul agreed as he released her nipple and devoured her mouth again.

The blasted cell phone kept ringing until she grabbed it, annoyance fueling her words.

"It's late, can't this wait until morning."

"Meara... you look beautiful. Naked and ripe and delicious. I wish it were me sucking on those chocolate-colored nipples. Soon it will be." The faceless voice snarled. "But you're *mine*, not *his*."

She screamed loudly and dropped the cell onto the rug, her frantic movements looking as if she had been dowsed with kerosene and lit on fire.

"*Shite!*"

Brutus immediately bolted to all fours and ran to the glass French doors barking into the darkness. She yelled and hopped off of her spouse's lap. Quickly, redressing as she bellowed

"It's... *him*... he can see us!" The terror in her voice motivated Paul to run to their bedroom on the second floor, returning within seconds with his service weapon.

"Stay here," he commanded. "Lock the door behind me. Brutus," he spoke calmly to the now wide-awake Rottweiler. "Guard the house."

Obediently, the massive puppy sat down in front of the sliding glass door, his dark ears cocked as if listening for something out of the ordinary.

"Call Koa, and then the police," her spouse ordered right before he disarmed the alarm, opened the backdoor, and ran into the surrounding blanket of darkness.

Quickly, she relocked the door, grabbed her cell phone, and made the call to Koa.

"Aloha," he answered sleepily.

"He's here!" she yelled into the receiver. "The bastard's here and Paul just ran out to find him! He's got his gun, Koa!"

"Stay inside! I'll be right over."

"Okay," she stated as she sat on the couch with Brutus sitting right in front of her, a low growl emanating from his throat. "What's wrong boy? Do you hear something?"

Their puppy left her, ran to the backdoor, sniffed the gap between the bottom of the door and the floor.

Muffled shouts could be heard from outside followed by a loud *pop* like a Fourth of July firework going off, only louder. Her breathing became shallow and for a moment she thought she might pass out. The waiting was killing her. Also not knowing what was happening outside didn't help the situation.

Brutus snarled, the hair on his broad back standing at attention. The dog jumped up threw his thick, muscled body at the backdoor, whimpered then ran back to where she sat on the couch.

Several excruciating minutes later, Paul and Koa knocked on the back door. Brutus ran over, his pug tail wagging playfully at the sight of her husband and his mountain of a cousin.

"I was so worried," Meara blurted.

Paul's face came into view first; several purplish-blue bruises were becoming visible on both cheeks and his jaw.

"What happened?"

"I caught up to him," Paul said holding his side as if he was in pain and then she saw it, the red stain of liquid that was quickly spreading across his shirt.

"Call nine-one-one," the calm SEAL ordered. "Tell them someone's been stabbed."

Carefully, Koa set him down on the couch before running to the downstairs guest bathroom for the first-aid kit.

"Oh, no! *Paul!*"

"Here, son," his father said handing him a small cup of water.

"Thanks, Pop."

Paul leaned back against the pillows and allowed Meara to take his hand in hers, the simple gesture making his heart tighten and his member flex beneath the covers. *Jeez!* At least he knew that even when injured his wife's touch still had the power to get him hard.

"Do you need anything else?" Meara inquired, worry-lines making her appear slightly older than her twenty-five years.

He shook his head.

"I'm fine," the injured officer replied with a wince.

"Of course, he's fine," Koa stated matter-of-factly. "I taught him well."

"Mahalo for that, *braddah*," Paul thanked again as he gave his cousin a shaka. "If it wasn't for all of those years you used me as a practice target, teaching me Brazilian Jujitsu and basic hand-to-hand combat moves, that guy would have killed me."

He stopped suddenly when he noticed Meara's eyes welling with tears.

"Princess, I'm gonna be fine," he verbally comforted his worried wife. "I promise."

He then kissed her inner wrist.

"Do you feel up to finishing the events of last night, Lieutenant Commander?"

"Yes, Sir," he answered trying to sit a bit straighter without tearing his stitches.

"Can you describe the perpetrator?" Sergeant Murphy questioned as he scribbled notes onto a pocket-sized notepad.

"He was about six-five", broad, muscular build, like Koa, but stockier... bulkier. He had a fist like a sledgehammer."

He remembered as he touched the bruise on his jaw like he could ever forget. He was going to kill the *sonofabitch* when he found him.

"Anything else stick out at you?"

"You mean besides the knife?" Paul countered sarcastically, earning him a scowl from the older man. "He was wearing a mask, but it wasn't a ski mask... it was more... *shit*... it's hard to describe. Everything happened so fast, it was pitch black, and there was something familiar about him... *fuckaduck!* It's hard to put my finger on. One minute I was circling the back of the house, the next he hit me from behind. The asshole just came out of nowhere."

"That's when he stabbed you?"

"Yes, Sir," Paul stated firmly. "I felt the blade, but the adrenaline was pumping through me and when he lunged at me again... I fought back."

"You said you injured him. Where on his body?"

"His left knee," the Navy man recalled. "I did a round-house kick to it, and it brought him down, at least for a few seconds anyway. He should also have a broken wrist. I thought I heard it crack when we were fighting."

Sergeant Murphy grinned before saying, "Remind me never to pick a fight with you."

"I don't understand why it was so dark back there," Paul scowled in annoyance. "I installed floodlights and motion sensitive infrared cameras, but nothing was on even though the internal alarm system was functioning properly."

"That's because he was able to disarm the external sensor for the lights and cameras," the seasoned policeman explained. "When the CSI investigators checked, the wires had been cut."

"I'll have to find a way to fix that," he huffed, running his hand through his hair.

"Did he say anything that would help us identify him?" the detective continued.

Paul shook his head, the fuzziness returning as the morphine drip on the IV reengaged.

"I... can't... remember. You look beautiful today princess," he flirted with the blurry figure in front of him. "Can't wait to... get you... alone..."

Then it all went black.

"*Mahalo*, Doctor Harris."

Paul heard Kai's voice then heard an unfamiliar female voice respond.

"He's gonna be fine," a soft feminine voice with a raspy quality retorted, but he couldn't quite place who it belonged to.

"Yes, thank you very much," Meara's lovely lilt brought him back to the land of the living, but with a pounding headache.

"No worries, he's tough, Missus Choy. I remember back in high school he'd always stand up for the underdog. He had a real smart mouth though, always got him in trouble."

"I remember once he tried to verbally humiliate this bully in elementary school when the older, much larger boy kept taking my lunch money," Noelani added.

"What happened?" Meara's question was laced with concern.

"He got his ass kicked, but it was still a heroic thing to do."

Kai and Meara laughed, the sound clearing his head a little more.

"I remember when he asked you out to the junior prom," Kai added jokingly to the female he didn't recognize.

"Yeah," the doctor replied, her voice filled with nostalgia. "I'm glad I said yes. He was the best kisser I've ever had. Not even my husband can out-do him."

"He was the *best* kisser you ever had?" Meara snorted in a very unladylike fashion. "He told me that women told him he couldn't kiss."

Paul forced his eyes open and could make out the pretty brunette who was shaking her head.

"I only told him that because I was so turned on that if he didn't stop kissing me... I would have... *ya know*," the doctor said playfully.

Meara and Kai laughed loudly.

"Should we let him know?"

"Please don't," Dr. Harris pleaded. "His head is big enough as it is."

"Definitely," his traitor of a wife and cousin said at once.

"You're extremely fortunate, Missus Choy."

"Thank you, Doctor Harris," his wife blushed. "I know."

"Hey," he grumbled under his breath. "Don't stop now. It's like hearing your own eulogy, but with the benefit of not being dead. Hey, there Maggie. So, I'm the best kisser you ever had?"

"See what I mean?" the embarrassed physician blushed. "That mouth always gets him into trouble. Behave or I'll have the nurse turn off your morphine drip."

"No, don't do that. I'll be good," he slurred, his tongue feeling heavy and like it was covered with slime. "Where's my wife?"

"I'm here," Meara replied. "You Casanova, you."

"I can't believe she made me think I wasn't a goo' kis… sir… *I'm soooo tir…*" The medicine began to kick in again.

"Is this normal, doctor?" Meara asked.

"It is," Maggie comforted. "The morphine will keep him comfortable while he heals. I'll give him a less potent pain reliever to take home. Tell him not to use it if he doesn't absolutely need to."

"I'll let him know." Meara smiled.

"He'll be here for another day then he's free to go home, but he'll have to take it easy for a few weeks," Dr. Harris informed the room in general.

"No worries. I have a ton of vacation and sick time hours accumulated," he said without care, waving his arm around strangely.

"Good." Dr. Harris smiled at both of them. "Your husband is fortunate the attacker missed his vital organs. I guess it's good that he's a deadly weapon himself."

"Yeah, Paul. Why didn't you ever tell me you had mad fighting skills?" his wife chastised in that all too adorable accent.

"I don't like to brag," his words slurred again.

"Since when?" Koa smirked from across the room where he was sitting reading a book.

"Since I'm now a married man," the heavily medicated officer scoffed. "The only mad skills I need are the ones in the bedroom."

Then he waggled his eyebrows suggestively.

"No!" Koa covered his ears with his hands. "Stop! T-M-I, brah. I don't need to hear about you and your wife doing the do."

"You mean having *'the sex'*," Aiden added mischievously.

"Stop!" The SEAL barked. "You're making me itch."

"Are you comfortable?" Meara asked her sulking husband, his rugged athletic form naked from the waist up as he lounged on their new king-sized bed. Brutus lay at the foot of the bed biting a thick rawhide bone watching them both intently.

"Not really." Her husband glanced down at the noticeable erection tenting the thin white sheet covering him.

"Put that thing away," she teased, blushing at his current state of arousal.

"I can't with my wife standing around in only a pair of see-through white panties and matching lacy bra."

"For Pete's sake," she admonished, quickly donning her robe. "Is this better?"

"Much," he chuckled then closed his eyes.

Glancing around the large master bedroom, Meara noticed how truly seamlessly their contemporary-styled space had come together. Furnished with a massive king-sized bed with hand-carved, mahogany headboard perfect for reading in bed, matching dark, espresso-stained dresser, two nightstands, and a matching armoire housing a forty-two-inch flat screen television set.

Throughout the room hung framed, original black and white photographs she took of different locations around London and

Scotland including Oxford University, several Scottish castles, and the Thames at sunset. She wondered if Paul had noticed she had hung up the photos.

Wow! The room looked amazing and beautifully decorated, especially on a shoestring budget.

She found her wide-toothed comb on the dresser and combed out her tangles while nibbling on a slice of multigrain toast, washing it down with a cold glass of freshly squeezed orange juice. Who knew living near the ocean could make you so hungry.

Outside the muffled sounds of the gently lapping waves against the shore combined with the happy shrills of overhead gulls serenaded her, beckoning her to go out onto the balcony, but she couldn't since the wooden floor planks still hadn't been replaced.

Releasing the lock, she pulled open the sliding glass door and looked out onto the small space. The view of the *Moks* from the balcony was incredible. Inhaling deeply, she reveled in the crisp, salt-scented breeze coming off the calm Pacific.

"Ahh," she sighed. "A girl could get used to waking up like this every morning, sated, content and cherished."

"Don't go out there," her husband's deep baritone startled her. "It's not safe."

"I know," she acknowledged while closing and relocking the sliding glass door then quickly arming the system. "I thought you had fallen back to sleep."

"So, you were planning to be naughty." His voice raspy with either sleep or lust, she wasn't sure of which, as his mesmerizing brown irises sparkled in the mid-morning light.

"I wasn't going out there. Not until Uncle Alfred fixes it."

"And when will that be?"

"He's working on a big project at the governor's mansion, so not until he's finished. After all, that is a paying job," she explained, and then smiled at all of the free help they had.

"We pay him," Paul interjected with a chuckle.

"Feeding him doesn't count," Meara replied then giggled for the first time since they returned home from the hospital.

Paul was driving her crazy trying to resume his normal activities including making love. She'd fought off his advances all morning and was utterly exhausted.

"Uncle Joseph and my dad are spending the night tonight, so no walking around in those delectable boy-shorts of yours." He gazed at her longingly. "Come here."

He smiled when she did what she was told.

"You must be feeling better because you're back to your regular male dominating self," she jibbed, gently touching his cheek.

He graced her with one of his sweet, boy-next-door, lopsided grins, making her insides turn to mush.

"Are you alright?" he asked holding out his hand toward hers. She placed her cold hand in his much warmer one, and the contact warmed her from the inside out.

She shook her head gently leaning against his shoulder.

"What if he stabbed you a little lower and to the left?" She stared at him, toffee eyes to chocolate brown. "I don't want to be a widow after only several months of marriage."

"I'm fine," he responded, and smiled again.

"You haven't given me babies yet either," she whined unashamed.

"Babies?" he gulped the word with wide eyes.

She nodded enthusiastically saying, "Yes, lots of adorably, chubby babies with your eyes and exotic good looks."

"I can definitely fill that order, but not so soon," he begged. "Give us a chance to enjoy each other first."

"I have to warn you though," his wife began, tilting her head to the side. "My family has a history of twins."

"Are you serious?"

"My mum's an identical twin and so are my brothers," she confessed. "So, there is a huge chance that I'll give birth to twins as well."

Paul touched her belly, rubbing his palm over her sensitive skin.

"Twins?" He grinned. "That would make life... interesting."

"Have I scared you out of fatherhood yet?" she teased.

"No. I'd love to see two little girls who look just like their mommy running around," he said with a smile. "Just not right now."

"I understand." Meara grinned too and sighed.

He placed a chaste kiss on her temple.

"Plus, I need more practice with the *making love thing*," the lieutenant mocked.

She rolled her eyes, his playfulness making her giggle.

"I think you've already reached the expert level at the *making love thing*."

He touched the tip of her nose with his index finger, the mere contact inciting her dormant libido.

"*Gonnae no' dae that*, Mister Choy," she whispered.

"Why?"

"Because—"

"Because, why?" Paul interrupted as he tucked her against his uninjured side then informed, "Because you're horny, like me."

He knew it wasn't a question.

The scoundrel of a man slowly pushed her robe off of her shoulders and quickly unhooked her bra. His warm palms massaging her shoulder blades with gentle circles.

"Uh huh," she groaned as he leaned into her and kissed her on the nearest shoulder. "But yer lookin' a bit peely wally."

"What does that mean?" He chuckled.

"You look sickly," she moaned with desire.

"*Ouch!*" he abruptly protested, and the pain in his voice immediately squashed her desires.

Quickly, she moved away, clutching her robe and bra, which were now hanging around her elbows, and then looked down at his pained expression.

"That does it," Meara growled. "I'm going to sleep in the guest room tonight."

His eyes narrowed.

"You can't be serious." His large hand clutched at his side in agony, and she felt her heart rate increase.

"I won't let you hurt yourself anymore, Paul. Doctor Harris said to take it easy for at least two to three weeks. That means refraining from sex."

"I refrained from sex for over—"

"Twenty-seven years," she interrupted. "I know. So, you shouldn't have any problems being celibate for a few weeks."

"I hate you right now," he teased. "Don't sleep in the guestroom. I won't try anything, I promise."

She looked at him with longing and then gave in.

"One inappropriate touch and I'm outta here," she warned with all sincerity. "Got it?"

"I got it."

Without another word, she turned on her heel and disappeared into the walk-in closet, quickly getting dressed in a pair of dark Bermuda shorts and a white gauze peasant top. She grabbed her *gutties* (otherwise known as sneakers), marched over to the dresser to retrieve a pair of ankle-length socks, and then sat down at the foot of the bed to put the items on.

"Where are you going this early?" Paul asked suspiciously before glancing over at the alarm clock. "It's only eight a.m."

"I have to get that special-order fabric from the office that I ordered a month ago. The thing finally came off of back-order status.

It came by UPS yesterday." He was about to say something when she added, "It'll be a skoosh."

"That means *'don't worry'*, right?" he smiled, getting used to her Scottish slang.

Impressed, she nodded.

"Dorian is picking me up and driving me to the boutique."

"Good," he sighed relaxing a bit more. "Do you have anywhere else you need to go?"

She smiled.

"Dorian is also taking me for *'messages'* and to the venue that is hosting the fashion show next month."

"Why can't my cousin do some of the leg work?"

"Because Spencer is home for a few days," his wife revealed. "And they wanted to spend some time together."

"Makes sense to me," he mumbled then held out his hand to her, pulling her down to him when she rested it in his palm. "Be careful."

"I will," she reassured, kissing him innocently. "I will."

"Thanks for shadowing me today, Dorian," Meara said, peering absentmindedly forward at the winding road.

"No worries, Missus Choy."

"I keep telling you, call me Meara," she insisted with a frown.

"Yes, Miss—, I mean, Meara," Dorian restated. "That's what I'm here for. At least until that brooding husband of yours is back on his feet."

She giggled as her mind flashed with images of her man resting in bed, going out of his ever-loving mind with boredom. The sigh escaped her lips before she even knew it was there.

"Don't worry." Dorian's soothing deep voice eased her apprehension. "Paul is a tough bastard. He'll be on his feet in a couple of weeks... good as new."

She smiled.

"All of the hits he's learned to take from Koa, I can't imagine he'll stay down for long. Not with a wife like you that needs looking after."

Meara's feathers were a bit ruffled at his rather sexist comment.

"I can take care of myself, you know. I'm not a wee lass waiting for Prince Charming to rescue me, ya know," she informed the beefy man, her Scottish accent sounding harsh and stronger than ever.

Her bodyguard frowned.

"I didn't mean to imply that you're helpless—"

"Good, 'cause I'm not," she reiterated hoping to cement her point.

The security expert smiled and nodded, and she smiled too.

Dorian's black Escalade pulled into the boutique's small parking lot and parked a few feet away from the backdoor.

"Wait here," the large, more than intimidating half-Hawaiian, half African American man stated sternly, his dark eyes serious. "I'm gonna take a look around if it's safe I'll come get you. If I'm not back in five minutes call the police. Here are the keys in case you have to leave without me. Five minutes."

She nodded, taking the keys from his large hand.

Like a jungle cat stalking its prey, he turned and headed to the back entrance, quickly unlocked the door using her key and disappeared into the building. In less than a minute he returned, a perturbed look covering his features which normally were ruggedly handsome.

"What's the matter?" she spoke low, her voice shaky. "Tell me, what's happening? It not a request, Dorian."

"Take a look." He held the door open for her, waited while she stepped inside a few feet and looked into the open storage room door.

She gasped before muttering a litany of swears; anger clawing at her belly like a wild thing. The blood drained from her face as she stared at her fabrics, swatches, and sewing necessities all destroyed and thrown around the room as if a tornado had touched down in the small space and turned it to rubble. Written on the wall in red spray paint were the words, *'Next time he won't be that lucky.'*

"What the hell is that?" She pointed to something in the corner propped-up against the wall.

Dorian pushed past her to see what had her staring in shock and picked up a small photo of her and Dorian leaving her house earlier that morning.

"Damn it!" His loud voice shook the walls, and she wondered how the plaster didn't fall right off. "This guy is like a ghost."

Meara took out her cell phone and called Sergeant Murphy, Noelani, and Koa who had taken a short leave of absence while Paul was out of commission. The whole group would be at the store as soon as they could.

"Are you gonna call your husband?"

She shook her head no.

"That's not wise at all, Meara."

"I'll tell him when I get home," she promised. "There's nothing he can do right now except worry."

"If you say so," he said, turning away from her before taking out his own cell and making a call. "Aloha, Jessica. I need two guys at the Choy residence, A.S.A.P. Tell them I'll brief them when I get to the house. Make sure they're armed. Mahalo, babe. I'll talk to you later."

"Is that—"

"My fiancée, Jessica. She's my receptionist and office manager." He smiled. "I like to keep it in the family."

She smiled back, but the nagging nervousness wouldn't dissipate.

Before she lost her nerve, she picked up her cell and speed dialed Paul who picked-up on the second ring.

"What's wrong?" he anxiously answered.

"H-he got in-into the store," Meara stammered, her breath was coming out in harsh, ragged pants.

"*Fuck!*"

"He destroyed the rest of the fabrics and all of our supplies." She steadied her voice as she spoke. "He also left me another present."

"Damn it to hell! What was it?" Paul's anger could be felt over the line.

She took a deep breath in before stating, "A picture of Dorian and me leaving the house this morning."

The former SEAL motioned for her to hand him the phone.

"Aloha, braddah. Two of my guys are coming over to keep an eye on the house. They'll be there in fifteen minutes. Koa knows them, but they won't bother you. They'll be driving an SUV like mine. Their names are Kyle Williams and John Reece, ex-military, highly trained and real bad-asses."

She left the room when a knock came from the front door of the shop. Noelani and Spencer stood holding hands looking mortified. Quickly, she unlocked the door and let them in, hugging them both before asking, "Why didn't you just open the door?"

Noelani shook her head.

"I lost my key, Meara. *I lost my key!*" Noelani's entire body was shaking.

Finally, it all made sense.

When the detective showed up, CSI unit in tow, combing through the debris with a fine-tooth comb, her body was finally calming down.

"Meara," the portly detective said, his eyes warm, but concerned. "This guy is really good, no fingerprints, no hair fibers, no nothing. It's like he's—"

"A ghost... I keep hearing that. It doesn't make me feel any better."

She wished Paul was here, but the man was still at home calling her every ten minutes to get an update. Just as the thought came into her mind, her cell rang again, and she glanced down at the screen to make sure it was her husband calling and not the psycho-nut-job-pervert.

"No clue who this guy is, honey. Would you like to talk to Sergeant Murphy?" She handed the man standing beside her the phone and walked out into the main lobby to sit with Noelani and her boyfriend who were talking heatedly.

"Sorry," she apologized.

"No worries." Spencer smiled and hugged her briefly, the scent of his expensive cologne tickling her nose. "Maybe you can talk some sense into her head. I sure can't."

"I'm not staying at your apartment with you and your two roommates," her best friend stated emphatically.

"You aren't gonna stay at your place alone."

"I'll stay at one of my uncles' house or Kai and Aiden's place," Noelani encouraged, kissing him briefly. "Don't worry so much, Spencer."

"Are you going out of town, Spencer?" Meara queried, grabbing a broom and dustpan from the hallway closet. "Another mission?"

He nodded in the affirmative, still holding his girlfriend's hand.

"Be safe."

He winked.

"I always am."

Noelani walked him out and returned a few minutes later.

"He's a good bloke," Meara complimented, her accent soft in her less agitated state.

"Yes, he's a very good... *bloke*," Noelani agreed.

Paul was going out of his mind with worry. His damn wife was still at the boutique with the police and Dorian, and he was holed-up in his bedroom being guarded by his father and uncle. He couldn't even sit up without help; much less help Meara who was probably on edge enough for the both of them.

"I made soup," his uncle informed. "You want some. It's nice and hot."

He shook his head.

"Come on, Paul. You have to keep your strength up."

"I'm not a child anymore, Uncle Joseph."

His uncle sat at the side of the bed, looking at him sympathetically.

"I know you're worried about this punk hurting Meara," Joseph soothed. "We all are, but don't you forget the Kapahu's are a bad-ass family, and we protect our own."

"Yes, sir," he stated, feeling a little of the tension leaking out of his body. Then he barked, making his uncle flinch. "I just feel so damn useless!"

"I understand," the other man nodded sympathetically.

"Paul," Meara's lovely lilt came from the doorway, her usually bright eyes bloodshot like she'd been crying.

She ran to his uncle first giving him a brief hug before coming over to sit next to him, wrapping her arms around his neck and beginning to cry. The tears rolling down her slender neck and onto his chest made him feel even more useless than ever.

"I can't take much more of this." She was sobbing now, completely undone.

"Shh," he comforted her as best as he could in this state, rubbing her arms as he held her, ignoring his burning wound. "I won't let anything happen to you, princess. Not a damn thing."

And by God, he meant every word.

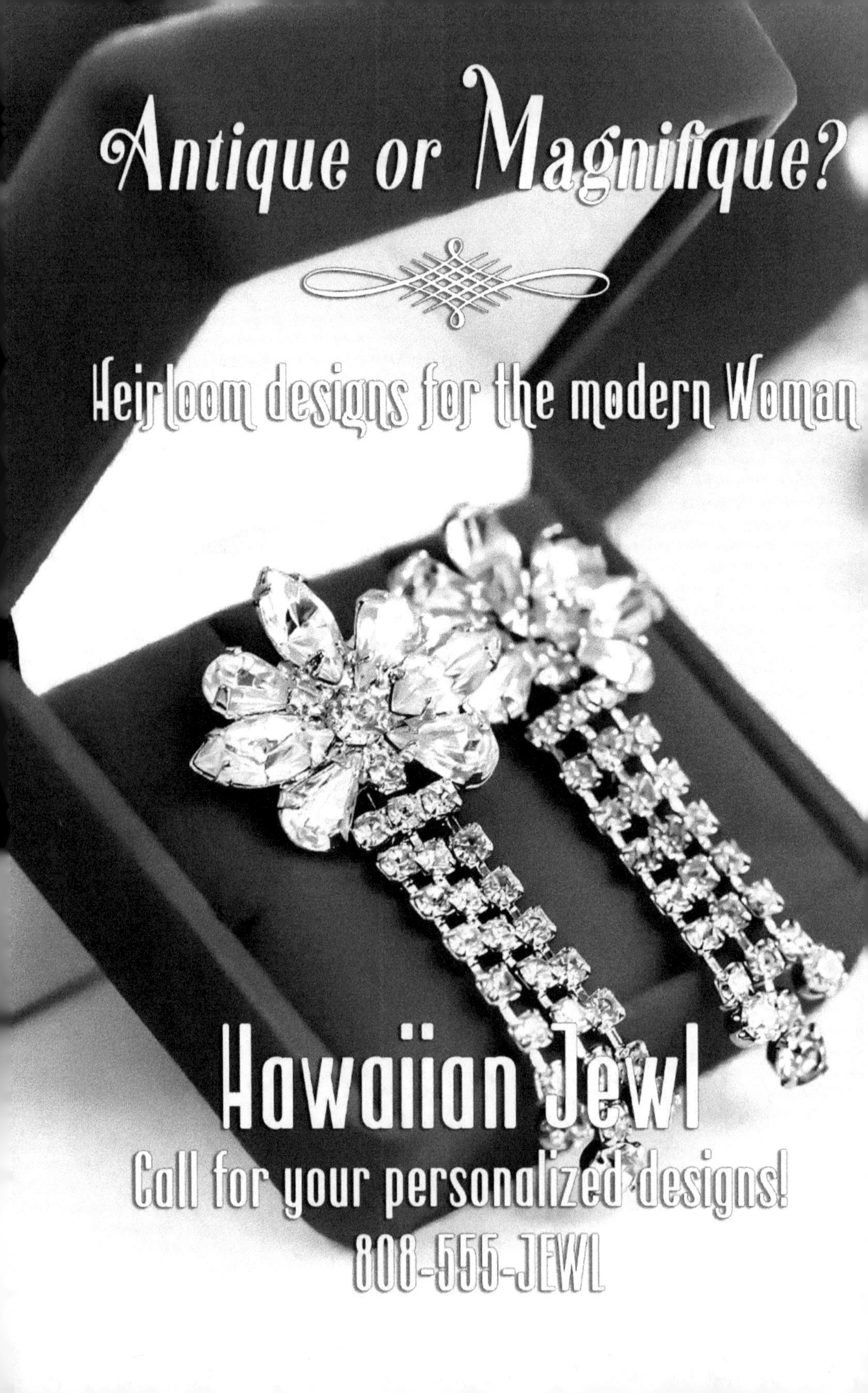

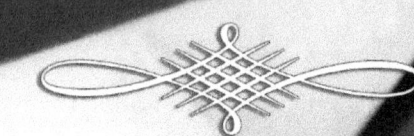

CHAPTER SIXTEEN

One month later...

"I can't believe we finally finished making the outfits for the fashion show," Noelani announced on an exhale as she sat beside her bestie stitching the last hem, and then hung up the garment to be steamed free of wrinkles.

"Me neither," Meara agreed as the tension left her shoulders. "I'm taking them home with me. There's enough security and ex-testosterone-male-warriors at my house to cover the President when he comes for his Christmas vacation."

She chuckled, feeling comfortable as well as safe with the hovering Dorian sitting in the back office reading the newspaper.

"I can hear you two."

They both laughed.

"Sir, yes, sir," they both answered in unison making him laugh as well.

"Where's your husband—?" Dorian began to speak but was stopped.

Meara held up her hand before counting down.

"Three... two... one."

Then she pointed to her cell phone resting on the desk. As expected, the slim smart phone housed in a purple protective case began to vibrate. She smiled, picking it up on the third ring.

"Hi, honey," she acknowledged the caller with a smirk and a sideways glance at her grinning best friend. "Where are you?"

"I'm leaving Kai's training room as we speak," her husband enlightened.

Kai, wanting to stay home with the kids and still work as a physical therapist, had recently started working from her home part-time. Paul was one of her first patients and she busted his *bawbag* to get him back in prime fighting condition.

Each day, they worked out for an hour before he came to pick her up from the boutique, relieving Dorian of his daily bodyguard duties.

"How was it today?" she inquired.

He chuckled softly; the sound sexier than anything she'd ever heard.

"Kai is a real pain in the ass, and bossy as hell, but she's fixing me up really well. I feel great. How about you?"

"I'm well," she enlightened. "We just finished the last outfit for the fashion show in a few days. I'm really nervous."

"I'm sure you and my cousin will be the talk of the show," Paul reassured in that way he had, instantly calming the butterflies in her stomach. "I should be there in forty minutes, give or take a minute. Traffic is a nightmare. Dorian won't leave you two alone."

"I know." Meara grinned. "He's going to take Noelani to Uncle Joseph's house tonight. Her bags are already packed. Spencer had to go out of town again."

"That guy works a lot." Her husband chuckled. "He needs to get a raise."

She sighed.

"I'll see you soon. Drive safely," she paused then added. "I love you, Lieutenant Commander."

"I love you too, Missus McBride-Choy."

Paul arrived exactly forty-two minutes later and rushed her inside the vehicle with all of the outfits for the fashion show. He kissed her, then briefly waved to Dorian and his cousin before leaving the parking lot.

"What would you like for dinner?" he asked, smiling at her in a wolfish way making her feel like she was the meal.

"I'm not hungry," Meara said, quietly looking into his handsome... no; handsome wasn't an accurate enough word. The man was male perfection.

A concerned expression appeared.

"Did something else happen today?"

She shook her head and his body relaxed.

"You have to keep your strength up, princess."

"I'll cook," she told, but then her mind drifted to all that still needed to be done before the fashion show.

"You look tired." Her husband frowned. "I'll cook."

"It's alright." She reached over and rested her hand on his upper thigh, the muscles below his basketball shorts immediately tensed below her teasing fingers.

"Don't do that," his voice sounded choppy.

"What am I doing?" Meara questioned with a pout.

"Playing with fire, little lady," her husband lectured with a wolfish grin, and then moved her hand and placed it on his rock-hard erection, the hidden appendage flexed as she held it through the material.

"I think I can relieve your tension, Mister Choy."

"Pop is spending the night, remember?" He grinned.

She frowned.

"I guess we'll have to be extra quiet then."

Dinner was delicious; homemade chicken stir-fry with Asian vegetables and steamed white rice.

"This is wonderful, Meara," Pop praised the chef then took another spoonful of everything making her feel appreciated and loved.

"I'm glad you like it," she responded, blushing, and beaming from ear to ear, wishing she had gotten something for dessert.

"You've outdone yourself," Paul hummed as he also helped himself to seconds, or was it thirds?

"Hey!" she chastised. "Don't overdo it. You're going to make yourself sick."

Paul looked up at her with a sheepish grin.

"You wouldn't say that if you saw the way Kai works me out. Believe me, I won't be stuffed."

"I'm going to start training again as well," she announced to both men who glared at her curiously.

"Start training? With whom?" her husband probed.

"Koa, of course," she replied, wiping her mouth with her napkin.

"You can train with me," her husband insisted.

"That's so not a good idea," she replied in a rush, shaking her head.

"Why not?" her spouse questioned while his father simply continued to eat his meal.

"Because, my dearest, you can be extremely bossy and demanding with me," Meara retorted, staring at him, daring him to deny it.

"I am not," he denied her remark like she knew he would. "Pop, am I demanding?"

His father said nothing as he continued eating his dinner.

"This is really delicious, Meara," her father-in-law stated with his mouth full of food.

"I promise not to be a tool," Paul stated sincerely.

"I'd rather train with Koa or even Adrienne."

Thrown for a loop, he studied her intently, eyes narrowed in thought.

"Train with me once," he challenged. "And if I drive you crazy, you can stick to the original plan."

She pondered it for a moment before answering.

"It's a deal," she repeated. "One time. If you get too uppity, I'll drop your arse."

"Agreed."

Both men cleaned the kitchen while she went upstairs to take a shower. Loyally, Brutus followed close to her heels, settling down right outside the bathroom door like a four-legged sentinel.

"Good boy," she praised, patting his large head, and scratching behind a floppy ear. "I won't be long."

In response, he whimpered and licked her hand knowingly.

Turning on the shower, she stripped down to skin and got in, stepping into the steady stream of warm water. With her eyes closed, she reached for her loofah and the container of body wash, but it wasn't where she had left it.

What the hell?

"Looking for this?" Paul's masculine baritone startled her.

He stood in the entrance of the shower holding the bottle of body wash in his right hand watching her intently, his tongue darting out to lick his bottom lip.

"What are you doing here?" Meara grilled, wiping water away from her eyes. "Where's Pop?"

"He's downstairs watching a movie on cable."

Everyone knew his father was a movie addict. He had a huge collection of DVDs and Blu-rays in every genre invented. The man even enjoyed the films that were complete box office flops. It didn't matter to him. He loved them all.

"I see," she said, looking around nervously.

"Why do you seem so anxious to be alone with me?"

"The last time we were about to make love, that limey bastard stabbed you," she said with a frown.

"Believe me, I remember." Paul grimaced, his hand instinctively moving to the injured area.

"Every time I close my eyes, I see you bleeding."

It was true. Since the incident, she hadn't had a decent night's rest. She would fall asleep well enough, but within an hour or so she would jerk wide awake. It was crazy that she could still function with only a couple hours' worth of sleep.

"He's not here, princess. We are all alone. Dorian's men are outside, one posted in the backyard the other in front and Pop is keeping watch with his Glock close by," he informed, stepping into the shower with all of his clothes.

She laughed at the sight of him soaking wet in his shorts and t-shirt.

"Get out you mad man." Meara blushed, admiring his physique.

"No one can see us or hear us here," he reassured. "The windows are frosted glass, and the running water will mask any sounds that you make."

"That *I* make?" she scoffed.

"Yup," he whispered. "Help me out of these clothes."

She hesitated for a moment, her eyes narrowing and glancing at where he had gotten hurt only a month prior.

"Are you strong enough?"

"Princess, if I felt any stronger, I'd be Superman," the confidently spoken words made her heart palpitate and her mouth dry.

"I don't know," she said with mock innocence. "You might not be up for the challenge. After all, it has been an entire month since you got *practice*."

"Don't you worry about me. I'm sure I'll pass the test." He took her hands and guided them to his shirt. "Undress me. I'm wounded, remember?"

"Whatever," she mumbled as she removed his t-shirt then hooked her fingers inside the waistband of his shorts and tugged them down.

"Step out, honey," she instructed, happy when he did what he was told. His erection jutted proudly away from his body. "I see you're ready to go, big boy."

"You have no idea, princess."

He grabbed her hips as he pulled her under the water with him, their bodies pressed firmly together.

"So soft. I forgot how good you feel."

"Then let me reacquaint you," she interjected mischievously, rubbing her beaded nipples against him, loving the way he responded.

He took the body wash and poured a dime-sized amount into his palm, rubbing his hands together until they were sudsy before slowly and meticulously soaping her skin. Starting with her neck and shoulders and working his way down until he ended at her breasts, which he took a few minutes making sure they were extra, extra clean.

"I think they're clean enough," she reprimanded, rolling her eyes blatantly.

He grinned continuing his journey further down cleaning her arms, torso, and stomach.

"Turn around, face the wall," he commanded holding her hips and maneuvering her until she was staring at the old-fashioned pink and sea foam green tile. "Put your hands on the walls and spread your legs... good girl, you look beautiful like this."

She pushed back against him feeling his hard member on her lower back. Her husband continued soaping her back, armpits, and then he began cleaning her buttocks slipping his thick digits into the seam, but not trying to enter her tight rosette.

"I've missed your lovely body, Meara." His voice sounded strained like he was about to lose all his self-control, that damn Hawaiian lilt doing strange things to her body.

"I've missed you, too."

Leaning her cheek against the cold tiles while the love of her life began to rub the folds of her sex under the false pretense of *cleaning* her. She heard him gasp as his cock came in contact with her slick entrance. Her mind was in a fog of lust when he finally kneeled behind her swiping his tongue over her cleft in a long, luxurious lick that made her entire body stiffen.

"Don't deny me for that long again, princess. I don't think I'd survive."

She nodded in agreement, widening her stance to allow him better access, an approving growl vibrated against her folds, the sensation almost making her knees buckle.

"I-I just wanted to make certain you were healed," she explained as he pushed two long, thick digits inside of her clenching channel.

"Ahh, I'm as good as new," he sighed against her inner thigh. "Do you feel me?"

"Yes," she whimpered as he continued his ministrations.

"I'm gonna make you scream my name, princess," he promised as he built her to the point of orgasm but stopped when her body almost found release.

"Paul, I need you," she begged as her body shook with frustration.

"I know," he stated as he began the mind-blowing pumping motion. "Just a little more teasing, and then I'll take care of you."

"I'll get even, Mister Choy." She glared at him over her shoulder then quickly added, "Payback's a bitch."

He gulped, eyes dilating until they looked completely black.

"Okay." He stood swiftly lining up the wide, purplish cockhead to her needy entrance. "Never say I don't give my wife what she wants."

His arrogant chuckle only added to her desire and then he was thrusting inside her, hard and fast and wonderful.

"Aye, that's it... harder... faster," she demanded, meeting every single thrust he gave her. "C'mon, Paul. I need more."

"Your wish is my command, princess."

With those words spoken, he started to ram into her sex like a man possessed. Reaching between her legs and rubbing her slick nubbin with a rough fingertip.

"I'm not gonna last much longer," he announced, loudly.

Her body suddenly stiffened, and a delicious wave of heat began in her belly and rushed down to her sex. She yelled his name as the orgasm struck her like a clenched fist, bowing her body as Paul plunged balls deep.

"I'm right... there with... you," Paul hissed through clenched teeth as he exploded inside her spasming channel, hot, liquid desire filling her body as well as her soul.

Her man, alive and well and making love to her just the way she wanted him to. It was all she wanted in life.

"Meara," he groaned on a whisper, right before pulling out and quickly turning her around to face him, hugging her like he thought she'd vanish into mist.

Silently, he rewashed her still tingling body, touching her like she was made of glass or something equally as delicate. Then he washed himself, turned off the water, and dried her then himself. Never once did he look her in the eyes until he carried her to their bed and laid her on top of the comforter.

He left again and returned wearing a pair of boxer-briefs and carrying one of his large Navy t-shirts, the kind that reached her knees and dressed her sans panties. She reached over and turned off the bedside lamp as he settled behind her, his groin to her buttocks. His nose found its way against her hair, and he inhaled deeply.

"Paul, what's wrong?" she asked unable to fight off sleep. "You're acting strangely."

"I don't think I could live without you," he sounded primal and raw. "I just want to find him. Find him and kill him."

"Don't think about it right now," she pleaded, wrapping his arm more securely around her waist. "Please, sleep… just sleep."

And they did.

"Damn it, Meara!" Paul growled. "Keep your hands up."

"They are up!" she insisted sternly, hitting him with her gloved fist, the unexpected motion snapping her husband's head back a little. A satisfied smile appeared on her face, and she filled with feminine pride.

"Lucky shot," he stated right before he lunged, striking her in the upper arm. She winced from the blow, but quickly readjusted her stance countering his next attack by side-stepping to his left. The swift motion made him lose balance as she swiped his legs sending him crashing to the padded floor of Koa's home gym.

"How was that?" she asked, helping him to his feet.

"Better," he frowned, "but not good enough. You keep dropping your left hand before you do your roundhouse kick, which tells your opponent what your next move will be."

"Sorry, it's been a while since I sparred," she stated dryly.

Paul grabbed her wrists and gently pulled her to him, encircling her shoulders in a firm embrace, inhaling deeply the vanilla scent of her shampoo.

"No," he said, "I'm sorry." Then he placed a kiss on the top of her head. "I don't mean to come across like a drill sergeant. I just want to know that if no one else is around to protect you, you can kick some ass on your own."

Slowly, her shoulders relaxed as she rested her cheek against his t-shirt-covered chest, the fragrance of sweat and Paul filled her with determination.

"Okay," she hastily acknowledged. "Let's get to it then."

She pushed away from his impressive form ready to show him what she could really do.

His brow hitched as he circled her like a caged panther, his muscles rippling beneath his sleeveless t-shirt.

"Show me what you can do, Missus McBride-Choy," he chuckled loudly.

"Are you sure?" Her eyes narrowed. "I don't want to hurt you."

"You won't," he answered humorously. "Tell me a little about this style of fighting."

"It's simple really," his wife explained. "Brazilian Jiu-jitsu works on the premise that most of the advantage of a larger, stronger opponent comes from superior reach and more powerful strikes, both of which are mitigated when grappling on the ground. This particular style of Judo emphasizes getting an attacker to the ground in order to utilize ground fighting techniques and submission holds involving various joint-locks and chokeholds."

"Sounds complicated," her husband muttered, still looking for an unprotected part of her body to attack. "It sounds like you know a thing or two about this."

She smiled wryly.

"I've been studying it since I was eight," she boasted. "And have competed in many tournaments."

"Should I be worried that you're gonna injure me?"

"Maybe," Meara responded with a grin, hoping she hadn't forgotten her martial arts.

"How does it work exactly?" Paul tried to kick her, but she blocked it before he spun and landed a backhanded slap against her facemask.

Anger immediately flowed through her veins, and she reminded herself that it was never a wise idea to let an opponent make you lose your cool.

"The gist of it is that a smaller person, me, has a better chance against someone bigger, you, on the ground."

Without warning, he rushed at her again with a series of fast jabs to the chest and upper body region landing several hits on her side, face, and arms. He darted forward aiming a direct hit at her abs, but she easily blocked and spun out of reach.

With cat-like reflexes, he jumped up off of the floor at least five feet intending to bring her down using a roundhouse kick, but the counter she used was a jumping sidekick that landed directly on Paul's broad chest making him stumble backwards a few feet. She smirked feeling a little too cocky at his surprised glare.

Quickly regaining his balance, he lunged again, but this time she blocked that punch along with a front kick before explaining.

"A more precise way of describing this would be to say that on the ground, physical strength can be offset or enhanced by an experienced grappler who knows how to maximize force using mechanical strength instead of pure physical strength."

"Koa never mentioned all of this to me. He just taught me the techniques and I hoped not to get beaten too badly." He smiled that seductive all-knowing smile of his. "I never thought I'd marry such a deadly person. Remind me never to piss you off."

He winked playfully before sweeping her legs, making her tumble to the ground.

Immediately, he pinned her to the mat using his large, heavy body to make her submit, but she kissed him on the nose right before using a guard, a specific move to maintain submission, and reversed their positions.

"Do you give up?" she asked, sitting on his chest like she belonged there.

He shook his head, bucking her off at the same time, repining her to the mat.

"I'm not the one who's in trouble, my love."

The smugness in his voice fueled her motions as she used a side-control to regain the upper hand.

"Stop being so arrogant, or you'll be sleeping in the guestroom with Brutus."

"Yes, dear," he replied as she got to her feet and helped him up. "I'm impressed."

The sexy, sweaty Hawaiian leaned forward and grabbed her around the waist hauling her against his heaving chest. He kissed her neck, licking a trail down to her collarbone.

"Wicked," she managed to say before he pulled her back down to the mat and began fondling her left breast over her sports bra.

Paul chuckled.

"We are supposed to be sparring not making out," she admonished playfully as he tried to pull down the thin straps of her bra.

Ignoring her statement, he bent his head and placed several wet kisses on the swell of her breasts.

"I agree," Koa snickered from the open doorway. "Stop playing around."

His cousin laughed at their embarrassed faces.

"It's my turn to see what you are capable of, Meara."

"What happened to the two of you?" Aiden asked as they met for their bi-weekly basketball game.

Paul winced as the man hit him on the arm on top of a rather large, purple bruise his wife had given him during their second round of sparring the previous day.

"Meara," he mumbled so no one else around would hear.

Aiden threw his head back and laughed loudly.

"Your *wife* did this to you."

He shook his head adamantly.

"What did you do to piss her off? Leave the toilet seat up again?"

"Nothing," Paul whined like an errant child.

Aiden's gray-blue eyes narrowed in disbelief.

"Nothing?" the man scoffed in disbelief. "I doubt that."

"We sparred yesterday."

"Ah ha," the other man said.

"I may have told her she was hitting like a little girl," Paul added as he rubbed the nape of his neck.

"Well, I guess that would do it. You are such a moron." The other man smirked.

Koa happened to walk-up at the same time.

"Did you know Meara beat the shit outta this guy?" Aiden questioned as he playfully slapped the Navy SEAL on the back making him wince. "What's wrong?"

"Absolutely nothing's wrong, braddah," his cousin lied unconvincingly to Aiden. "I got hurt during training."

"That sprite beat the shit out of both of you?" Aiden looked at him then at Koa then back to him, shaking his head sympathetically. "I don't know whether to laugh or cry for you."

"Damn it, Aiden!" Koa cursed. "Don't let her adorable body, and supermodel face distract you, she fights like a cage fighter. No holds barred, no holding back either."

"Get outta here," Aiden guffawed, waving them off like gnats. "There is no damn way *Meara* could do that much damage."

Koa raised the hem of his shirt to reveal several dark bruises on his abs and side, his brow hitched defiantly.

"I didn't airbrush these things on."

"Hello, guys." Meara's soft Scottish lilt wafted across the court making every guy within a hundred feet stop, look, and drool.

His wife looked beautiful in a pair of white shorts, gray tank top, and tennis shoes; her long hair pulled back in a low ponytail. He heard both Aiden and Koa groan and he shot them both dirty looks.

"That's my wife," he reminded.

"We know," they replied together adjusting themselves in their shorts.

Koa looked down at his sneakers.

"We're married, not dead. Plus, Adrienne's away for two weeks for a seminar in Maryland."

Aiden looked over his shoulder at Meara's fast approaching form saying, "Since Kai started her own business, she hasn't been in the mood lately."

"Pervs," Paul ridiculed, punching both men on their shoulders at the same time.

"*Ouch!*" They yelled in unison making him feel better.

Eagerly, he walked over to her, pulling her in for a quick kiss.

"Is everything alright?"

She quickly nodded her head.

"You forgot your water bottle." His spouse grinned and patted his butt. "It is hot today. I thought you might need it. I don't want you getting dehydrated."

"Hi, Meara." Aiden rushed up and planted a wet kiss on her cheek. "You're looking lovely today."

"Thanks," she said, a blush creeping across her face. She dropped her keys and bent to grab them the same time Aiden did the same, causing them to bump foreheads, hard. "I'm so sorry, did I hurt you?"

"No, I'm fine." Her new cousin-in-law rubbed his head trying to alleviate the pain.

"I get a little clumsy when I'm nervous," Paul's wife confessed.

"Why are you nervous, princess?"

She glanced around the court and his eyes followed her movement. He wasn't surprised that every male on the court was brazenly studying his spouse. Possessively, he grabbed her around the waist, pulled her against him and planted a mind-blowing, full-on, tongue-wrestling kiss on her.

When he finally released her, she managed to respond.

"What was that for?" she asked with a smile.

"It was just for being *my wife*," Paul said, much too loudly then looked around giving the men still staring dirty looks.

Everyone turned away and began chatting among themselves.

"That's what I thought."

She laughed.

"You are so territorial, honey." The heated look in her toffee eyes warmed his entire body.

"I love you," he reminded firmly. "And I'll kick the ass of anyone willing to challenge me."

"Feisty. I like it when you're possessive," she purred right before kissing his bottom lip. "I'll have to thank you properly later."

Her suggestive words made him growl.

Aiden cleared his throat regaining their attention.

"Meara, these two bozos said that you gave them all of these war wounds." Aiden grinned. "They're kidding right?"

One perfectly shaped eyebrow hitched.

"What are you trying to say, Lieutenant Kaplan?"

Aiden's lips thinned. He knew it was never a good sign when someone called him by his title. Especially if it was someone of the opposite sex.

"Um," he glanced around at his teammates, but they only looked away. "It's just that you are beautiful and—"

"So, beautiful women can't fight big, hulking, brainless—sorry guys—men. Is that what you're implying?" Her Scottish brogue was almost too thick to understand, but her annoyance could be seen from outer space.

"That's not what I meant, exactly," Aiden backtracked, knowing he'd put his foot in his mouth.

"I think she should give you a demonstration of her fighting skills. Don't you, cousin?" Koa requested matter-of-factly as Paul nodded in agreement.

"I don't want to hurt you, Meara," Aiden stated.

"You won't," she insisted then graced him with a feral smile that made him swallow the little spit that still remained in his mouth.

What happened next was epic!

"*Ouch!*" Aiden squealed like a piglet, grabbing the bag of frozen peas out of his brother-in-law's hand. "Stop poking me on the bruise."

He growled low in his throat at the snickering sailor watching him intently.

"I'm so sorry, Aiden." Meara handed him a plate of spaghetti and meatballs and a glass of apple juice. "I didn't mean to hit ya that hard. Ya just made me angry tis all."

Her Scottish lilt, soft and alluring, and deceptively charming when they all knew she was a deadly assassin.

Paul smiled to himself. His wife really was perfect. Beautiful, smart, and dangerous.

"The garlic bread is finished," Koa announced.

"Could you please take it out and slice it?" Meara instructed. "Do you have a breadbasket?"

"I have a plate," Koa replied with a smirk.

Meara chuckled.

"That will do."

"Paul, how's the salad coming along?" Aiden asked from his seat.

"It's ready," the younger man replied, rolling his eyes. "Mahalo for the help, *brah*."

Then he rested the bowl of salad in the middle of the table, while Koa did the same with the garlic bread.

"No worries," Aiden said as they all sat down on the lanai of Koa's house to eat the dinner Meara had prepared.

"*Kolohe,*" Paul scolded with mock disgust.

Aiden's mouth opened in protest.

"Is it my fault your wife injured me?"

"Yes," he said, glaring at Aiden's surprise. "Next time, take our word for it that she's a ninja."

"*Mahalo* for cooking dinner," Koa stated as he twirled his fork, picking up a heaping mouthful of spaghetti. "With Adrienne out of town, I was gonna order a pizza, but this is so much better."

"Yeah," Aiden agreed after swallowing. "Kai and the kids are on a play date with some of the other Navy wives. I was gonna make a PB and J before you injured my sandwich-making arm."

He winked playfully.

Paul pulled out her seat for her before sitting down beside her at the outdoor dining table. The waning sunset dipping low into the horizon casting long shadows across the beach below.

"I have to go to Annapolis in two days," her husband informed as he took a bite of his dinner.

"How long will you be gone?" she asked, taking a bite of the freshly baked bread.

"A week," he added. "I want you to come with me."

Shaking her head, she reminded, "The charity fashion show is the same day that you leave. I can't miss it."

"Then I'm not going," he replied sternly.

"Paul, it's important for you to go. Don't burn bridges. Koa can stay with me until you get back since Adrienne's away."

"I can't," Koa spoke with his mouth full. "I'm leaving on a mission in the morning. I won't be back until late Monday evening."

"Alright, I'll stay at Aiden's place," she conceded with a broad smile.

Aiden shook his dark locks.

"No can do," the man responded, shaking his head. "Kai and the kids and I are visiting my dad in Maryland for a week."

"You have to come with me." Paul rested his fork on his plate. "I won't allow you to stay alone... unprotected with this psychopath still out there."

"You won't a-*allow* me," she gasped. "Is that what you said? *You* won't allow *me*..."

"I just remembered the basketball game on cable tonight," Koa rambled as he grabbed his plate and drink.

Aiden still sat holding the bag of frozen peas on his shoulder.

"There's no game tonight," he responded off-handedly.

"Yeah, there is." Koa nodded toward the house.

"No, there is not," Aiden snapped, grabbing another slice of bread.

"Aiden," Paul spoke calmly. "Get inside the house so I can talk to my wife... please."

"I gotcha."

Aiden stood suddenly, seized his plate and glass as well, then quickly followed Koa inside and closed the glass French doors behind him.

"Why do you have to argue with me about everything?" Paul huffed. "Do you think I want to come home and find your dead body lying in our house?"

"Of course not, but I thought I proved I can take care of myself," she whispered to no one in general as she stared at her half-eaten dinner.

"You did," Paul sighed. "But that doesn't mean this guy is gonna come after you with empty hands. Suppose he has a knife or a gun for God's sake."

"Then your dad can stay at the house with me. Dorian's guys will be there too."

"I don't know, Meara."

He tugged her into his lap and buried his nose in her shiny locks.

"Why don't you let Noelani take care of the fashion show this time?"

"There's a lot of prep work to be done. It's too big of a job for one person," she said right before taking a bite of the half-eaten meatball on his plate.

"You'll keep Dorian at your side at all times?"

"Every single minute. He can even watch me pee if it will make you feel better," she joked sarcastically which made him narrow his eyes.

That made her snort.

"I'll do everything he says. I promise." She crossed her heart. "Whatever he says."

"Alright. May I enjoy my dinner now?" he questioned as he began devouring his food once again with his wife still on his lap.

CHAPTER SEVENTEEN

The boxes were heavier than she remembered as she and Noelani loaded the rental van. Their outfits were already at the venue with the models, and they were bringing a few last-minute sewing supplies just in case something needed repair during the show. It would suck to be unprepared at such a monumental event in their young careers.

"We didn't forget anything, did we?" she asked her best friend and Spencer who were mentally calculating their items.

"No," Spencer said with a large, rare grin on his face. "I think you two have managed to pack every sewing supply known to man."

Noelani kissed her boyfriend's cheek before turning to her and saying, "Are you riding with us to the Marina?"

"Sadly, I'm under strict orders not to leave Dorian's side."

"Got it," Noelani stated approvingly. "We'll meet you there in twenty minutes."

She nodded before getting into Dorian's SUV, fastening her seat belt, and then hitting the speed dial button on her cell phone.

Paul picked up on the first ring.

"Is everything going well?" His voice sounded deceptively unemotional as he spoke, making the butterflies in her stomach feel more like ten-pound vultures. "Where's Dorian?"

She turned to look at her bodyguard who looked straight ahead at the crowded Oahu streets.

"He's sitting beside me," Meara divulged with a smile. "We're heading to the Marina for the show."

"Remember, you have to be within arm's reach of him," Paul reminded then paused. "No wandering off alone or with anyone you don't know. Is that clear?"

"Crystal," she whispered. "I'll take care of myself."

"Promise?"

"I promise. Cross my heart and hope to—"

"Don't finish that sentence," he commanded, his voice sounding gruff. "I love you more and more with each passing day. You know that don't you?"

She giggled at his overbearing demeanor, the one she'd grown to love as much as the man himself.

"Ditto."

"The show was fantastic girls!" Mrs. Devlin hugged them both as she exited the runway, her sea foam green, Christian Dior sheath dress elegantly showing off her fit body. "Because of your designs, the organization raised over one hundred thousand dollars. I can't tell you what it means to me. Thank you so much."

"Mahalo for letting us showcase our work for such a worthy cause," Noelani spoke first.

"Yes." Meara glanced nervously toward the nearly empty room. "Thank you so much."

"No need for sappy words. You two will be showcased in every national fashion magazine in America. Your business is going to need to expand in the near future." The older redhead winked. "I hope you're both ready to become fashion moguls."

"I'll see you out," Spencer said, leading her to the nearest exit. "I'll be right back."

"Meara," Dorian called from across the room. "I'm getting you out of here."

"Sure," she agreed then glanced down at her naked ring finger. "Damn it!"

"What's wrong?" The security expert jogged over to where she and Noelani were standing.

"I took off my wedding ring when I was fixing the hem of the bolero when it got torn," she hissed. "I must have left it in the dressing room."

"I'll get it for you," Dorian interjected quickly.

"It's alright." She smiled. "I'll grab it and meet you at the car. I'll be quick. I promise."

Dorian's body stiffened immediately.

"I don't think that's wise. I'll go with you."

"What about Noelani?" Meara queried, her stomach turning into a large, nervous pit.

"What about me?" Her friend's ears perked up.

"Who's going to protect you?" The thought of her cousin getting hurt because of her made her stomach clench again.

"Spencer," Noelani said without hesitation. "I'll go out to the car and wait for him."

"Lock the doors," the overprotective Scot commanded, while giving her friend a brief hug goodbye.

Noelani winked.

"I will. See you tomorrow."

"Goodnight." Meara's smile wavered slightly.

"Let's get your ring." Dorian preceded her to the dressing room where her ring rested on the small vanity table near the sewing machine.

Without hesitation, she ran forward, retrieved her ring, returned it to her ring finger and turned to show him the most important piece of jewelry she had ever owned, back in its rightful place.

"See? No harm, no foul." Her grin made him grin as well.

He began to say something when the lights went off.

"What the fuck?" Dorian cursed just as he was struck from behind, and his large body crumpled to the linoleum floor like a discarded tissue.

It was then that Meara saw the dark figure behind him blending into the blackness. The gasp that tore from her chest felt as if she had also been physically struck.

"It's nice to finally meet you, face to face, so to speak."

Instinctively, she stepped back trying to put as much distance between her and the Goliath-figure cloaked in black.

"What do you want?"

"Isn't it obvious?" The voice sounded garbled and distorted. "You."

Before her mind could examine her options, he lunged at her, but she side-stepped using his own momentum against him to bring him to the floor. Swiftly, she leaned over, punched him in the face twice before she felt him grab her ankle and tug her down.

"No need to try to escape," the person explained. "I only want to touch you... to make love to you."

Her eyes widened in panic as the thought of being raped almost made her vomit all over her would-be-attacker. Using her legs in a scissoring motion, she managed to kick him in the face. The man immediately released her in order to protect the area. Using the opportunity to her advantage, she jumped up and ran away quickly.

"You're out of your bloody mind!" she screamed at him as she ran back to Dorian's unconscious body.

"You'll like it. Just don't fight me." The ominous figure stood, lunged forward, and knocked her off of her feet, causing her head to slam against the cold hard surface. Her vision instantly blurred.

Before she could formulate a thought, he was on top of her tearing and ripping her new, red pantsuit. The sound of the fraying material brought her back to reality and she brought her knee up and hit him dead in the groin. With a mighty roar, he rolled off of her swearing and writhing in pain.

Wasting no time, Meara bolted up kicking with all of her strength at the maniac's ribcage, a loud animalistic howl filled the room urging her to strike again, but this time she kicked at his head.

"Meara," she heard a soft whimper from Dorian who was now staring up into her frantic eyes. He tossed her his gun and she fired at her assailant, but her hands shook so badly she missed as her attacker ran out of the nearest exit into the night.

"Dorian!" she yelled as she bent down to retrieve her cell phone, quickly dialing.

"Nine-one-one, what is your emergency?"

"My name is Meara Choy," she gasped breathlessly. "I'm at the Honolulu Marina. I need help. My friend's been hurt!"

It took the Honolulu police eight minutes to arrive on scene at the marina; it was the longest eight minutes of her life.

"Mister Matthews is going to be fine. He has a big lump on the back of the head, and he may have a concussion, but other than that he's gonna be alright." The middle-aged, female medic explained as she also applied antiseptic to the bump on Meara's head that was bleeding.

"Will he have to be admitted to the hospital?" Mr. Choy, aka Pop, asked with concern.

"Unfortunately, yes," the lady said simply. "With a concussion, they'll want to keep him overnight for observation. It's standard procedure."

"Of course," she mumbled under her breath, her legs shaking so much she thought they might buckle under her weight. "Where's Noelani?"

She scanned the area frantically. The realization she hadn't seen her friend in over a half an hour made her nervous.

"Uncle Joseph took her home," Pop informed. "She was waiting in the car when all of this happened."

"Noelani shouldn't be alone." Her stomach tensed with concern for her best friend's safety.

"He's not after her," the officer reminded.

"What about Spencer?" The question was like a heavy weight. She didn't want anyone to get hurt because of their association with her. "He walked Missus Devlin to her car then disappeared."

"He's a military guy," the officer prompted. "He can take care of himself. I'm concerned about you, Missus Choy."

"*Bugger!* I hope that maniac didn't hurt Spencer." The tears started freely falling and she wished that Paul was with her and not in Maryland. "Has someone called Paul?"

"I did," Pop answered. "He's taking the first plane out of Annapolis. Should be here as soon as he can."

"How did he take the news?"

"He cursed a blue streak, asked about you then hung up to call the airlines."

"Meara, can you tell me anything about your attacker?" Sergeant Murphy inquired; pen poised above his notepad.

"He was tall, Koa-sized tall, bulky and strong as an ox."

"Anything unique about him?"

She thought for a moment, her skull burning as the local anesthetic wore off.

"He used one of those speech modulators to disguise his voice." She touched where the lump was and winced at the slight pressure of her fingers. "His cologne was stifling; he practically doused himself with it."

"I'm assigning you a squad car until we find this bastard. No arguing, Missus Choy."

She smiled appreciatively.

"Pop is staying with me. Koa and Aiden are out of town, but I'm fine. I don't need—"

"Don't worry," her father-in-law practically growled, the sound telling her he wasn't taking no for an answer. "I'm not leaving your side."

The unmarked black Chevy sedan followed her and Pop back to her house and parked out front. Dorian's men patrolled the front and back yards and Brutus stood guard inside. As soon as they were safely inside, she locked the door and set the alarm.

"I'm gonna shower," she informed her father-in-law as she headed upstairs. "I won't be long."

"Are you hungry?" The concern in his voice was clear. "I can fix a light meal... breakfast for dinner maybe?"

She shook her head no.

"I'm not hungry."

"Okay," Pop smiled weakly, anxiety filled his wise brown eyes, eyes that reminded her of Paul's, and her chest began to ache with longing.

When she got to her bedroom, she locked it behind her and headed straight for the bathroom. Stripping her clothes off of her body as she went, quickly turning on the shower to a neutral setting, not too hot, not too warm. She stepped under the spray and began to sob.

She had no idea how long she stood under the steady stream, but when she finally pulled herself together her fingers and toes were wrinkled like prunes.

Feeling more at ease, Meara turned off the water, and hurriedly dried and dressed in a loose-fitting pair of sweatpants and one of Paul's t-shirts he wore to play basketball, inhaling deeply as it came over her head. It still smelled of him.

She found her brush on the dresser and sat at the edge of the bed brushing out the knots, carefully avoiding her wound, and then headed toward the door when her cell phone rang. Glancing at the screen, she saw it was Sergeant Murphy calling and she let out a deep breath she didn't even know she was holding.

"Hello?" she answered.

"Missus Choy, this is Sergeant Murphy. Sorry to disturb you so late, but I have some news for you."

"What's the news?" She felt a sudden chill in her bones even though the night was humid and balmy.

"It's about your ex-boyfriend," the officer spoke softly.

"Roger? Did you catch him?"

There was a long pregnant pause.

"We found his body about an hour ago," the man informed with a strained tone. "Near Sand Island, a single gunshot to the back of the head."

She gasped losing her balance and landing hard on the floor on her buttocks.

"Say again."

"He's dead, Missus Choy. The coroner says he's been dead for months now. Someone beat him up pretty badly before they... well, let's just say, it wasn't a quick death."

"What do you mean?" Her mind started to spin, and her stomach lurched unexpectedly.

There was a long silence before the detective revealed more disturbing news.

"He's missing one of his fingers."

"*No!*" she gasped, air rushing out of her lungs. "What's happening?"

"I want you to stay put, got it?"

"Yes, sir," she agreed.

"My officers are watching the house and you've got two security guards with you, right?"

"Aye."

"Damn!" Sergeant Murphy sighed. "I don't know how you got on this guy's radar, but he's latched onto you pretty good. Be safe and keep the doors locked. Is your father-in-law with you?"

"He is," she whispered.

"Good. I'll check on you in the morning."

"Thank you."

She hung up, still sitting on the floor, when the phone rang again. It was Paul this time.

"Paul?"

"Aloha, princess," his voice was a strained whisper. "I'm boarding the flight right now. I'll be in Honolulu in about eight hours."

"Paul," she spoke through sobs. "They found Roger's body a few hours ago. He was shot execution style. Sergeant Murphy called right before you did."

"What?!"

"It's not, Roger," Meara repeated in a haze. "He's been dead for months."

"Where's Dorian?"

"At the hospital, he has a concussion," she explained, her head beginning to throb. "They're holding him for observation. He put up quite a fight with the doctor on duty, but his fiancé convinced him it was for the best."

"Damn it! Where are the guys?"

"Downstairs, outside, there are also a couple of police officers as well, and your dad is here too."

"Alright," he said on a long, frustrated sigh. "Don't leave the house."

"I won't," she reassured.

"Let me speak with Pop."

"Okay," she complied, heading toward the bedroom door. "He's downstairs."

As she reached for the doorknob, the lights went out, and her heart instantly began to pound in her ears and her breath caught in her throat.

"What's wrong?"

"The lights just turned off," she whispered.

"Can you get to the window to see if the police officers are still there?"

"I'll have to leave the bedroom to check."

"Take my gun," he ordered. "It's in a locked case under my side of the mattress. The combination is our anniversary, month, and year."

Speedily, she ran back to the mattress and rummaged around blindly until she felt the smooth plastic case Paul's gun was housed in.

"I got the case." The words felt like sandpaper over her tongue.

Without delay, she punched in the numbers and inhaled sharply when the case snapped open, her eyes widened like saucers.

"It's not in the case," she mumbled, staring into the empty plastic holder that should have held Paul's service weapon.

"What do you mean it's not there? I cleaned it before I left and put it back in the holder. It has to be there!"

A tear rolled down her face as the realization hit her like a two-by-four. The stalker had been inside her house.

"Savior." The single word of a prayer lifted up to the heavens like an offering. "He was in our house."

Goosebumps appeared on her arms, the hairs at the nape of her neck stood on end, and her tongue felt as if it was numb.

"Where's my dad?" Paul's voice calmed her enough to focus on the present.

"Downstairs with Brutus," she answered mechanically.

"There is a baseball bat in the closet. Go get it."

She jogged to the closet and searched until she found the vintage *Louisville Slugger* autographed by Jackie Robinson. The bat was probably worth a small fortune.

"I have it."

"You'll need to go downstairs to check on Pop, but first you'll need to go to the guest bedroom window and make sure the police car is still out front. Can you do that?"

She swallowed down the bile that was slowly creeping into her esophagus.

"Yes, I can do that," she gulped her fear. "I have to make sure Pop is alright."

"Don't hang up," Paul instructed with a soothing tone. "I'm gonna call Sergeant Murphy on the other line. Put the phone in your pocket... do you have a pocket?"

She looked down at her sweatpants.

"I've got pockets," she repeated robotically.

"Put the phone in your pocket, whatever happens make sure he doesn't know it's on you. If he takes you out of the house, the police can track him with the GPS. I'm gonna call my CO at Pearl-Hickam and have him send a chopper to the house."

"I'm gonna be fine," she steadied her voice.

"Meara?"

"Aye?"

"Whatever you do... don't let him take you out of the house. Do you understand?"

Her brain suddenly began working again and dread threatened to overtake her.

"What did you say?"

"I said make sure he doesn't take you out of the house."

"I know."

"Meara," Paul's voice was a painful whimper. "I love you."

"I love you, too. Don't ever forget it."

The short walk across the hallway to the guest bedroom was the longest, most frightening walk of her entire life. Her breathing was coming out in choppy pants, the loud, raspy sound filling the space like an invisible fiend. Moonlight filtered through the sheer curtains helping her to see the street below, but there wasn't a police car parked there anymore.

What the fuck! Fear accosted her feet, turning them into lead weights as she stood motionless in the room debating her next move.

If the officers weren't there, then most likely Dorian's men weren't there as well, and she was on her own to find Pop and get them out of harm's way. Taking a deep breath, she steeled herself and left the protection of the room, heading downstairs, feeling her way through the hallway, down the staircase, and into the main living room.

"Pop," she called out in a loud whisper. "Pop, where are you?"

Only deafening silence greeted her.

"Brutus... come here boy. Come to me." She heard a small weak whimper and ran toward the sound.

The sight she saw made her vomit in her mouth. Her beloved Rottweiler was bleeding from his side, the copious amount of liquid seeping into the second-hand area rug.

"Brutus, stay still," she comforted. "Help is on the way."

"Is it really?" The deep baritone startled her causing her to scream. Stumbling backward she hid the bat behind her, the feel of smooth wood giving her strength.

"How did you get in here?" Meara blurted the first thing that came to mind as she noticed the alarm had been disarmed from the inside and it appeared to be working properly.

"Mister Choy let me in," he replied smugly.

"He wouldn't do that."

"But he did."

"I have a gun and I know how to use it," she bluffed, holding the bat tighter. "Leave now if you want to live."

He laughed wholeheartedly, the sound like fingernails scraping against a chalkboard.

"You mean this gun?" The intruder held up Paul's weapon, and when she saw it the air rushed out of her lungs like they'd been punctured by a sharp object.

"How did you get that?"

"I picked it up the last time I was here," he stated matter-of-factly. "You can have it back if you want it."

He threw it to her and smiled when she caught it.

"I took out the bullets; I wouldn't want to get shot... accidentally."

"I can assure you it wouldn't be an *accident*."

"Always so feisty, Meara." He chuckled. "That's what I love most about you."

She inched slowly toward the alarm hoping to activate the panic button.

"Tsk, tsk, tsk," the man stated dryly. "I wouldn't do that if I were you. I'll snap your neck like a twig if you make another move toward that keypad."

Immediately, she stilled.

"Where's my father-in-law?" she prodded, trying to focus on her attacker's voice since he was hidden by the engulfing darkness. "I said, where is, Pop?"

"I left him in the kitchen resting." The arrogant man smirked, and she realized he was in the southeast corner of the living room near the entertainment center.

"What did you do to him?" she asked weakly, not truly wanting to hear the answer, terrified to hear the answer. "If you've hurt one hair on his head, I'll—"

"You'll what?" he shouted at the top of his voice; the sound familiar to her ears. "Kill me? Is that what you were going to say, Meara? You'd kill me to save your precious Pop."

"In a heartbeat," she growled. The room seemed smaller with this figure in it and her skin crawled at the familiarity she felt with him. It was one of those déjà vu moments that you just couldn't place. "Where are the officers and the bodyguards?"

He chuckled like one of those cheesy bad guys in a cartoon, the ones with the handlebar mustaches and black hooded cloaks.

"It's amazing the equipment you can buy online. I, for example, bought a police scanner, at an amazingly low price. Do you know what I used it for?"

She shook her head no.

"I called those officers pretending to be dispatch and sent them on a wild goose chase to the other side of the island," he bragged proudly. "Clever, right?"

The tight sensation in her chest wasn't a good sign.

"And what about the other men?"

"I killed one of them." The person shrugged. "The other one is unconscious, tied up at the side of the house."

"I d-don't understand," her pained whisper sounded like a rush of air as she racked her brain for something to say. "Why are you doing this?"

"All I've ever wanted to do was love you, protect you," he explained. "From the moment I saw you I knew you were the one for me."

"You're insane!" she barked taking another step back but halted when the figure stepped out of the shadows toward her. "Don't come any closer."

The need to flee barreled down on her like an avalanche, but she stood her ground sweeping the area for anything that could slow him down. After all, she was no fool. He was a big fellow, at least 6'5" from the size of him with a burly, muscular build. She'd need to be smart to survive. Her sparring match with Koa suddenly came to mind reminding her that she wasn't completely helpless.

"How did we meet?" she continued, trying to lower his guard.

He moved a little closer.

"A mutual friend introduced us."

"Really?"

"Yes," he said stopping abruptly. "I love you, Meara. I just want to be with you. Let me be with you."

"How can you be with me when I've never seen your face?"

"You want to know who I am?"

"Of course," she lied, knowing the darkness would mask her deception. She cleared her throat before asking, "Did you hurt Roger?"

"Roger, your ex-boyfriend? Of course, I did," he proclaimed proudly.

"Why would you do that?"

"Because he hurt you!" he snapped. "He cheated on you and reported you to the Immigration office. I killed him for you. He was useless anyway, the way he begged and pleaded for his life. No backbone at all."

"Thank you for protecting me," she spoke with quivering lips. "Roger wasn't loyal, but you didn't have to kill him."

"I enjoyed killing him," the figure informed. "It was fun."

His words made her cringe, but she had to get close enough to him that she could get a good swing at him.

"How can you say that?"

"I did," the obviously unhinged male said gruffly. "He wasn't going to stop until he got you back."

"But I wasn't his to get back. I'm married to Paul, remember?"

She remained calm, trying to make him act irrationally.

"No." He shook his masked head. "Roger's actions made you marry Paul to stay in the country."

"I love Paul," she stated gently. "I would have married him regardless."

"I met you first," he insisted. "You were supposed to be mine. Not his!"

Meara nodded defiantly.

"You! Are! Mine!" He yelled.

"Let me see your face," she urged. "Let me see who you are."

"No," he stated. "Not yet... not yet."

Slowly, he walked toward her until he stood a foot away, his strong cologne stifling her. The expensive scent had been in her house, in her boutique before. She knew her stalker. She knew him well. She was friends with him...

"*Fuck!*" she yelled, her hands trembling like she was a junkie. "*Sp-Spencer?*"

With that acknowledgement the man pulled off the mask and smiled like a Cheshire cat.

"Smart girl," he smirked. "I've wanted to tell you for so long."

"Spencer," she repeated, trying to comprehend her situation. "You love, Noelani."

"I thought I did," he stated dryly, a look of guilt marring his face. "But then I met you and we fell in love—"

"I'm not in love with you," she spat the words, hands starting to sweat.

Shock took over at his misunderstanding of her feelings towards him.

"Paul is the only one I've ever loved," Meara added, her blood pumping loudly in her ears.

"After I kill Paul, you'll see things differently." Those words hit her as if his hands had struck her.

"No," she replied, willing herself not to faint. "I won't let you do that."

"Honey-pie," he snarled approaching her cautiously. "If you don't come with me right now, I'll kill everyone you've ever loved: parents, siblings, anyone I can track down."

"You are a monster," she snarled at him.

"No," he reassured with an almost childlike smile. "I'm on a mission to find the perfect partner, a soul mate to spend the rest of my life with."

As he spoke, he took another small step and that was all she needed.

Gripping the handle tightly, she side-stepped and swung, hard. So hard that she heard a crunch of bones as it contacted his head. The roar that escaped his throat was that of a tortured beast ready to disembowel its victim.

Again, she hit him, but this time on his knee, bringing him down to the floor. Readjusting her grip, she raised her arms for another swing, but he struck out with his fist. The impact against her jaw snapped her head back and to the side making her release the bat. Her only weapon clamored to the hardwood floors and rolled out of sight under the sofa.

"Bitch!" Spencer yelled, snarling, and growling at her as he grabbed hold of her right ankle and pulled her down, pinning her body under his.

"No!" she pleaded as his strong hand tugged her sweatpants down around her thighs. *"No!"*

She kicked and punched wildly, finally landing several blows to his temple. He released her and she quickly scrambled to her feet, pulling up her sweats while running toward the staircase.

As her foot touched the bottom stair, she was struck from behind, catapulting her down and forward so that she lay on her stomach across several stairs, her knees resting on the floor. Her legs were roughly yanked open wide before calloused hands jerked her pants down again revealing her naked buttocks and vulnerable sex to the leering giant lowering himself.

His semi-hard erection brushed her buttocks and she stiffened, trying desperately to buck him off. A hard blow to the back of the head stilled her as her vision blurred and her breathing slowed. Spencer's body was completely over hers now, his warm, alcohol-scented breath brushing against her ear.

"You're tough to get alone, Meara. I've been trying for months now to tell you... show you how I feel about you, but that nuisance of a husband of yours was always around."

"Get off of me, Spencer!" Her fear began to overtake her senses as she pleaded, "Don't do this. We're... friends."

"I'll make it good for you, baby. I promise," the murderer whispered as he kissed her on the temple then licked the shell of her ear, finally sucking her earlobe into his mouth.

"*Stop!* Please, stop!" Desperation was becoming a solid entity inside her mind making her short life flash before her eyes. *"Get off of me!"*

Spencer ran an eager hand over her hips and felt the small object in her pocket.

Shite!

"What do we have here?" He fished the cell phone out of her pocket before putting it up to his ear, his weight almost crushing her. "Hello, Paul."

Spencer hit the speaker button so she could hear.

"Motherfucker!" Paul growled with uncontained rage. "The police are on their way and so are some friends of mine in Koa's SEAL team. If you have half a brain, you'll leave before they get there!"

Spencer chuckled, the sound grating against her already frayed nerves.

"I'm Special Forces, remember? I'll fuck your wife, kill her, then sit down for a cold beer and still be outta here before they arrive."

"You are one sick bastard."

"Well, we can't all be perfect."

"Paul!" she cried as loud as she could with the weight of Spencer's body pushing her onto the stairs.

"If you hurt one hair on her head, I swear I'll make it my life's mission to hunt you down like the dog that you are. Do you fucking hear me, Spencer?" Paul hissed. "When I'm finished with you there won't be anything left to fit in a coffin or cremate!"

"Idle threats, son," he sneered, but his voice was a little unsteady. "You are on a plane over the Pacific, right? You can't save her."

He ran his empty palm over her heated skin roughly kneading her buttocks.

"Her ass is amazing: soft, but tight and firm," he rasped.

"Get your hands off of her!" Paul roared with desperation and contempt.

"Goodnight, my friend. I have to go fuck your wife now," he mocked then hit the end button. "You feel so good, Meara. I've dreamt of this for all these months and now I'm going to have you."

"No!"

Her body stilled as the fogginess from the blow began to clear. Suddenly, she reared up, head butting him in the nose. With all of the force she could muster, she twisted her body around and punched him again in the now broken appendage.

"*My nose!*" Spencer screeched as he held both hands over his nose, blood streaming down his face, writhing in agony. "You fucking broke my nose!"

Pulling up her pants with one hand, she ran up the stairs making it to her bedroom without falling or bumping into something. She slammed the door hard, locked it and glanced around the space hoping to see a way outside.

Then she remembered Uncle Alfred hadn't fixed the balcony planks yet. It was her only chance. This was her only way out. Kill or be killed. And she certainly wasn't going to be killed. Not without a fight anyway.

Running on pure unadulterated adrenaline, she unlocked the sliding glass door leading to the balcony and slid it open as far as it could go, then hid behind the curtain panel next to the opened door. Her breathing was choppy and loud, but she thought about seeing Paul again and growing old together surrounded by chubby grandchildren and it calmed her immediately.

The loud banging and swearing coming from the door startled her and she willed her body to remain completely still. A loud crash sounded just as the door was kicked open; splintering wood flew across the room like a bomb had just exploded.

"We were gonna be so happy together!" Spencer roared; his rage obvious. "But now I'm gonna fuck you and then kill you, or kill you then fuck you... haven't made up my mind yet."

The sick bastard!

"Do you know what I did to that bodyguard?" he taunted. "I slit his throat. Do you know why?"

Silence greeted him as she held on to the last bit of her commonsense. Her plan had to work, or she would be at his mercy shortly and his promise to rape and kill her was not an idle threat. His footsteps echoed through the space coming closer and closer to where she hid behind the thin fabric.

"Because he fought back," the highly trained soldier snarled his words. "Just like you're doing right now."

Her palms began to sweat, and she clenched her hands into tight fists to keep her fear under control.

"Meara?" he called out. "I'm gonna find you."

His voice was further away somewhere near the walk-in closet.

"If you come out now, I promise I'll make it quick... painless."

She took a slow steadying breath as the silence played against her psyche.

Where the hell was he?

"I'm gonna find you, honey-pie," he sang out like a schoolboy at recess.

Then suddenly, he was standing beside her on the other side of the curtain, his breath loud as he stared out of the open glass door.

"Fuck!" he exclaimed loudly stepping out onto the balcony.

The primal instinct to survive fueled her movements as she punched him in the back through the curtain, lunging his heavy body farther out onto the balcony. She jumped up landing a flying sidekick to the middle of his broad back. The impact pushed him against the rotten wooden railing surrounding the shabby area and the sound of wood beginning to snap and splinter was like music to her ears. With the added weight, the planks below him gave way and he fell through, his body from the shoulders down dangling in mid-air as he tried to regain a hold on the fragile, moldy planks.

"You fuckin' bitch!"

In a blind rage, he grabbed her ankle pulling her out with him, her extra weight was the final catalyst. The entire balcony squeaked and whined just before the worn, rusty bolts holding the structure to the side of the house ripped out and they were both plummeted downward in an avalanche of broken wood and flailing limbs.

Meara heard the loud, disturbing sound of bone snapping as the deafening thud sounded when she hit the ground, and then the world turned to black.

The hubris of individuality is often expressive, but a definitive pride comes from the knowledge obtained by reading books.

Belen Bookstore empowers the mind and spirit to travel to destinations only imagined, to live the lives one cannot comprehend, and to open discovery to the furthest reaches of imagination.

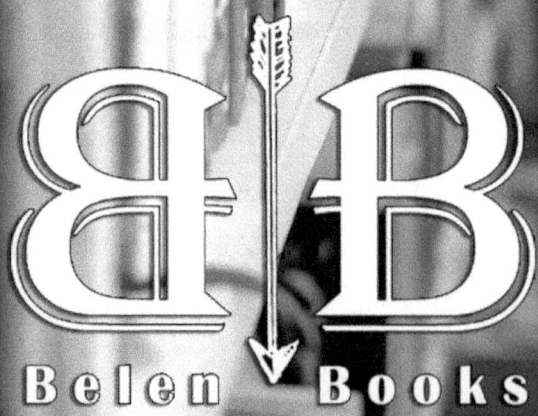

www.belenbookspublishing.com

CHAPTER EIGHTEEN

"She's coming around."

Meara heard Paul's strained voice to her right side, but she couldn't *will* her eyes to open.

"Princess," he pleaded softly. "Wake-up."

"Please, Meara, wake-up."

Daddy? Was that her father's voice?

With all of her determination, she forced her eyes open, glancing around the crowded hospital room. Paul and her father looked down at her intently, their eyes bloodshot and puffy. Several days of stubble on their faces reminded her of where she was.

"I'm in the hospital, aren't I?"

"Yeah," Paul replied stiffly, his eyes welling with unshed tears.

"How long have I been here?" she groaned softly.

The room went silent.

"Two days so far," Paul relayed. "The entire family has been waiting for you to wake up."

"Where's Spencer?" She sat up abruptly, almost ripping the IV out of her arm. The sting clearing away the medicine induced fog in her brain.

"He's dead," Paul spoke calmly as he gently placed her back onto the mattress, even though his eyes were shadowed with anger.

"Apparently, when you fell off the balcony you landed on the sand." She recognized Sergeant Murphy's voice coming from the foot of the bed. "Fortunately, he landed on a table saw blade. The thing almost sliced his spine in half."

Looking out, she saw his smiling face, eyes red-rimmed as well.

"Good, he deserved it," she said trying to sit up, but the strength to perform the simple task eluded her. "What's wrong with me? I can't feel my wrist."

"When you fell, you landed on your left wrist," her husband informed. "It's broken. You're wearing a cast to keep it immobile while it heals. You also have a concussion from the fall and a fractured fibula which is also in a cast. That will take time to heal as well."

He leaned over and brushed his warm lips over hers. The tenderness made her eyes well-up, and she desperately held back the tears.

"Relax, sweetheart," her father's thick Scottish accent tickled her ears.

"Daddy," she whimpered when her father's hands grasped her good arm.

Her father's tears began to fall.

"You're here," she moaned at the sudden sharp pain in her wrist.

"Shh, me Bonnie lass," her father stated, planting a brief kiss on her forehead. "Save your strength."

She couldn't hold back the smile when she said, "You've always hated airplanes."

"I still do," he smirked, his bright blue eyes glistening under the harsh fluorescent lights. "But I needed to make sure your husband had you well taken care of."

"Where's Mum?"

"She's in the cafeteria fetching coffee, she's out of her mind with worry," he said, kissing her again. The sweet gesture made her heart clench. "She can never sit still."

"How's Pop?" She braced herself for what was to come but was reassured when Paul graced her with a grin.

"He's fine. Spencer knocked him out and tied him up in the kitchen."

"And Brutus?" Her stomach instantly knotted as she remembered her puppy bleeding from the stab wound. "Is he alright?"

"He's doing much better. The vet stitched him up, no vital organs were hit. The little beast is being pampered by the veterinary assistants as we speak."

"I can't wait to see him," she giggled. "And Noelani, how's she holding up?"

"Of course, she's shaken up," her husband informed with a frown. "Uncle Joseph found her at her place. Spencer drugged her and left her tied up to a chair. Thank God that was all he did. She feels guilty about not seeing through Spencer's charade."

"We all do," Meara informed with tears.

Paul kissed her again.

"I'm pure done in," she suddenly announced in a heavy Scottish drawl as the pain medication was delivered through her IV. "I'm gonna take a little nap."

"That's a good idea, princess," Paul agreed as he kissed her lips again. "I'll be here when you wake up."

"O... k..."

CHAPTER NINETEEN

"I'm well," she said, rolling her eyes, knowing her mother couldn't see her through the cell phone.

It had been a week since her parents returned to Scotland. Their incessant calls were driving her crazy. She'd never admit that she secretly loved all of the attention.

"Are you taking it easy?" her mum asked. "The doctor said you needed to rest for at least a couple of weeks."

"Mum, it's been two weeks already," she reminded, holding back a chuckle. "Paul hasn't let me do anything. I'm stuck in this bed like a prisoner in solitary confinement."

"Good, I gave my new son-in-law permission to spank you if necessary. So, you must behave."

Meara didn't have the heart or the nerve to tell her mother that Paul actually liked spanking her, and she *really* liked being spanked.

"Yes, mum, I'll behave myself," she giggled mischievously.

"I'll talk to you soon."

"Give my love to Dad and the boys, yeah?" Her accent reared its head.

"I will... kisses to all of your Hawaiian family."

"Bye, Mum." Clicking the end button suddenly felt overwhelming.

"Was that your mom... again?" Paul's deep baritone with its sultry Hawaiian lilt made her jump.

Smiling, she replied, "She calls me at least twice a day and my dad is worse. My brothers are planning to visit after I've healed up, if it's alright with you of course."

"Of course, the more the merrier. We've got plenty of space."

He rested a tray with a bowl of steaming udon noodles in broth with chunks of white meat chicken and a medley of baby vegetables on the bedside table. Eagerly, she reached for the bowl with her good hand and began to eat the delicious concoction.

"Mmm," she sighed on a moan. "I'm going to be spoiled after all of this."

Her husband stood at the side of the bed watching her eat, lust made his brown eyes turn black.

"Sergeant Murphy will be over in about thirty minutes," Paul quickly informed. "You should get ready."

"Sure!" She ate faster, loving the savory dish. "I won't be long. Will you come for me when he's here?"

Paul nodded then turned toward the walk-in closet.

"What's the matter?" his wife questioned his retreating back when his shoulders slumped.

"Nothing's wrong," he lied, and she could tell he was lying by the strain in his voice. "I just need a shirt."

He disappeared into the closet and returned shortly wearing one of his blue T-shirts with the Navy logo on the front.

He looked gorgeous and her heart and sex clenched at the same time. Need filling her in a sudden rush. Her panties were instantly soaked.

"Take a shower with me. You can wash my back?" She swung her legs over the side of the mattress, and then remembered the cast.

He swallowed hard.

"No," he answered too quickly for her comfort, his gaze fixated on the object holding her lower leg immobile. "You're still healing. I don't want to hurt you."

She pouted giving him her most seductive glance before saying, "I'm healing. I just need some TLC from you."

"Later," he swiftly countered then gave her a wink and left the room.

What the hell was that all about?

She finished her food then showered, brushed her teeth, and dressed in a pair of black yoga pants and one of Paul's T-shirts that fell to her knees; his scent was still on it. Without care or precision, she put her hair up in a messy bun and went downstairs to the living room where Paul and Sergeant Murphy were sitting discussing something of importance.

Paul looked up first, an uneasy smile on his face.

"I was just coming to get you."

"Sure," she said coolly avoiding eye contact. The sergeant stood, giving her a quick hug before she sat beside her husband on the couch, carefully, leaning her crutches against the coffee table.

"It's good to see you, Missus Choy," the older man said sincerely.

"It's good to still be seen," she muttered teasingly, but neither man smiled. Clearing her throat she asked, "What brings you by, Sergeant?"

He coughed, cleared his throat nervously then answered, "We ran a background check on the lunatic who did this to you."

"Spencer Davis," she clarified.

"Turns out that was just an alias," Sergeant Murphy corrected. "His name was Samuel Spencer... Army ex-Special Forces... dishonorably discharged from the military about a year ago."

"Dishonorably discharged, why?" She looked at the two men their expressions grave. "Spit it out, damn it!"

Paul spoke this time. "While he was stationed in Germany, five young women went missing within a year and a half."

"Bugger!" Her stomach immediately began doing somersaults.

"Spencer... Samuel, whatever," Paul's words escaped in a low growl as he spoke. "He had dated all of them and was suspected in each case, but they couldn't find any proof to arrest him. So, they discharged him instead."

"Were the women ever found?"

Both men shook their heads.

"Pieces of them were found... two of the women that is, but the others just... disappeared," Murphy added on a loud exhale. "His M-O, apparently, was to stalk his victim first, then introduce himself. He'd date someone for a while decide if she was worthy..."

"Let me take a wild guess... no one was ever worthy," she said sarcastically, taking the detective aback.

"No, no one ever met his high standards, except—"

"Me," she gasped in horror. *"Great!"*

"Noelani went through his things and found pictures of all of his victims, including you and her."

"D-dear f-father," she stuttered.

"Your best friend was the original target, but for some reason he wanted you instead." The sergeant's face went pale at the thought. "Noelani was blessed he didn't kill her as well."

"She's pretty shaken up," Paul added. "The thought of losing you has been eating her up inside."

"Is that why she hasn't come to visit me?"

Paul nodded then added, "I think the guilt over her loving Spencer and finding out that he's done so many awful things hasn't been easy on her."

Meara grimaced.

"I don't blame her for anything that freak did to me. As far as I'm concerned, we were both victims."

"Good, because I needed to hear you say that." Noelani whimpered from the doorway, her face sullen and her eyes red and swollen. "I'm so sorry, Meara."

Her best friend ran to her, giving her a tight hug, both of them crying and whispering soothing words to each other as the men shifted uncomfortably in their seats.

"I love you like a sister, no matter what," she reassured her overwrought friend.

Noelani sat beside her on the couch pushing Paul over.

"I found this hidden in his things." She handed the worn, brown leather journal to the detective. "I read as much of it as I could. The things he described were too horrible to finish, but I think you'll be able to find all of the women he's... harmed."

"You mean the other three?" Murphy's eyes narrowed when Noelani shook her head.

"I mean... the other six." The pain in her eyes was enough to make Meara begin to shake uncontrollably.

Paul stood to embrace her, but Noelani beat him to it. She encircled her shoulders, squeezing her gently.

"I'm so sorry," his cousin wailed hysterically. "I don't know what else to say, Meara."

"It's not your fault. Please, stop apologizing," she stated as they hugged each other back... hard, allowing the tears to resume their escape.

Noelani straightened suddenly then informed, "He also describes what he did to Roger McVicor in the journal as well. I'm glad he's gone for good."

The finality shook every soul in the room to their core.

"The world is definitely a safer place," Meara grumbled under her breath.

"Good boy, Brutus." His beautiful wife lay on their king-sized bed playing with their currently licking monster of a dog. "That's a good, boy."

Meara rolled around the bed in her favorite white tank top and white cotton bikini panties. Her hair spilled around her shoulders in a long, thick espresso curtain, the sight of her so carefree and playful made him smile.

"Hey, Brutus," he said loudly. "Stop slobbering all over my wife."

The dog stopped as he understood and jumped off the bed settling on the area rug at the foot of the bed.

"Jealous?" his wife teased in that tone he loved so much.

"Extremely," he said, sitting on the mattress, his eyes instantly roaming over her lush curves. His cock flexed inside his boxer-briefs.

Meara tilted her head to watch him as was her habit.

"I didn't think you cared anymore," she accused without heat. "You haven't touched me in weeks."

"You were injured," Paul patiently explained, and then gently touched her cast with his fingertips.

He heard a subtle moan escape her lips at the simple contact before she rushed at him pinning him beneath her body. She lowered her mouth over his sealing their lips together as her tongue demanded entrance into his mouth.

"Kiss me, damn it!" she insisted when he refused to let her in.

Guiltily, he pulled away, holding her at arm's length. The need in her eyes breaking his heart wide open.

"I can't."

"Why?" her voice raised an octave.

Suddenly, he pulled her against his chest, holding her securely, and breathing in his favorite vanilla scent.

"I n-never asked you what happened after he hung up on me," Paul stuttered, his heart breaking.

The realization he saw in her eyes hit him like an unexpected slap to the face. She understood now that he thought she had been raped.

Sweetly, she took his face in both hands, holding his chocolate gaze with hers.

"He didn't rape me," the words flowed out of her in a stream of relief that carried her back to a simpler time when lunatic exes and stalker, dishonorably discharged, ex-Special Forces, murderers didn't exist. "Is that what you thought happened?"

He nodded, squeezing her tightly to the point where she couldn't breathe.

"The last thing I heard was him saying those... things and hearing you screaming when he touched you. All I could picture was—"

"He didn't... he tried, but I fought with every ounce of strength I had," she confessed with a loud sniffle. "All he did was touch me."

"I never should have left you alone," her husband blurted as guilt radiated off of his stiffened form, hands clenched tight at his sides.

"It wasn't your fault," Meara soothed, pushing away to look at him again, a lovely, bright smile gracing her full, pouty lips.

"I'm your husband. I'm meant to keep you safe and protect you from all of the shitheads out there, but instead, I trusted that fucker! I played basketball with that murderer!" He rambled through all his fears. "Ate Sunday brunch with him, trusted my cousin to be with him... suppose he had hurt her too."

He covered his face with both hands like a small child.

"I didn't want him to be dead," Paul confessed angrily. "I wanted to kill him myself."

"I know... I know," Meara spoke softly as she took off her tank top and pushed him until he was flat on his back against the mattress. "You kept me calm. The thought of seeing you again motivated me to fight even harder."

She kissed him chastely on each cheek, his chin, and finally his mouth.

"The vision of growing old and fat with you surrounded by beautiful grandchildren made me stronger," she boldly admitted. "My future with you, made me want to live."

He felt his entire body relax, the tension seeping out of his limbs and a heavy weight being lifted from his soul.

"Take off your shirt," his wife instructed, her voice harsh with desire. "I want to see all of you."

"I never thought I'd hold you again." He heard himself say as he took off his shirt and threw it on the floor beside the bed. "I pictured landing at Honolulu Airport greeted by the police telling me that you were dead."

"I'm not," she said smiling, her fingers rubbing his nipples with small circular patterns. The tender touch making his member spring to life. "I'm right here, with you, safe and sound and horny as hell."

She winked as she lifted off of his hips.

"Take off your pants... isn't that better?"

The little minx leaned forward, taking his over-stimulated cock into her mouth, sucking the engorged head like a Popsicle or a lollipop.

"Still as delicious as I remember," she joked.

"Meara," he moaned, her tongue now running down the sides of his painfully hard shaft.

"I don't want to wait to have children, Paul," her words were firm and unyielding. "This incident reminded me of how fragile life is and that there are no guarantees any of us will live a long, full life. We've got to be happy when we can… live and love for the moment, because it can be taken away in a heartbeat."

"I thought you were on the pill?" he asked curiously.

Meara smiled seductively.

"I haven't been able to take them with the medication I was taking, remember?"

She laughed when he pulled off her panties, carefully avoiding her cast, revealing her wet sex.

Leaning up, he kissed her tenderly on the lips, dipping inside her hot mouth licking and nipping and tasting her unique sweetness.

"I guess we should start trying then. I'm aiming for twins. We'll have to do everything… *twice*," he informed with complete sincerity. "It'll be our newest project."

He arched his brows mischievously.

"After all, *'Project Lieutenant'* worked out so well," Paul added with a chuckle.

Meara nodded in agreement.

"Make sure that these lessons last a really long time," his gorgeous spouse taunted humorously.

He laughed before giving her beaded nipple a long, wet swipe with his tongue.

"So bossy, my Scottish princess," her handsome Hawaiian husband countered. "But lucky for you, today, I'm taking requests."

The End

BRITISH & SCOTTISH WORDS AND MEANINGS

Arse – British slang for ass, bottom, backside, bum

Bampot – Scottish slang for fool, idiot

Bawbag – Scottish slang for balls, scrotum, bollocks

Bird – British slang for woman

Hen – Scottish slang for woman

Bloody hell! – British slang for "Damn it!"

Bugger off! or *Bugger* – British slang for "Fuck off" / "Fuck"

Cheeky – British slang for rude, feisty

Lass – British slang for young girl, young lady

Messages – Scottish slang for groceries, food supplies

Minx – British slang for a sly woman

Pos h – British slang for fancy

Quine – Scottish slang for young girl

Yon – Old English for location, over there

Phrases

"Gonnae no' dae that!" – Scottish slang: 'Don't do that!'

"Haud yer wheesht" – Scottish slang: Shut up!

"Yer lookin' a bit peely wally" – Scottish slang: 'You look pale or ill.'

COMING SOON FROM L. D. K. JOHNSON

Honoring Noelani

Episode #4 of The Kapahu Series

AVAILABLE FROM L. D. K. JOHNSON

Kapahu Series

Standalone Novels

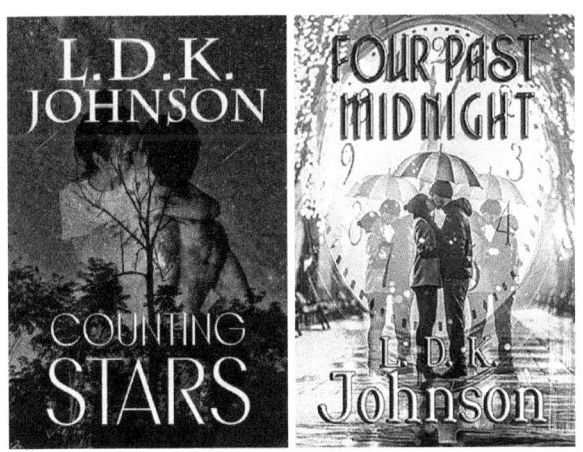

Available Everywhere!

www.belenbookspublishing.com

ABOUT THE AUTHOR

L. D. K. Johnson is an American author hailing from the East Coast of the U.S., where she enjoys spending time with family and friends when she is not sitting in front of her laptop writing the next book that comes to mind. Her favorite things in life are chocolate, creamer (not necessarily coffee), and anything D.I.Y. related.

L. D. K. Johnson first made her mark on the writing scene with her beloved contemporary erotic romance books, The Kapahu Series, set on the beautiful Hawaiian island of Oahu. Ms. Johnson followed with Counting Stars, Four Past Midnight, and the first installment of her adult Fantasy series, Lup Teren (Wolf Land Series).

After a several year hiatus from writing, L. D. K. is ready to jump back into the fray; wowing fans with sexy new stories, but not without a reintroduction of her prior books in a new home.

www.ingramcontent.com/pod-product-compliance
Lightning Source LLC
LaVergne TN
LVHW010303260326
834688LV00044B/1433